HIDDEN IN THE KEYS
The Complete Series

SAGE PARKER

PUBLISHING

ISBN: 9798794887495

To Connie, for everything.

CONTENTS

PART ONE

CHAPTER 1

Julia stood with her back to the window as she finished up the few dishes she had used that morning. She was distractedly drying the cup and staring absently at the open cupboard, oblivious to the amazing views outside her kitchen window. It was in fact the very view that had attracted her to this house in the first place. The minute she had walked in with the realtor and seen the view, she had envisioned herself and Frank drinking warm cups of coffee in front of the large bay window, talking and laughing while admiring the beautiful ocean just outside.

However, since moving to Longboat Key Island a few short months ago, most of the time she had been taking in the view by herself. Although Frank had retired as promised, he still seemed to have many loose ends to take care of and spent a lot of time away from their little beach house attending to *business*. Julia tried to be understanding, but she had hoped that he would try a little harder to enjoy their retirement together.

She put the last of the dishes away and glanced impatiently at her phone again. Still no return message from Frank.

She saw a few emails from some potential clients in the area though, asking her if she had any open sessions. Before they moved to the Keys, she had dutifully told all her clients back in Ohio that she was no longer in business and referred them to other Reiki specialists. But when Frank had continued his habit of spending long hours away, she decided to put out some feelers in the local area, hoping to help fill her time while he was gone.

Sighing, Julia walked over to the small desk she had set up in the corner of the family room. She loved the open feel of this little beach house. She could see from one corner of the main floor to the next and had taken great

1

pains to furnish their home in a cool and beachy, minimal palette. The perfect atmosphere to relax and unwind.

Julia sat down and began to answer a few of her emails – responding to questions but still unwilling to commit to any sessions just yet.

When she heard someone at the front door, she jumped up excitedly.

"Frank?" she called out. Rushing to the front door, she flung it open, smiling in anticipation.

Standing up awkwardly, the UPS man gave her a sheepish grin. "Uh, hello, Mrs. Masterson. Sorry to disturb you. I just thought that I would set this package inside as it's marked fragile and contains food. Thought it could spoil out on the front porch."

Julia glanced down at the package on the ground in front of the main door. It had to be the cookies from their local bakery back in Ohio. She had almost forgotten that she had ordered them. The shop did not often send cookies through mail, but Julia had insisted and paid extra. She had been so excited on the phone to the owner, telling her how she would surprise Frank with them this weekend on their special trip.

Frowning slightly, Julia bent down to pick up the box, doubting the surprise she had planned for the weekend would even happen now.

The UPS man stood back a bit, watching a range of emotions cross Julia's face. The couple had moved in a few months ago, and since then, he had delivered several packages to the house. He was a married man, and relatively happy in his marriage, but he was still a man. He took every chance he got to admire Julia's beauty. He watched her long dark hair cascade over her face as she bent down to pick up the package. When she stood, he saw that her clear blue eyes seemed unusually troubled.

"Is everything alright, Ma'am?" he asked.

"Oh yes, it looks just fine," Julia answered, interpreting his question to be concerned with the condition of the package. "I bought these for my husband, and I'm sure he will be tickled pink when he sees them." She smiled reassuringly at him, showing a set of perfect teeth, and he wondered again how such a beautiful woman had ended up here with a man who looked so much older.

As he smiled back at her and walked out to the front porch, he gave her one last glance and hoped she was alright.

Julia carried the package into the kitchen and opened the box, appreciating how carefully the store owner had obviously packaged the cookies. Sighing, she glanced down at her phone again but only found a blank screen staring back at her. She wondered if maybe it was time to cancel the plans she had so carefully made for the weekend.

Their 25th wedding anniversary was the next day, and Julia had planned an incredible surprise that had been in the works for the past month.

She and Frank had been walking along the docks admiring all the boats, and he had seemed extremely excited by the big catamaran sailboats they had seen. "Will you look at that, Julia?" he had exclaimed happily. "That thing is huge and doesn't look like it rocks around at all! Now that is something I could see myself touring around in!" Julia had looked at him in delight and surprise.

That very day, after they returned home, Julia had booked a catamaran for the two of them for their anniversary, ordering champagne and a fancy on-board dinner to surprise him. The cookies had been an afterthought; he had remarked how he missed them one day while they were talking about Ohio.

Now, as she put the cookies away, she tried to calm her racing mind. It seemed wrong that he would choose the weekend of their anniversary to leave without a word. Even though he was away often, in the 25 years they had been married, Frank had never missed their anniversary.

She sat down at her kitchen table, looking out at the waves gently lapping onto the shore. The ocean looked exactly as it had the day they decided to retire and move here.

She remembered how she had cried that day, telling Frank that she was done with their marriage and could no longer continue the life they were living. Frank had walked towards her and uncharacteristically put his arms around her, holding her close.

"Come on now, Julia, don't talk crazy. I brought you here for the vacation you wanted, didn't I?" he had asked.

Julia had looked at him incredulously.

"I booked this vacation as a surprise and dragged you here kicking and screaming," she had remarked bitterly. "Why don't you get it, Frank? You're always gone and I'm alone just sitting around waiting for you. This is not the life we talked about when we got married." She sobbed and grabbed a tissue, trying to gather her composure.

Frank turned to face her, but no words came out.

"I have been waiting for over 20 years for you to get your act together," she complained. "First it was *let me build my career*, then *let me build this business venture*, then to let you spend time with the kids, then you needed time alone to decompress. I've tried not to complain but it never ends Frank!" Julia knew she sounded whiny and petulant, but she couldn't seem to stop the words from coming out once she had opened the flood gates.

"I can't do this anymore Frank," she repeated, her eyes and nose red and swollen from crying. "We either work on our marriage together, or I leave." She still wasn't sure if she had even meant it when she had given Frank that ultimatum, and she was certain he would be angry at her outburst, but Frank had looked at her dumbfounded and for once had been at a loss for words.

"Julia, you know we can't get a divorce. That would be completely against my beliefs and religion. You can't mean that."

Julia had stared at him stupefied. "You can make two children with another woman and not marry her, but you can't get a divorce?" she had asked, not quite comprehending what she had just heard.

"You know how my family is, Julia. Divorce is not an option. That's why Jane and I couldn't get married. The family never accepted her, and they were convinced our relationship wouldn't last. I couldn't marry her knowing it would end in divorce."

He had held her at arm's length, looking at her squarely in the face. "The family loves you, Julia. You're bright, attractive, and accomplished. Everything my family ever wanted for me. We have to stay together!" he had proclaimed petulantly.

"Your kids certainly don't love me." Julia had looked squarely back at him in a rare show of defiance. "If we are going to make this work, then something has to change."

That's when Frank had taken her in his arms and swore to her he would change. They were looking out over the gently lapping water when he had told her they would move to the ocean, just like she had always wanted. He would retire and spend the rest of his life making things right between them again. As long as she didn't leave him, he would work hard on himself and make her happy.

Julia had leaned back against him and desperately wanted to believe him, just like she had when he first proposed. Back then, she had been so in love that she ignored the red flags and trusted his word instead. Since then, she had dedicated so much of her life and herself to him that she really wasn't sure that she could leave him if it came down to it.

True to his word, Frank had dutifully followed her around on her house hunt, agreeing with almost all her choices and wishes. He allowed her *carte blanche* when it came to decorating, only minimally complaining about how she was spending money. Julia really started to believe that Frank was being sincere this time.

Understandably, he still needed to close out his businesses and clear up loose ends, but she had been so excited and busy planning their new life, she had barely noticed when his old habits had gradually begun again.

Julia stood up, frustrated at her line of thought. She grabbed a light windbreaker and headed out to the beach, determined to try and regain some of her equilibrium. For most of her adult life, she had been able to channel her energy and her thoughts into a calm and meditative mood when needed, but the last few days had felt different. Her energy felt wild, and she felt a terrible panic that she had never felt before.

Walking down along the shore, she tried desperately to quiet her mind and embrace the sun, the wind and the gentle waves. Julia felt the tightness in her stomach and her heart was pounding hard against her chest. She tried to squash the rising tension in her body and was failing miserably. She reasoned with herself that it was not unusual for Frank to just disappear, it happened all the time.

This time was their anniversary though, and it felt different.

Sitting in the sand, her legs crossed in her usual lotus position, she tried hard to meditate. She breathed in the salty sting of the ocean, felt the scratchy grit on her thighs where they touched the sand, and listened to the soft splash of the waves as they ebbed in and out on the shoreline. *Breathe in, breathe out*, she thought to herself.

But no matter how she tried to remain zen, she couldn't shake off this overwhelming feeling.

"Curse you, Frank!" She shouted out loud, springing up from her position. She flung off the jacket she was wearing and frantically looked around at her serene surroundings. Today the sun wasn't gentle and warm; it was just a hot blob and irritating. The sand was not warm and welcoming; it was just itchy and gritty. She looked back to their house, hoping against all odds to see Frank standing there looking for her. All she saw was the empty deck, hazy in the heat of the sun glancing off the hot beach.

"Where are you, Frank?!" she called out, frustrated. Desperate to do something and not knowing what else to do, Julia started to walk towards the Pier about a half-mile away. She walked, and then jogged, before breaking into an all-out run until she reached the Pier, sweaty and exhausted. Breathing heavily, she looked out over the water, ignoring the curious looks of the people around her. She knelt in the sand, exhausted, and prayed like she had not prayed in a long time. She asked God for guidance and the wisdom to know what to do next.

CHAPTER 2

The phone on her nightstand buzzed incessantly as Julia tried to wake up and orient herself to her surroundings. She remembered falling asleep on the couch last night, too tired and worn out for her nightly, before-bed ritual. The room spun as she looked around and wondered how she had ended up in her own bed. Granted, she had consumed more wine than she usually did, but she didn't think she was blackout drunk.

Groaning at the effort and holding her head, she looked down at her phone, hoping for the thousandth time that Frank was finally reaching out to her, but she didn't recognize the number that popped up on her screen.

It had been six days without a sign from him, and he had missed their anniversary yesterday. Even for Frank, that was unusual.

She had decided last night that enough was enough. It was time to find out where he was. Julia had watched enough crime shows to know that the police generally didn't look for grown men who were often away on business, and was sure Frank would be back before she had 'overreacted' and filed any kind of report. But she still needed answers.

The only other option she could think of had been to call Frank's children and find out if they had any idea where their father was. Just as Julia had feared, the call had not gone well.

"What do you mean you don't know where Dad is?!" Cynthia had screamed at her. "How can you not know where your own husband is? Have you done something? What have you done to chase him off?"

Mary had tried to calm her sister down. "Now come on, Cynthia, you know how dad is. If Julia knew where he was, I'm sure she wouldn't be calling us right now." She then addressed Julia. "But it is really odd that you only chose to call us now... it's been five days... shouldn't you be a little more concerned?"

"Yes, well, no. This isn't the first time he's left for days... but it's our anniversary today, and he has never missed it before. I was hoping that maybe he had been in touch with one of you or your mother, and you might know something." Julia had felt as if she were on the defense from the moment she picked up the phone. "Please just call me if you hear from him."

"Who cares about your anniversary? My father is missing!" Cynthia had yelled into the phone. "I can't believe your whining about your anniversary when our dad is missing!"

"That's not what I meant..." Julia tried desperately to explain herself. "I just meant that's why him not being home is strange this time. He's been gone longer before, just... not on our anniversary."

"Seriously, Julia?! Can't you stop thinking about yourself for even a minute? What are you going to do about finding our father?" Cynthia had worked herself up into a rage, and Julia was not sure Cynthia was even listening to anything she was saying right now.

"I'll see what I can do in the morning. I'll call the local police station and see if they can help me," she said, trying to calm Cynthia but regretting her decision to call the girls. "Just please let me know if you hear from him."

Mary chimed back in. "We need to check the hospitals. What if he's hurt or something?"

"I did call all the local hospitals before our anniversary a few days ago. There was no record of him being admitted or any local incidents. He could be anywhere though, and I don't know where else to look." Julia felt like she needed to justify her every move since Frank had left. They didn't seem to want to hear that their dad often pulled such a disappearing act, reappearing days later as if nothing was out of the norm.

"Please, Julia, you have to do something to find him." Mary's voice sounded scared, and it reminded her of the few times she had come to Julia as a little girl when she had been frightened by a storm.

Cynthia's angry voice cut her off. "You had better do something quick and find him, Julia, or I will take matters into my own hands and it won't be easy for you then."

Cynthia had abruptly hung up the phone and Julia had been left staring at the blank screen, confused and incredulous at how the conversation had ended. She put down her phone and started to question why she had not tried harder, and sooner, to locate Frank. Never mind that his disappearances were a normal habit of his. This time had felt different, and she wondered if she should have done more.

That's when she had pulled out the wine, trying to calm her nerves and figure out what her next move should be.

Now she tenderly eased herself out of bed, regretting her decision and cursing every winemaker in the area. As she sat on the edge of the bed, she clasped a pillow to her pounding head and started sobbing. "Why Frank, why? Why do you always do this to me?" she cried into the pillow. "I've tried so hard to be a good wife. What more can I do?"

The loud pounding coming from her front door roused her from her self-pity. She wrapped a fluffy robe around her and walked gingerly to the door, finding it hard to control the queasiness in her stomach. Opening the door cautiously, she found herself looking directly at a very broad chest.

She carefully lifted her head, squinting in an effort to shield her bloodshot eyes from the blinding sun, and looked into the face of a very tall, well-dressed and stern looking man. Standing next to him was a female uniformed police officer.

"Mrs. Masterson?" The tall man inquired, taking in her red eyes, disheveled hair and apparent disarray.

"Yes, that's me," said Julia, feeling the knot tighten in her stomach. Her heart pounding almost as much as her head. She didn't want to hear what she thought they were going to tell her, and she was certain that she was going to lose the contents in her stomach right there and then; on that tall man's shiny and expensive looking shoes.

"My name is Detective Brody Barker, and this is Officer Klein." Julia looked over at the officer and tried her best to smile, desperately trying to stop herself from throwing up all over her newly painted front door.

"I was wondering if we could come in for a moment and talk?" The detective pushed his way slightly into the doorway without waiting for an answer. Officer Klein stood politely at the door, looking pointedly at Julia and waiting for an invite.

Julia eased back slightly, holding her hands over her mouth, as much to hold back the nausea, as trying to contain her shock and dread.

"Oh dear God," she said silently. "This is about Frank, isn't it? What happened? Have you found him?"

CHAPTER 3

Brody Barker walked into the open living area of the house, taking in the empty wine bottle, and the half-full glass still sitting on the coffee table marred with wine rings.

"Celebrating something, Mrs. Masterson?" he asked, looking at Julia critically while retrieving a pad and pencil.

Julia looked around at her cluttered living room. Normally a very neat person, she was appalled at how her living room looked right now. Her coffee table was stained with wine, her throw pillows were strewn around the room and blankets were half on and half off the couch. She had a vague memory of getting herself tangled in the blankets last night as she got up to angrily launch her pillows at the wall.

"No, of course not. I was upset… not celebrating. I guess I might have had a little too much to drink last night."

Brody took in her swollen, red-rimmed eyes and the pallor of her face. Judging from how the living room looked and her hungover demeanor, she was probably a booze hag and drank every night, he thought to himself. He wrote a few notes in his notebook and waited curiously for Julia to start talking. In his experience, if you waited long enough, they always itched to say something.

"Why are you here?" Julia looked from Brody to Officer Klein, trying to read the expressions on their faces. "Have you found Frank? Do you know where he is?"

Brody watched Julia closely, trying to read her face and looking for any signs of deception or nervousness.

"I am assuming you are referring to Frank Masterson, your missing

9

husband?" he asked Julia, his eyes never leaving her face.

"Yes, of course. My husband, Frank." Julia perched on the edge of her couch, trying to decide if the tight knot in her stomach was from anxiety or the wine – or both. She cursed herself for drinking too much. Her head felt heavy and numb, and she was having trouble coherently gathering her thoughts.

She looked over at the detective who had not stopped watching her since he had first walked through her door.

"Why are you here?" she asked again. "How did you know my husband was missing?" Julia closed her eyes and rubbed her head, trying to clear the fuzziness in her brain to make sense of what was going on.

"Well, it is true we don't seem to have a missing person's report from you, Mrs. Masterson." Brody walked over to the kitchen table and pulled out a chair. "Do you mind if I take a seat? I'd like to ask you some questions." Brody sat down without waiting for an answer from Julia.

"Yes, of course," Julia said, flustered. This was not how she had expected the morning to go. She had planned to go to the police station and file a report, now she was confused and feeling very uneasy.

Julia saw that Officer Klein was still by the doorway, casually standing at attention with her hand just inches away from the formidable looking gun she had holstered on her hip.

"Please, take a seat if you'd like. Can I get you some coffee or something?" Julia looked from the detective to Officer Klein and back again. She wondered what the protocol was for entertaining the police.

"I think we are fine for now," Brody answered for both of them. "Why don't you take a seat and maybe we can get on to some questions. You look a little shaky, Mrs. Masterson."

As Julia sat down, she could feel the bile in her stomach churning and her head throbbing. *Curse that red wine*, she thought. Right then and there, she swore she would never have another drop of alcohol.

"Did you say your husband is missing? Exactly how long has he been gone?" Brody held his pencil over the notebook he had placed on the table, poised and ready. He watched as Julia shook her head slowly a few times as if trying to clear her mind. *Or maybe she was buying time to come up with a story*, Brody wondered.

"I guess it's been about six or seven days now. I'd have to go and look at the calendar," Julia answered truthfully, despite feeling sicker and sicker. All she wanted was to stop with these games and for them to tell her if Frank had been found. "Do you know where he is?" she demanded, looking back and forth between the detective seated at her table and the officer parked by her door. "Please, if you know anything, let me know. I've been worried sick."

Still not taking his eyes off her face, Brody answered accusingly, "I'm just curious, Mrs. Masterson. If you were so worried, why didn't you come to the station and file a missing person's report?"

Julia looked down at her hands guiltily.

"I was going to go this morning," she said, not looking up and feeling like her head was going to burst.

"Hmmm, I see. Do you think it's a little odd that a wife would wait for six days before actually starting to look for her husband?" Brody's voice remained cool and calm as he asked his question. He tried to keep his face expressionless and void of any accusation. In his experience, it was helpful to appear non-judgmental during questionings.

Julia looked at the cool and composed face the detective was displaying and swallowed hard, wishing desperately she had just gone to bed last night and trying to keep the bile that had now risen to her throat at bay. "My husband has a habit of leaving for a few days at a time. Usually business stuff. Unfortunately, this is not that unusual for him."

Brody was writing in his notebook as she spoke, and didn't look up as he asked, "And yet you said you were worried sick about him when we first walked in? If this is normal behavior, why would you be worried at all, Mrs. Masterson?"

Julia took a deep breath and swallowed hard. Her hands and face felt clammy, and her normally lustrous hair was stuck in clumps to her sweaty forehead. She stared at the detective's face in confusion, wondering where this line of questioning was going and how this would help find her husband.

Brody took in her confused gaze and decided that if he were going to get any real answers this morning, he would have to do a little prompting.

"I was just wondering, Mrs. Masterson, why Mr. Masterson's two daughters, who apparently live in Ohio, needed to file a report about their missing father when you live here with the man and did not find it necessary to file one?"

Julia stared at the detective, trying to comprehend what he was saying. All the while, the contents of last night's supper, combined with the wine, finally made a heroic last-ditch effort.

The vile mixture forced its way into Julia's throat, before expelling its contents right there on her newly refinished hardwood floor.

Brody Barker jumped up, startled, as Julia suddenly sprung up from her seat and hurtled herself towards the bathroom, slamming the door shut behind her.

Officer Klein reflexively put her hands to her gun and ran after Julia, followed closely by Brody. Brody was about to bang on the door and demand that Julia open it, when it became apparent from the sounds coming through the door what had prompted Julia's hasty exit.

Officer Klein grinned at Brody and backed away from the door, in a feeble attempt to give the woman a little privacy. "Looks like Mrs. Masterson is not a very good drunk," she remarked.

"Maybe there are a few more empty bottles lying around?" said Brody, looking around. "Why can't these early morning interviews ever go smoothly? I haven't even had my first cup of coffee yet," he grumbled miserably.

He looked at Officer Klein hopefully. "Ok Kate, in your experience, how long will this little stomach cleansing session last?"

Kate grinned even broader, delighting in Brody's discomfort at the situation. "Don't get your hopes up, Brody. I doubt you're going to get much out of her for a while. Unless, of course, you want to question her while you're holding her hair back?"

Brody groaned loudly. "Why always me?" he moaned. "Why do I always get stuck with the drunks?" He walked to the kitchen table and settled in for a long wait. "You might as well head back out on patrol, Kate. There's no sense in both of us wasting an entire morning waiting for her to sober up."

CHAPTER 4

Julia woke up on her bathroom floor with her head resting on some of the fluffy new towels she had recently bought. For the second time that day, she tried to orient herself and figure out how she had ended up here, and just like earlier that day, she cursed all the winemakers in the region; this time even those in the state were added to the list.

Struggling to her feet, she looked in the mirror and groaned at her own reflection. Her eyes were red and swollen and her hair was matted and stuck to her face. She opened her mouth and examined her teeth and decided her breath would probably wake the dead at this point.

Still trying to figure out exactly what had transpired that morning, what time it was, and where on earth her phone was, Julia decided that the best course of immediate action was to take a shower and attempt to look and feel a bit more human.

A little later, after a long and rejuvenating shower, Julia wrapped herself in a fresh towel she had grabbed from the linen closet. Her hair hung long and wet around her shoulders, but at least she smelled clean again. She had scrubbed her teeth until the fuzzy feel on them was finally gone and she shook her head experimentally, delighted that the pounding in her head had stopped.

Still wrapped in her towel, she ventured forth in search of her phone, determined to call the police station and find out what they knew about Frank's whereabouts.

When Brody heard the bathroom door open, he glanced up. His seat at the kitchen table had provided him with a magnificent view of the ocean as well as a clear view of the bathroom door. Watching Julia's towel clad figure emerging, he almost whistled at her well-toned frame and her long legs peeking out from under the short towel. He felt his pulse quicken a bit and wished he was waiting here for her under different circumstances. As she approached, still holding her towel tight, she kept her head down, seemingly looking for something.

"Aaaaah!" Julia screamed when she saw the detective sitting at her table, almost dropping her towel in her fright. "What are you doing here?!" Julia demanded.

Studying her face carefully, Brody let the question linger for a few seconds before answering. "Waiting for you to finish being sick."

Julia saw her phone sitting on the table next to the detective and snatched it up quickly. "Oh, uh, I thought you would have left by now." She looked around for the female officer, wondering if she was still standing guard at the door.

"I told Officer Klein to leave and continue her shift," Brody remarked, noting down Julia's reactions, and how strongly she clutched her phone. "We weren't sure how long it would take for you to compose yourself, and Officer Klein had some pressing matters to attend to."

Julia clutched her towel closer and looked at Brody suspiciously. "And you don't have anything more pressing to do than wait for a woman to sleep it off?"

"No, Mrs. Masterson, there is nothing more pressing on my schedule today than finding a missing man."

Julia's breath caught in her throat and she felt the same tightness in her stomach she had felt for nearly a week. There was something about the detective's tone that made her feel uneasy.

"No? Maybe not. Although, I'm not sure how you sitting at my table all morning will help find Frank. And I assure you, detective, I'm as anxious as you to find my husband."

Without the constant threat of her stomach losing its contents, and with her head a little clearer, Julia finally felt bold enough to look the detective squarely in the face. What she saw were a pair of clear, dark eyes staring coolly back at her, set in a chiseled, well-defined face, with lips that, at the moment, were in a straight and uncompromising line. She found herself wondering if Detective Barker ever smiled.

"It would have been very bad press if I left you passed out on your bathroom floor in your own vomit and something happened to you, Mrs. Masterson," Brody said matter-of-factly. "It's my duty to ensure that anyone who needs help gets it. I hope that you weren't too attached to the towels I placed under your head?" Brody queried.

His eyes never left her face, although Julia thought she sensed a slight hint of amusement in his voice.

She blushed slightly, envisioning the broad-shouldered, well-dressed detective crowded in her bathroom, shoving towels under her head while she was unconscious.

Julia started to back out of the kitchen towards her bedroom, a sick feeling of anxiety forming in the pit of her stomach. "If you'll excuse me, I'd like to go and get dressed now." As she continued to back away from him, his eyes never left her, making her feel like a trapped fly struggling to get away from the watching spider ready to pounce.

"Of course, but please don't be too long. This would not be the time to decide to run any errands Mrs. Masterson, if you know what I mean. My time is not completely unlimited, and I would hate to have to come and find you to finish our conversation." Julia shuddered slightly at the barely veiled threat and hurried to throw some clothes on.

A few minutes later, she had thrown on a pair of shorts, a t-shirt, and wrapped her long dark hair in a loose bun. She had grabbed a bottle of sparkling water and had offered the detective one as well. To her surprise, he had accepted this time. *So, he is somewhat human*, she thought to herself.

As Julia sat across from him at her kitchen table, Brody pulled out his notebook and his pencil once more. Watching him perform this ritual again and studying the plain number two pencil, Julia wondered out loud, "Do you ever use the eraser?"

"Pardon?" he asked, looking at her without a trace of humor.

"Never mind." Julia shook her head. "Let's just get started. I'm anxious to know if you know anything about my husband's whereabouts?"

"If you don't mind, and with all due respect Mrs. Masterson, I have waited the entire morning and half the afternoon to get this going. I would prefer to be the one asking the questions."

Julia shrugged her shoulders, attempting to look nonchalant despite the tension starting in her neck.

"Let's start at the beginning again, shall we?" Brody looked at her with one eyebrow slightly raised, not really expecting an answer. "When was the last time you saw your husband?"

Julia wrinkled her forehead slightly, trying to think. "The last time I saw him was Sunday morning last week. I was out running and he left before I returned. I texted him and asked where he had gone. I had planned to make us lunch and wanted to know if he would be back in time."

Brody watched her silently, waiting for her to continue.

"He said he had some sudden and urgent business to take care of and not to wait up; it might take a while." Julia sighed and continued. "I pestered him a bit about when he planned to return and why he had left so suddenly. He has been leaving more and more often and for longer periods of time again, and I was frustrated and wanted some reassurance that he wouldn't be gone long this time."

Brody looked up from his notes. "And what did he say?"

Julia looked down at her hands sadly, "He was angry and wouldn't give me an answer. He accused me of stifling him, being selfish and not letting him take care of his business. I have the texts right here." Julia picked up her phone and handed it to him.

Taking the phone, Brody began to read the texts; he jotted down a few notes here and there. "I see there is nothing after this day other than outgoing texts from you to him?" Brody looked at her curiously and handed her back the phone.

"No, I haven't heard back from him."

"Tell me, Mrs. Masterson, how did your husband leave that day? I saw a car in your carport. Did he have his own car or was he picked up?"

"I'm not really sure," Julia said, trying to think back. "I guess I assumed at the time he had just taken an Uber. We only have one car for now. We had agreed two cars was a waste of money seeing as we planned to retire and would probably do everything together." Julia smiled bitterly.

Brody continued to scribble in his notebook. "So, you don't know where he went, exactly when he left or how he left?" he asked, looking up with a frown on his face.

"No, I guess I don't," Julia said, a bit defensively. She looked at Brody, her eyes challenging him to doubt her. "Look, I know that sounds a bit strange, but it's happened so often that I just don't question it anymore. It's just become part of our married life."

"And how long have you been married, Mrs. Masterson? You do, of course, know that, right?" Brody did not attempt to hide the frustration and sarcasm in his voice.

"Of course I know that," Julia answered, somewhat irritated at his tone and insinuations. "We have been married 25 years as of yesterday. It was our anniversary."

Brody looked at her, surprised. "Your anniversary? Was it common for your husband to leave you alone on your anniversary?"

Julia shook her head vigorously. "No, that's just it. That's the one day we always spent together, no matter what. One time Frank even flew back from China on short notice and on a very expensive flight, just so he wouldn't miss it! That's why it was so strange when he didn't come home or answer my calls or texts. I had a whole day planned for us and even bought him some special cookies and had them delivered from Ohio. I still can't believe he didn't come home."

Julia felt tears welling up in her eyes but willed them away. This was no time to show weakness or cry. She needed the detective's help to find Frank.

"And how did that make you feel, Mrs. Masterson? I certainly would have been upset if I had gone to so much trouble to plan a special day and my husband didn't show up."

Julia thought back to her frantic run on the beach and her uncharacteristic outbursts. "Yes, I guess I was a little angry and disappointed. Everyone has their breaking point."

Brody closed his notebook and gave her an odd look.

"Yes, Mrs. Masterson, that's been my experience as well. As you say, everyone has their breaking point."

Brody rose from the kitchen table, stretching slightly, feeling stiff after having sat for so long.

Julia looked up at him, a bit panicked. "Wait, what now? How do we find him? What happens next?" Julia watched his face, hoping for an answer. She wasn't sure if she saw pity, disdain, or suspicion in his face.

"Mrs. Masterson, I am wondering if maybe you know the answer to that question better than any of us." Brody looked down at the pale figure in front of him, wondering if she and her husband were pulling some kind of scam or if she was possibly solely responsible for his disappearance.

"Your husband's daughters called us this morning, asking us to look into the suspicious disappearance of their father. It seems they are convinced that you might have a lot to do with his disappearance and know where he is."

Julia gasped in disbelief. "What? They think I have something to do with Frank's disappearance? That's ridiculous! I just spoke with them last night. I told them I didn't know where he is."

"Maybe so, Mrs. Masterson, but until we get this cleared up, I'm asking you not to leave town for any reason without letting me know. I suspect until we find out what happened to your husband, we will be spending quite a bit of time together."

CHAPTER 5

Brody sat in Kate Klein's cruiser, his shirt sleeves rolled up, exposing strong forearms. He lifted the binoculars to his eyes yet again.

"Do you think she offed him?" Kate asked, stealing a glance at the well-built, handsome man sitting in her cruiser.

"I don't know what happened to Frank Masterson, Kate, that's what we're here for. To follow the leads and see where they take us." Brody put down the equipment and rubbed his tired eyes.

He had been following Julia around for two days now and had come up with nothing. He prided himself in solving his cases quickly, but this one had stumped him. There had been no sign of life from the missing man for at least 8 days now – no cell phone pings, no credit card charges, nothing. And following Julia Masterson around was also yielding nothing. She had not done anything out of the ordinary.

He picked up the binoculars again, looking for Julia in the crowd of people below. He and Kate had watched as she took off on a run and continued to observe her from a distance when she returned nearly half an hour later. She proceeded to strip down to a bikini, and Brody watched her as she dove into the ocean and swam with the current in a way that looked almost majestic.

"That was quite a run she took," remarked Kate. "I guess that's how she stays in such great shape. She could teach us a lesson or two."

Brody just grunted and looked over at Kate. She was one rock-hard, muscled female and very proud of it. Brody doubted that, regardless of her excellent running style, Mrs. Masterson could hold a candle to Kate Klein when it came to physical fitness.

Brody shifted uncomfortably again in the heat. He hated this kind of surveillance. He wasn't cut out for long hours of sitting around doing nothing and he resented that he had been assigned this case. In his opinion, it was probably a simple open and shut scenario. Either the husband had had enough and had run off, or the attractive Mrs. Masterson didn't want to be married anymore and pulled a Black Widow move on her husband.

Either way, the case was lackluster at best and Brody was frustrated at his own inability to solve this case quickly and move on. He had been pulled off a human trafficking case he had been working on for months, and he was bitter about having to solve a domestic dispute instead.

"Why do you think the chief is so hot about a missing person's case anyway?" asked Kate, taking the peel off a ripe banana and shoving it in her mouth.

Brody shot her an annoyed look. She had been munching on fruit all morning and her chewing, coupled with the smell of hot overripe fruit, was starting to get on his nerves. He had discarded his jacket in the back of Kate's cruiser, but he was still hot and irritated.

"Who knows? It's an election year. He always goes all cock-eyed during election years. I guess it doesn't look very good when a respectable businessman goes missing on his watch and the perp might get away with it."

Kate laughed at the quip and threw her banana peel out the window.

"What?" she said, catching Brody's sharp look of disapproval. "It's biodegradable."

Brody opened his car door and got up, stretching his long, cramped legs. "I'm going to take a walk and get a closer look; check if I can see or hear anything of interest," he said to Kate. In truth, he doubted he was going to discover anything new today, but he would go crazy if he had to sit in that car for another minute.

"Suit yourself," said Kate. "Want me to stick around for backup or head out for some patrol work? I can drop your jacket in your office when I get back in," Kate offered.

"Yeah, you head on out," said Brody, already walking away. "I doubt I'll need any backup with Mrs. Masterson."

"Don't be too sure about that," mumbled Kate under her breath, "that might be what her husband thought before she took him out." And with that, Kate started up her car and peeled out of the parking lot.

Brody strolled along the short boardwalk, trying to look casual. Even so, he knew he stood out with his shiny black shoes, slacks and rolled-up shirt, but he needed to get out of the car. One of the reasons Brody liked to work alone was to get away from the incessant babble a partner inevitably forced on him. His best ideas happened when he had a clear mind and no one buzzing in his ear. There had been one exception to that rule – one partner he had worked well with many years ago. Brody shook his head, trying his best to suppress memories of his ex-partner from his mind.

Leaning casually against the pillar and doing his best to stay in the shadows, Brody watched as Julia Masterson emerged from the water. Her body glistened alluringly as she slowly sank into a lotus position, arms resting on her knees with her palms up, as if either offering or accepting something from some unknown force.

Voodoo witch, thought Brody, resenting the way his body was responding to hers. He had looked up her bio and found out that she was some kind of Reiki master. Apparently, she had a number of clients and people willing to pay good money for her services. He had tried to look up what Reiki was but had only managed to find out it had something to do with some kind of energy stuff that sounded a lot like supernatural hocus pocus to Brody. He was not the most church-going Christian in town, but he nevertheless liked to steer clear of any witchy stuff. Down here in the Keys they had their fair share of cults and warlocks, and it never ended well.

Despite his mistrust, he was fascinated at the stillness she was able to maintain, seemingly oblivious to her surroundings. He enviously wondered what that must feel like. For years now, Brody had been fighting against an inner unrest and anger that he seemed to be losing control of. He had started to think he might need to go to some kind of counseling after all or risk losing his temper and end up doing something he regretted.

As he watched her, a breeze picked up slightly, blowing her long dark hair away from her face, and exposing a small, perfectly formed nose and a finely chiseled profile. Brody absently let his mind wander and imagined himself walking over and discussing meditation with her, allowing her to gently move her hands over his body, drawing out the bad energy and letting the warm sun take away any lingering tension left in him. As he let his imagination have free reign, he wondered if she were the type of woman who would agree to a little afternoon romp and what a nice distraction that would be for him.

"Stalking a new love interest?" A voice next to him commented.

Brody was startled out of his idle musings but forced himself to remain immobile. He was embarrassed that he had been caught so unaware, and it took a bit of effort to remain nonchalant.

Not wanting to let on where his mind had been, he casually turned to look at Krystle Davis, the local reporter and a past love interest. "Hardly. Probably more like a Black Widow." He was disgusted at himself at how Krystle had been able to sneak up on him and was determined to sound as offhand as possible.

"Interesting," said Krystle raising her eyebrow slightly with interest. "So, what's the scoop on her then?"

"Come on, Krystle, you know me better than that." Brody gave her a slight smile. Krystle was a short, attractive blonde woman with a very voluptuous build, and she knew how to use her assets to her advantage.

Krystle just shrugged. "You know how I am. Once a reporter, always a reporter. Never hurts to ask."

Krystle bumped slightly against Brody with a suggestive smile. "If you're not stalking and if you're not on the clock, maybe you'd be interested in a little afternoon recreation? You know, for old times' sake?"

Brody looked down at the woman gazing at him suggestively, half tempted to take her up on her offer. Watching Julia for two days had certainly stirred up some desires in him and Krystle might just be the one to take care of those urges. He had been avoiding Krystle, knowing that she was interested in a much deeper relationship than he wanted despite the casual attitude she tried to portray. He was hoping to avoid muddying the waters even more.

Somewhat reluctantly, Brody shook his head, "Sorry Krystle, not today. I am still on the clock, and I've got a lot on my mind. Besides, I thought we had decided last time that it wasn't a good idea for either of us to hook up again?" Brody grinned down at her.

After he had not answered some of her calls, she had left a message saying they should probably not continue their occasional trysts. She had told Brody that as a reporter it was a bad career move for her to be seen with a cop. People might not trust or open up to her anymore. Brody suspected it had more to do with him not taking her calls, but it was fun to throw it back in her face now.

"Suit yourself cowboy, but women do change their minds you know. You know where to find me if you change yours." With that, Krystle gave him a sly wink and walked away.

Brody shook his head slightly at Krystle and continued to watch Julia sitting on the sand. She slowly stood up and stretched out a bit still seemingly oblivious to anyone around her. She shook out the shirt she had discarded after her run and pulled it over her head, shaking out her long hair as she reached down and slowly stepped into her shorts.

Then, looking directly at him, she started walking in his direction.

"Are you planning on stalking me for the rest of my life, or maybe at one point you will start looking for my husband?" Julia looked up at him, challenging him to deny he was following her.

Brody casually pulled away from the pillar he was leaning on and looked directly at Julia, "Maybe I'm doing both?"

Julia expelled an aggravated breath and looked Brody directly in the eye. "Look, I don't have anything to do with my husband's disappearance. I am as confused as you and even more desperate to find him. You just following me around will not solve anything because I don't know where he is. Instead, maybe it would be more useful for us to work together to find him?"

As Julia was delivering her speech, she raised her hands, almost beseechingly to Brody, and now she let them fall helplessly to her sides.

21

Watching her face and body language, Brody almost believed her, but the detective in him was still wary. He had seen too many cases of the spouse pleading innocence and turning out to be a cold-blooded murderer.

Considering her suggestion, Brody thought back to his hours in the hot and cramped car, sitting next to a sweaty Kate Klein, munching on overripe fruit. That had yielded him absolutely nothing. Spending time with Julia Masterson seemed eminently more appealing. Besides, if she allowed him access to their house and Frank's personal belongings, he might finally find something there that would lead him to the missing man. It was unconventional, but it was a golden opportunity to get to know her and her motives.

"Ok, deal," Brody said warily. "But if we are going to get to the bottom of this and find your husband, you need to be straight with me and answer my questions. No matter how personal."

Julia licked her lips nervously. She didn't really relish the thought of opening up about Frank and her marriage secrets, but she could think of no better alternative. She nodded her head slowly in agreement, saying nothing.

"Great," Brody had a slight smile on his face, finding he was actually looking forward to spending time with her instead of following her in a hot car, sweating like he was in a sauna.

"I'll pick you up for dinner at six. That will give me a chance to get some background on you and your husband tonight, and we can start combing through some of his paperwork in the morning."

Shocked, Julia looked up at him. "Look through his papers? I wouldn't dare look through them. That was one of Frank's strictest rules."

Brody stared at her, incredulous. "For God's sake Julia, umm… I mean Mrs. Masterson. The day your husband disappeared, for whatever reason, he gave up his rights to privacy. If we want to find him, we need to do some good ol' fashion detective work and start at the beginning."

Julia still seemed a little hesitant but nodded in reluctant agreement. "Maybe you're right, and it's ok. Call me Julia. I guess if we are going to spend time together, it makes sense to lose some of the formality, detective."

For the first time, Julia saw Brody Barker smile a genuine smile. It traveled all the way up to his eyes, slightly accentuating laugh lines that she hadn't noticed until now. She wondered if maybe he had laughed more when he was younger, and what had made him appear so jaded now.

"Agreed. Call me Brody. I'll walk you up to your house and call a car to come and pick me up from there." Taking her arm gently, Brody proceeded to guide her back to her house.

*

Later that afternoon, after a long, hot shower to help soothe her nerves, as well as clean off the sweat from her run, Julia looked at the clothes she had laid out on her bed.

What exactly does one wear to a dinner with a detective? She wondered.

She had been on several dates with her husband, albeit fewer in the last few years, but it had been decades since she had been to dinner with a strange man.

Picking up a cute little black dress, Julia quickly discarded it back on the pile. This isn't a date, she chided herself. Julia sat down on the edge of the bed and looked at her clothes reflectively.

So exactly what is this? She thought to herself.

An interview? A collaboration of sorts, or was this an interrogation? Cupping her head with her hands and resting her arms on her knees, Julia shuddered. How had her life, that a few weeks ago had seemed so simple and finally full of promise, turned into such a mess?

It seemed like only yesterday she had booked the catamaran trip for Frank and excitedly chosen all his favorite dishes for their anniversary meal. She had been so full of hope and anticipation when she had called his favorite baker in Ohio and ordered his favorite cookies. What had gone wrong? What had she done?

Julia's mood fluctuated between anger and humiliation as she thought about how she had been so certain that with just a little effort on her part, she could make Frank happy and be the attentive husband he always promised he would be.

Did you play me? Why, Frank, why? Where are you?

The questions kept screaming around in her head until she stood up and shook her head in frustration, trying hard to rid herself of the worry and self-doubt.

Julia looked at her clothes and grabbed a loose-fitting, light blue, slightly floral shirt that cinched at her waist. Slipping it on, she looked at herself in the mirror and thought, this will do. It flowed easily to her calves and was modestly cut. Grabbing a belt to accentuate her waist, she hastily threw it back on the bed.

What if he's lying and plans to arrest me tonight? Will they let me keep the belt? Instead, she grabbed a warm cashmere sweater. *It might be cold in a jail cell,* she thought wryly.

Sitting at her makeup table, she looked at her pale face. She had not been sleeping well since Frank had left. She tried to think back to the last morning when she had gone for her daily run and Frank had left. Why had it felt different this time, and why had she had this overwhelming sense of foreboding ever since he had left? And more so, why on earth had she not acted on it and reported him missing earlier? Would that have changed anything? Would they have already found him and would that have avoided the cloud of suspicion that now hung over her?

Moaning slightly and rubbing her head, Julia tried to empty her mind of all the why's and what if's. She had learned long ago it did no good to live in either the past or the future. The only control she had was in the now. So, what then had she been thinking when she had suggested she spend time with a detective who thought she was probably a kidnapper, or worse yet, a murderer? Shaking her head at her own folly, she tried her best to apply enough makeup to at least cover the fear gnawing deep in her gut and showing in her eyes.

Unaware of the inner turmoil his suspect was going through in the house, Brody sat outside in his unmarked car a few houses down, watching her house. He was dressed casually, as befitting a casual dinner with an old friend.

Best to keep her at ease and lose some of the formality, he thought.

Taking a last look at the front door to make sure no one was entering or leaving, he glanced down one more time at the notes he had jotted in his notebook. He would try not to pull it out during dinner. He hoped to get her to speak freely, and an open notebook would probably not be helpful.

Had she and her husband tried to pull off some insurance fraud? Had their plan somehow gone bad, or was Frank going missing part of a big plan? Was Frank Masterson still alive, and if not, was she responsible? Could she possibly have hidden his body somewhere and had she had help?

The questions kept running through his mind. She seemed too innocent and vulnerable to be a cold-hearted murderess, but he knew if she were involved in any way, she had to be cunning. He absently wondered how many bottles of wine it would take to get Mrs. Masterson drunk enough to start talking

CHAPTER 6

Brody sat across from Julia staring at the almost empty bottle of wine belligerently, almost daring it to say something to him. His plan of getting Julia drunk and talking had backfired royally. He had ordered red wine, remembering the brand on the bottle he had seen sitting on her coffee table at their first meeting. After pouring her a generous glass, he also poured some in his own glass, hoping to make her feel more at ease by joining her. Unfortunately, either Julia didn't drink much after all, or she was the most controlled booze hag he had ever met.

After the initial few sips, she had stuck to mainly sipping her water. He had occasionally attempted to top off their glasses, hoping to encourage her to drink, but the end result was most of the wine had ended up in his own glass. Brody could hold his beer like any good cop on the beat, but give him some wine or champagne and his brain started turning into that of a 16-year-old at his first binge drinking party.

His initial questioning had been rudimentary; he already knew most of the answers from studying the couple's bio. It was amazing what was out there on the internet without even having to search very hard. He decided it was best to keep the questioning to a minimum and maintain a casual and friendly conversation. He didn't trust his own tongue at the moment. He found himself concentrating less and less on her answers and more on losing himself in fantasies of what the evening could have brought had it been under different circumstances. Annoyed with himself, he shook his head to clear out some of the cobwebs created by the wine and tried to focus on why he was here.

Julia gazed out over the water, oblivious to the beauty of the sunset and deep in her own thoughts. Brody had chosen a cute little clam place on a dock sitting directly over the water. The seagulls were busily and loudly flapping around the tables, hoping to snag some scraps. Normally, Julia would have loved the place, but today, the pungent odor of fish permeating from the kitchen was causing Julia's already nervous and queasy stomach to churn. She could sense Brody studying her and turned her attention back to the man sitting across from her.

"Penny for your thoughts," Brody said, trying to encourage her to talk without coming across as aggressive, and feeling incredibly foolish for the childish saying right after the words left his mouth.

Julia had the decency to smile at him at least. "I guess it's just slowly becoming real to me." Julia gave a slight shrug of her shoulders. "I think a huge part of me still believes that he is going to come home at any moment and act like nothing abnormal has happened."

Brody studied her face and asked, "Has anything abnormal happened? You keep insisting it's not that unusual for him to leave for long periods of time?"

Glaring at him slightly, Julia answered, "Yes detective, this is abnormal. Even for our marriage. For one, I do not usually sit at a small, romantic little dinner table with a strange man and spill family secrets while my husband has been missing without a word for over a week!"

Brody had the decency to look slightly chastised. "Sorry Julia, I didn't mean to seem unsympathetic. It's just that you said numerous times that your husband often went AWOL and I'm naturally curious why this time is so different for you." Brody searched her face and demeanor, looking for any tell-tale signs of deception or discomfort.

"Well, it's not unusual for him to be gone, but he usually checks in with me at least every couple days. It's been over a week now and I haven't heard a word from him."

Julia clasped her hands together, looking down. "This is also the first time that his girls have claimed to not have heard anything from him. I guess I never thought about it, but he must have kept in more frequent contact with them than I thought." Julia looked at her clasped hands pensively, silently wondering if there was anyone else that Frank had kept in contact with and what else she didn't know.

As if reading her mind, Brody asked, "Was Frank having an affair Julia?"

The question hit her like a ton of bricks, and she looked up at him, startled that he had read her thoughts.

"I don't know, detective. I never thought about it being a possibility before now. Frank has always been so busy, much too busy to spend time with me anyway, that I always assumed he would be much too busy for anyone else. Now, I'm starting to wonder. Maybe he was so busy *because* he was spending time with someone else." Julia angrily brushed away the tears she felt welling up in her eyes.

I will not cry or show weakness in front of this detective, she thought, frustrated with herself.

Brody instinctively reached out and put his hand over Julia's cold clenched fingers. She might be a suspect in her husband's disappearance, but right now, he couldn't help feeling a little sorry for the lost looking woman sitting across from him. Her hands felt small and weak in his, and he rubbed his thumb over them absently.

"I'm really sorry, Julia, I don't want to upset you, but we have to follow all the avenues right now if we want to find Frank. The bottom line is that a man is missing and no one has heard from him for almost 10 days. His daughters suspect foul play, and until we find him, I will be forced to ask you a lot more uncomfortable questions."

His hand had felt warm and comforting just a moment ago, but now Julia snatched her hands away from his. "I know that," she said sharply. "You have a job to do, and I have a missing husband to find." She looked at him desperately, her eyes softening slightly. "It's just all so surreal. I can't seem to stop sea sawing between being angry at him leaving and worrying about where he might be."

Brody's ears perked up slightly at her admission of her anger. Finally, an emotion he could understand. Could this be the motive he had been looking for? "It must have made you angry a lot, having him run out on you all the time. I know I would have been furious with my ex if she had just taken off without telling me."

Julia looked at him curiously. "So, you've been married and divorced? Do you have any children, detective?"

"Yes, we were blessed with three kids. Two boys followed by a little princess." Brody smiled fondly at the thought of his daughter.

"The divorce must have been hard on them. What happened? You don't seem like the type of man who would just walk out on his responsibilities." Julia's face showed only true concern without any judgment, and since Brody couldn't detect any trace of malice or even just idle curiosity in her, he continued.

"It was hard on them, I guess. It's always the kids who suffer in a breakup. Our story was the same story as hundreds of other cops. Too much time spent on the job; too little spent with the family. Add to that the constant threat and tension of worrying about whether I would be coming home at night, and I guess it all just got to be too much for her. One night she had my bags packed and just asked me not to come back." Brody spoke matter-of-factly, not letting on that it had been one of the worst nights of his life.

"Oh no, that must have been an awful shock." Julia sat wide-eyed, trying to imagine what it would be like to come home from a dangerous job to find your bags packed and your home closed to you. "What did you do then?

27

Where did you go?"

Brody just shrugged his shoulders, trying to remain nonchalant. "I went and crashed with another cop for a while. My story is not unique. Cops always take in other cops, and we probably took in our share of thrown out cops while Holly and I were still together too. We never thought it would happen to us, but I guess it's inevitable in my line of work, and to be honest, it was kind of a relief."

"What? Leaving your kids and family was a relief?" Julia was puzzled. "How is that even possible? I think I would be devastated. I always wanted children, but Frank already had two and he didn't want any more. I think I would have gone insane if he had taken them from me."

Brody filed that piece of information away in his mind for a later date and continued. "Holly didn't take the kids away from me. She was always a great mom and let me see them whenever I wanted, and whenever they wanted to see me, they could. To be honest, I think we all got along better after the divorce. I made more of an effort to see the kids, and I didn't feel the pressure of disappointing Holly all the time."

Brody stopped short and watched for Julia's reaction, marveling at how she had turned the tables on him and had questioned him.

Her face looked attentive, and she seemed to be genuinely trying to understand what it had been like for both him and Holly at the time.

"I guess I just can't understand how two people who committed to one another can just divorce and give up. That was one of Frank's highest commandments. Absolutely no divorce. It goes against everything our church taught us. When two people commit in marriage, it's for life," she quoted.

Brody bristled at what he thought were very judgmental words. "Maybe divorce is not the ideal solution, but it is sometimes the best solution in some cases. At least we are both still here and one of us didn't end up missing." He remarked coldly.

Julia's face paled and she stared at him in shock. "I have nothing to do with my husband's disappearance," she said, in a very clipped tone. Sliding her chair back, she stood up and said, "I believe that the conversation is over for tonight, detective. Like I said before, I don't believe your accusations are getting us any closer to finding my husband. Please stay and enjoy the rest of your evening. I'll request for an Uber to take me home."

Brody stood up as well, regretting his stupid outburst and blaming the wine for his lack of professionalism. "Look, Julia, I'm sorry. That's not what I meant. I guess maybe the divorce is still a touchy subject for me. Let me just drive you home and, tomorrow, we'll start going through some of your husband's papers and see if we can find any clues as to where he might have gone."

As Julia stood there, undecided on what to do, she realized just how tired she really was. She didn't really want to go through finding and waiting for an Uber, but she also didn't want to talk about Frank and her relationship anymore; she certainly didn't want to go through his papers tomorrow. Sighing in resignation, she finally relented. "Fine, let's just go. I'm tired and I just want to go to sleep and forget this nightmare, at least for tonight."

Julia stood on the curb and waited for Brody to pull the car around, wondering what she had done to deserve this mess and how she was ever going to find Frank. When Brody pulled up, he got out to open the door for her and she slid in gratefully, sinking back against the soft leather of the seat and closing her eyes.

Watching her out of the corner of his eye, Brody wondered how much of her fatigue was an act and how much was real. *She certainly did look worn out,* he thought.

He tried to imagine what it would have been like for him if Holly had just disappeared on him, and how desperate he would have felt. He found himself resisting a strong urge to reach over and take Julia's hand in his. He shook his head and focused back on the road.

People don't just disappear, he thought. There is a reason and a resolution to every mystery and in his experience, the most logical answer was usually the right answer. The innocent looking Julia Masterson had to have had something to do with her husband's disappearance.

CHAPTER 7

The following morning, Brody sat at Frank's desk in a fairly organized office located at the back of the house. His head felt clearer than the night before, and he decided that wine and questioning a suspect was a mix he would steer clear of in the future.

Julia perched on the edge of an easy chair, nervously tapping the side of her coffee cup. "Are you sure this is necessary? One of Frank's strictest rules was that I never enter his office or mess with his papers." As she spoke, she kept glancing nervously at the door to the office, as if expecting Frank to come bursting angrily through the door at any minute.

"Yes, it is necessary. These papers might hold the key to where Frank went, or at least, may point us in the right direction to look." Brody didn't look up from the papers he was studying. Julia could revoke her permission for him to look through the papers at any time. From what he could see, it seemed that Frank Masterson had dabbled in quite a few financial endeavors, and Brody was eager to follow up on them. "You said you never come in here?" he asked, now glancing up briefly.

"No, there was no need. Frank was an accountant. He always took care of the finances. If I received any checks from clients, I just deposited them into our account. He gave me an allowance, and if I needed more money for something, he gave me access to our credit card."

Brody looked at Julia incredulously. "You mean in 25 years of marriage, you never once paid a bill or looked at your bank account?"

"No, like I told you, Frank was an accountant. He took care of our finances so there was no need. He prided himself in taking care of us and I never lacked anything, so I just let him."

Brody shook his head in disbelief. *Who spends 25 years never writing a check or looking at a bank account?* He wondered.

"I was young when I met him. I think I might have been looking for a bit of a father figure and he jumped right in from the beginning and took care of me. He made me feel safe." Julia wasn't sure why, but she felt the need to explain herself.

Still looking through the papers on the desk, Brody asked, "Where did you two meet, exactly?"

Julia smiled a bit at the memory. It seemed like so long ago, and she had been so young. "I was still in college. Frank was tutoring a bunch of us students."

Baffled, Brody looked up. "There's a course in college for Reiki, and Frank was tutoring it?" he asked, skeptical.

Laughing at the thought of Frank teaching Reiki, Julia said, "No, of course not. I was taking accounting courses at the time, and Frank was earning extra money tutoring."

"So, you were taking accounting when you met Frank?" Brody leaned back in the chair, eyeing Julia quizzically.

"Yes, why is that so strange? I was actually quite good at it," Julia said defensively.

"It just seems like quite a jump to go from being an accountant to practicing voodoo or witchcraft or whatever. I wonder what Frank thought of your switch in careers? I bet he wasn't too happy about it?"

"I do not practice voodoo or witchcraft," Julia said, looking at him coldly. "Maybe you should look into it before you judge wrongly or too harshly. A few Reiki sessions might do you a world of good. You seem very tightly wound. Perhaps after the sessions, you wouldn't jump to the wrong conclusions so quickly."

Brody looked directly at Julia, meeting the challenge in her eyes. "I don't jump to conclusions. I follow the facts and just go where they lead me."

Julia exhaled loudly, frustrated. "Even though I have told you over and over again I don't know where he is, you still think I have something to do with Frank's disappearance. If you keep looking in the wrong places, we may never find my husband." She looked at Brody, exasperated. "Maybe they should just send over a different detective. One without any preconceived ideas."

"Except that's not how it works, Mrs. Masterson. I was assigned this case and I will solve it." He looked at Julia smugly. "If you recall, I'm only here because Frank's daughters called in a suspicious disappearance. You, ma'am, did not even file a report. Clearly, your husband's disappearance was not that alarming a few days ago."

Julia stared at him, dumbstruck. "That is not true! I was planning to file a report the morning you showed up! I just never got the chance."

"Was that before or after you had your little celebration? Seems to me you were a bit too hungover that day to have made it to the police station."

Julia opened her mouth to protest, but then shut it. It was true. She would have been in no condition to file a report that day. *Why hadn't I just followed my gut and gone to the police earlier?* She thought.

Disgusted, she just said, "You have no idea what I intended to do or what I have been going through. Let's just get on with this and find my husband. The sooner we do that, the sooner you can leave me alone."

Julia stood, her arms crossed, her shorts showing off her tanned legs, and looking at him with a mixture of anger and desperation. At that moment, Brody wasn't sure if he wanted to throw her in jail or take her in his arms and guide her to her bedroom. He looked back down at the papers he had on the desk and cursed under his breath. What had gotten into him lately? Maybe he needed to give Krystle a call after all. And why did Black Widows have to be so enticing anyway?

Looking up from the papers she was skimming through, Julia sighed and stretched tiredly. She had been hunched over Frank's and her finances for hours and had found nothing unusual. Frank had always paid everything promptly and she didn't see any unusual bills. Her anger at Brody had already worn off and she wanted to make amends. "We've been at this for hours; I think I'll go and make us some coffee."

"Mmhmm, sounds good." Brody was busy laying papers in distinct little piles. *Something just doesn't quite add up,* he thought. There seemed to be missing links.

While Julia was in the kitchen, Brody pulled out the desk drawers and started searching underneath them, feeling along inside the desk and under the drawers.

Bingo.

He pulled out a key that had been taped under a drawer.

He looked up as Julia walked in with two steaming mugs of coffee. "Do you know if Frank has a safe around here?"

Puzzled, Julia set the mugs down.

"No, I don't think so. I don't recall a safe when we moved in, and I don't remember him buying one. There's the little fireproof box I showed you, but you already looked in that." Julia pointed to the little gray box sitting next to him on the floor.

Brody shook his head. No, that wasn't what he was looking for. That box had not been locked and only contained Julia's passport and some deeds and papers for joint bank accounts. Just the normal stuff couples would normally share. He suspected the key he just found opened something much more exciting.

Thanking Julia, he took the mug and stood up, looking around the room critically. *It could be here in the house, but it could also be somewhere else entirely,* he thought. He looked down and examined the key more carefully. It did not seem to have the markings for a safety deposit box. This key looked like it belonged to a home safe.

Julia came over to see what he was examining.

"Where did you find that?" she asked curiously.

"Taped under the drawer. Have you ever seen it before?"

Julia looked closely at the key. "Yes, I think I might have actually." She took a minute to think, wrinkling her brow slightly. "One day, it was laying on the desk out in the living room, and I put it in that desk drawer, so it wouldn't get lost. I went out for a run, and when I got back, Frank was so mad me. He thought I had hidden it from him apparently." Julia grimaced slightly at the unpleasant memory. "I guess he never thought to look in the drawer."

"Did he tell you what it was for?" Brody was still holding the key and scanning the room carefully.

"No, I asked but he was upset with me for moving it and never answered me. He just kept reminding me not to ever touch his things, and then he went into his office and I never saw it again."

"Hmmm," said Brody, looking even more critically around the room. "There's a good chance that what we're looking for is in this room then."

Julia followed his gaze, trying to look at the room more critically herself, as if she were a stranger who was unfamiliar with her surroundings and looked for anything unusual or out of place.

"The bookshelf!" Julia suddenly exclaimed.

Brody looked at the shelf that Julia was pointing to – it was not an overly massive piece of furniture, light and airy like the rest of the decor in the house.

He looked at Julia dubiously. "What about it? I don't see anywhere where a key like this would fit." As he spoke, he walked closer to the shelf and examined its contents.

Julia shook her head, "Not on it," she agreed. "Maybe behind it?" She walked over and started pushing slightly.

"Frank let me buy every piece of furniture in this house, including the desk and the rest of the furniture in here. He didn't comment on any of it. The only thing he insisted on was that we buy a bookshelf, and it had to have wheels."

Brody looked down and saw that the shelf was indeed sitting on 4 rustic-looking wheels, which at first glance, seemed to be decorative. He helped Julia push the shelf, the wheels squeaked slightly but they moved. When they had pushed it aside, they saw the shelf had covered a door.

"Oh wow, there's a door here. I don't remember that being here when we bought the place. Of course, I was more focused on the rest of the house, the office was always going to be Frank's domain anyway."

Wiggling the doorknob, Brody remarked, "It's locked, of course."

"The key?" Julia looked at him inquisitively.

Brody shook his head. "No, it's too small to be a door key. We can always take the door off its hinges, but do you want to see if you have any keys that fit in it first?"

Julia thought for a moment and then walked out and returned with a few keys, each on separate key chains. "Some of these are marked and some aren't. I guess we can just try them all. We kept all the extra keys in the desk in the living room. That's why I put the one you found in the drawer also."

Brody was doubtful that any of the keys would fit, but started trying them anyway. None of the unmarked keys fit the lock, but then Brody took a closer look at one of the labeled keys. "Do you have a basement here?"

"No. I don't think any house this close to the ocean has a basement. Why?"

"Because you have a key here marked *basement*," said Brody, as he put the key in the lock.

Both Julia and Brody watched in anticipation as the door clicked and Brody pulled it open.

"It's just a closet," said Julia, disappointed and trying to see inside through the darkness.

"That's probably why you didn't really notice it when you moved in," remarked Brody.

Leaning in slightly, Brody pulled a string attached to a single overhead bulb. The closet filled with the harsh fluorescent glare of the bulb.

"And there it is," said Brody triumphantly, looking at the safe that took up most of the closet space.

Julia stared at the safe, dumbfounded. "I don't understand. Why would he have that? I've never seen it before."

Watching her carefully, Brody thought he detected true confusion in her expression. *Either she has never seen this before, or she is one really good actress,* he thought.

"Well," Brody held out the key. "It's your house and I don't have a warrant, so it's your call for now. Do we open it?"

Julia glanced nervously to the door of the office, looking guilty. "Yes, I guess we had better look and see what's in it. It might give us some clues as to where Frank went."

As Brody opened the door to the closet wider and struggled with the key to the safe, Julia felt her stomach and chest tighten in apprehension. She felt like a school kid who had found her parent's secret stash of wine and was about to drink it. One of Frank's major rules was that she stayed out of his private spaces. She had rarely disobeyed that rule, not wanting to incur his wrath.

"Here we go," said Brody, swinging open the door to the big safe.

Julia's eyes grew wide as she stared inside it. Stacked on the top two shelves were what appeared to be rows and rows of gold bars.

Brody let out a low whistle, "He's got a regular mini Fort Knox in here."

Shaking her head in disbelief, she couldn't draw her eyes away from the gold. "I had no idea. Where did he get all that? How did he get it in here without me seeing it?"

Brody bent down and examined the lower shelves of the safe. He started pulling out stacks of files and what looked to be financial portfolios. "These might give us some answers," he said.

He picked them up and transferred them neatly to the desk. Julia was still staring into the safe at the gold incredulously. She had never seen so much gold in one place. *Where had Frank gotten all of this?* she wondered.

Brody coughed, clearing his throat and trying to draw Julia's attention to the desk. As she pulled herself away from the safe and over to the desk, Julia's hands started to grow icy and her stomach and chest constricted so tight she was finding it hard to breathe.

Brody looked at her concerned, "Are you alright? Here, sit down," Brody pulled out the desk chair for her. "Should I get you some water?"

Grateful, Julia sank into the chair and nodded. Brody returned a few moments later and handed her a glass of water. She took a huge gulp, closed her eyes and tried to breathe evenly. When she had gathered herself a bit, she looked at Brody with a tense and panicked look.

"I don't think we should look through these." Julia pointed at the stacks of files lying on the desk.

"What?! Why? We are going to have to if we want to find out where your husband is." He eyed Julia suspiciously.

Julia wasn't looking at Brody, though. She was looking at the stacks of folders with trepidation. "What is all of this?" she murmured silently.

Finally, she looked up at Brody. "I can't just shuffle through his private papers. He will be livid." She looked at Brody beseechingly, willing him to understand.

Brody studied her again. She looked so forlorn and shaken as she sat there in front of the mountain of folders. The detective part of him also noted she had said he would be livid. So, she either believed or she knew that Frank was still alive.

Shaking those thoughts away for now, he knelt down next to Julia and held her icy hands in his big warm ones.

"I can understand that you want to respect your husband's privacy," he said gently, "but we don't know where he is or what kind of trouble he might be in. If we can find him, we can help him if he needs it."

Julia's body shook even more. "Oh! What could he have gotten himself into!" she sobbed. She looked down at Brody with tragic eyes. "We have to find him. We have to help him," she said finally.

But instead of looking through the folders, Julia suddenly crumpled, pulling her hands away from Brody and bringing them to her eyes, sobbing uncontrollably.

Awkwardly, Brody stood up next to her and started to lightly pat her on the shoulder. "There, there Julia. Stop crying. We'll find him." His words only seemed to cause her to cry even harder. She crumpled down further into herself, her shoulders shaking violently, her body wracked with sobs.

Brody stood there, looking down at her and not knowing what to do. He had never been good at handling others' emotions and he was at a loss.

Finally, he awkwardly and slowly knelt next to her, pulling her down with him onto his lap, and held her like that. He cradled her against his chest, holding her like he used to hold his daughter when she was young. Julia curled into him and continued to sob inconsolably. They sat there for another five minutes or so, until Brody's shirt was soaked with her tears.

When her crying finally subsided, they just sat there for a little while longer. Julia found comfort in the safety and strength of Brody's arms, while Brody relished the soft feel of Julia's body against his, feeling an overwhelming urge to protect her.

"I'm sorry. I think I've soaked your shirt." Julia finally sat up, looking at Brody sheepishly and trying to slide gracefully off his lap.

Brody's lap felt empty and cold where she had sat and he reluctantly helped her to her feet, pulling them both up.

"No worries, it will dry." He looked down at her concerned face. Her eyes and face were red and swollen, but despite her disheveled looks, he still found her immensely attractive.

"I'm ok now. I don't know what came over me. I'm sorry you saw that." She didn't look at him directly, slightly embarrassed at her unsophisticated break down. She shuddered one last time.

Still trying to hide her discomfort, Julia said, "I'll just go and clean up a little and bring us some fresh coffee. You can go ahead and get started if you like."

Brody just nodded and watched her walk out of the office, his arms still aching to hold and comfort her. Discomfited at his own feelings, he found himself looking up at the ceiling, "God, please don't let her have anything to do with her husband's disappearance," he said, in a feeble attempt at a prayer.

CHAPTER 8

As the afternoon wore on, Brody was engrossed in the stacks of folders and portfolios. A clearer picture of Frank Masterson was starting to form in his mind, and he wondered how well Julia really knew her husband and how he would tell her about the information they had just discovered.

Julia had agreed to let Brody look through the papers, but she couldn't bring herself to do the same. It had felt like too much of a violation of Frank's privacy, and she feared what he would do when he found out. Instead, she had shuffled through the same old bills and checks she had been looking at all morning, not really seeing what she was looking at.

Her mind wandered back to early in their marriage, and to the first time she had seen the full power of Frank's wrath. They had had a short and intense courtship. Julia had done well in her classes and was just about to graduate when she had met Frank. She had been unsure and scared about her future at the time, uncertain what she would do with her life once she left the safety of the campus. Frank had seemed like such a steady and safe alternative to a lonely and frightening life in the big city.

His mother, father and sister had welcomed her with open arms. He had seemed kind and attentive, and above all else, safe. When he proposed, she had eagerly accepted, glad to have a direction and purpose in her life again. The wedding had been a small but glamorous affair. Frank's children had not attended. In fact, at that point, she had not even known Frank had children.

She found out about his children a few weeks into their marriage. Frank had left the house and she had been shopping online for some new bedding. Frank had urged her to leave her job, so she had not worked since they got married. He had promised to provide her with whatever she needed, and right then, she had needed a credit card to complete her purchases. She had walked into the office, looking in the drawers where she had seen Frank put the credit cards in the past. Instead, she found canceled checks, handmade cards, and pictures of two girls that looked remarkably like Frank. Stunned, she looked through all the drawers, until she found what seemed to be at least 10 years' worth of Father's Day and birthday cards to Frank from his *daughters*.

Frank had walked in and seen what she was looking at, and his face had turned from shocked to furious within moments. When she asked for an explanation, he screamed at her that she had no right to invade his privacy. He had grabbed her by the arm and dragged her off to the guest bedroom, locking the door and telling her she would need to stay in timeout until she repented and apologized. She had yelled and pounded the door, demanding for an explanation and begging to be let out, but finally, she had just worn herself out.

Frank had returned with a plate of food later that evening, asking if she was ready to apologize yet. She had still been confused and angry and demanded to be let out immediately with an explanation of why he had never told her about his children. He had looked at her coldly and said if she acted like a spoiled and ungrateful brat, she would be treated like one, and walked back out. Over the years, she found if she did not anger Frank, their marriage remained relatively peaceful and calm, even blissful at times, and she had become a master at appeasing him.

Julia roused herself from her memories and looked at Brody, sitting on the chair with a serious and concerned face. She had not told Brody this, but besides insisting on the bookcase, Frank had also insisted their new home have a spare bedroom.

Brody looked up and caught Julia staring at him with a curious look on her face. He smiled at her reassuringly but wondered how much, if anything, she knew about what all these folders contained.

"Any clues?" she asked, finally walking over to the desk.

"Julia." Brody began cautiously, "Did you know that Frank was providing for multiple families?"

Julia visibly paled.

"Multiple? What do you mean by multiple? Of course, Frank has been taking care of his girls and their mother since they were born. And he's been providing for us as well. Is that what you mean by multiple?"

Shaking his head, Brody looked down at the notes he had scribbled on a pad in front of him. "No, Julia, I mean multiple. I see as many as four or five families here. And I've only been looking for a few hours."

Julia started to shake slightly. "Why would you say families?"

Pushing a well-used handwritten ledger towards Julia, Brody answered, "Is that what your husband told you? Right here, look. Family A, B, C and D, and then here is the name Masterson Family."

Uncomprehending, Julia looked down at the neatly written, precise looking ledger. It was clearly written in Frank's meticulous handwriting and all the entries were painstakingly recorded. Each column belonged to a particular family, showing all expenses and payments – very much typical of what Frank would have done.

"Maybe he was supporting families in need, like charity cases or something?" Julia looked at the ledger hopefully, looking for some clues that Frank was just being philanthropic. As she looked closer at the ledger, Julia gasped. "Where was he getting all that money from?" she wondered out loud.

Brody was rifling through some other folders. "We'll have to keep searching to find that out, I suppose." Glancing up at Julia, Brody asked, "Was your husband the philanthropic type?"

Julia gave him a rueful smile. "Hardly. Frank was a firm believer *in you reap what you sow*. He took care of his kids because he created them and felt strongly that it was his duty to take care of them."

Cautiously Brody looked at Julia and said, "I guess we can probably rule out charity cases then?"

Julia looked down at her hands, crestfallen. Silently she whispered, "Yes, that's not the explanation for all this then."

Brody couldn't resist the urge to get up and take her in his arms again. "It's going to be ok Julia; we'll get to the bottom of this."

He gently stroked the hair cascading luxuriously down her back and cradled her head against his chest.

Julia leaned against his strong chest, trying to take comfort in the arms that were holding her close. With her head sideways against his chest, Julia could see through the open door and out her big picture bay window. She watched the waves of the vast ocean crashing in and out with the surf.

Still resting her head against Brody's broad chest, Julia whispered, "Where are you, Frank? What have you done?"

PART TWO

CHAPTER 9

It was dark outside and Julia was having a hard time seeing through the dense fog that had formed over the ocean. The waves splashed up higher and higher up her legs, as she struggled to wade through the rough waters. Her heart was pounding at 90 miles a minute and her eyes strained in the darkness, looking for her husband. She thought she could see a faint outline of a man up ahead and she called out frantically, trying to catch up to the vague figure. The waves grabbed at her legs, making it almost impossible for her to move, and she could feel herself being sucked into the ocean further and further. Panicked, she cried out for help, but the figure just kept going.

In the distance, she could hear the faint sound of beeping. As she struggled to keep her footing, her heart threatened to pop out of her chest and she felt herself being pulled into the ocean until the waves were pressing on her chest. The beeping sound grew louder and louder, and Julia flung herself towards the shore in a desperate attempt to get out of the pounding waves threatening to drown her.

Julia woke to find her legs helplessly tangled in her blanket, and her body doused in sweat. Her alarm was beeping incessantly on the nightstand next to her. Trying to calm her ragged nerves, she breathed deep and reached over to turn off the alarm. She looked around her bedroom, shaking off the last remnants of the nightmare.

Julia untangled her legs from the blankets, reached for the glass of water next to her, and took a long drink. Ever since she had realized her husband was missing, she had been having the same nightmare on repeat for the past two weeks. She always woke up drenched in sweat with her heart pounding in terror.

Looking over at the clock, she saw it was 6:30. The sun was just starting to glow a pale pink over the horizon. She sat on the edge of the bed, attempting to gather her thoughts and composure. Julia had always been an early riser, but the sleepless nights and nightmares from the last two weeks had left her sluggish, and she was relying more and more on the alarm to get her up in the mornings.

She wrapped a robe around her thin shoulders and padded into the kitchen. She had set the timer on the coffee maker the night before, and it had faithfully done its job. The rich aroma of freshly brewed coffee permeated her kitchen and she gratefully poured herself a cup and sat at the table by the huge bay window overlooking the vast ocean. She and Frank had only moved here less than six months ago and this view was one of the reasons she had bought the house.

As she sipped the hot coffee, Julia shivered slightly in the cool dawn. She contemplated throwing on her yoga pants and either going for an early morning run along the beach or greeting the morning with some yoga stretches. For most of her adult life, her morning ritual had been either a run or yoga, often both. But the last few weeks had been different. Today, she sighed and leaned back in her chair, cradling her coffee in two hands. Like yesterday and the day before, she could not muster the strength or the will to go about her morning rituals. Today would be no different.

As the sun slowly filled her house with its cool, pinkish glow, Julia glanced around the house. Just a few short months ago, she had been filled with such anticipation and hope as she carefully picked out the furniture and decorations. They had brought very little with them from their old home in Ohio.

The old house in Ohio had been large, opulent, and much too stuffy for Julia's taste. Frank already owned the home when they met and had not allowed her to make many changes in the 25 years they had lived there.

It had been different here in the new house. Frank had allowed Julia free rein when decorating. The result was a beautiful light and airy house and she had felt truly comfortable and at home for the first time in their marriage.

Julia got up, cradling her hands around the coffee cup. She wandered around their home, examining some of the little details she had incorporated into the aesthetic of the house and circled back to stand in front of the big window.

Had Frank been as unhappy here as I had been in Ohio? She wondered.

For the first time in 25 years, she had felt free and happy, and had been so preoccupied with creating their new life here she had not even asked him if he also liked it. Maybe she had been too self-consumed to notice his unhappiness or dissatisfaction.

The buzzing from her phone pulled her out of her reverie. She glanced down at the phone and saw that it was Brody, the detective who had been assigned to her husband's missing person case.

"Good morning, Brody, how are you?" Julia put the phone to her ear while setting her coffee cup on the table.

"Morning Julia, I hope you slept well."

Julia didn't mention her nightmare. "Fine, thank you. Any news this morning?"

Brody had been checking in with her fairly regularly since he had taken the case, but this morning was earlier than usual.

"I was wondering if you had some time this morning. I have some things I'd like to go over with you and some questions I'd like to ask."

"Yes, of course. Just give me an hour and I'll be ready." Julia sighed.

More questions, she thought.

She didn't understand his work of course, but it seemed that the detective spent an awful lot of time asking her questions. If she knew where Frank was, she would tell him. Maybe Brody should be out following leads, and not asking her so many personal questions.

Back at his cubicle, as he hung up the phone, Brody absently let himself imagine how Julia probably looked right now – the tousled hair and pouty mouth, eyes probably still puffy from sleep. He felt the now familiar tingle of anticipation in his stomach at the thought of seeing her later and tried to ignore the feeling. He took a final glance at the papers scattered on his desk and wondered how much Julia knew about what he had discovered. He couldn't help but wonder if she would be shocked when she learned what was in the papers. He glanced down at his watch and stuffed the papers into a brown leather satchel.

Just enough time to grab some breakfast at the local diner, he thought as he got up.

*

Julia was still shuffling through the papers and ledgers that were now strewn about on Frank's desk. She looked up at Brody every now and then and the confusion on her face was clear.

"I don't understand. There are so many accounts, and they're scattered all over. It isn't like Frank to have such a muddle with his finances. He is usually so concise. Where is all this money coming from?"

Brody shrugged his shoulders. "I don't know. I haven't been able to find that out yet. I'll keep digging, but honestly, he has hidden his trail with so many bends and turns. With accounts in so many countries, I'm not sure I can unearth exactly what is going on." Brody impatiently pushed some ledgers towards Julia. "What about these Julia? Do you know any of these people? Do you recognize any of the names?"

Julia reluctantly looked at the ledger. The names were all neatly written at the top of the pages above columns of numbers with dollar signs. She only recognized the name of the mother of Brody's children, Jane Harper, and what she supposed was herself, Julia Masterson. There were three other names, all female, and she did not recognize any of them.

"You think he was sending all of these women money, don't you?" she asked Brody, the anguish clear in her eyes.

"I think that all the evidence points that way, Julia, yes."

"Maybe they're relatives or old friends?" Julia looked up at Brody, desperately looking for an alternative explanation.

"We've already looked at all of his relatives. These women are not related to him. Unfortunately, we only have their names to go on. We don't have any addresses or even the state they live in."

Julia nodded, but she was still in shock at the thought of Frank supporting four other women. Of course, she had known he was sending money to Jane, to help take care of his children, but the sum shown on the ledgers far exceeded anything she had ever imagined. She had never really asked him about it, and he had never complained about sending her money.

"Listen, Julia, I know this is hard, but we need to follow up on these women. One of them might be the key to what happened to Frank."

"You mean he might be shacking up with one of them?" She looked at Brody defiantly, daring him to deny the possibility.

"Anything is a possibility at this point, Julia. We just need to follow all of the leads."

In truth, Brody did not believe that Frank was just shacked up somewhere with a woman. There was no evidence of any movement on any of the accounts since Frank's disappearance and Frank's cell phone had not been used either. He had not told Julia yet, but they had found records of another cell phone, also registered to Frank. There had not been any recent activity on that phone either.

Brody watched as Julia absently shuffled through the ledgers; although it was clear she was not really reading them. Her eyes had an absent and haunted look to them. He still couldn't decide if it was from despair or guilt, and he struggled with just how much to tell her.

Finally, Brody asked, "Did you know that Frank had a second phone, Julia?"

She looked at Brody with her eyes wide in shock. "What!? Why would he need a second phone? You mean like a business phone?"

Brody shrugged his shoulders. "We think he was using it to call Jane Harper and the other women on the list. We're still trying to trace some of the numbers on it to see if we can figure out who was on the receiving end. We believe some of the calls were made to some offshore banks as well."

Julia leaned her elbows on the desk and cradled her head in her hands. She was finding it hard to comprehend this new bit of news.

"I just don't get it. Frank was always so strait-laced and such a rule follower. He was almost nerdy and boring. How could he have kept all of this from me?"

Silently, Brody wondered the same. It didn't seem plausible that Julia could have been blind to what Frank had been doing.

"Well, the further we dig, the more complicated your husband's life seems to get, that's for sure."

Brody started to gather the papers back together and stuffed them into his satchel. It was clear that he was not going to find the answers he needed here. What Brody still needed to figure out was whether Julia was hiding something or whether she really didn't know.

"Think about the names Julia. If anything occurs to you, call me and let me know. We are trying to set up an interview with Jane Harper in Ohio. I'd like her to take a look at some of the names as well and see if she knows any of them."

Julia looked at Brody disappointed that he was leaving already. Since Frank's disappearance, she had felt lost and often lonely. She didn't have many friends here yet and it would be odd to strike up a conversation about her missing husband with a total stranger. There was something comforting about having Brody around and being able to talk about her concerns with someone who knew her situation.

"You're leaving already?" she asked.

Brody recognized the lost look on her face. His mother had had the same look after his father had died when he was a teenager. She had often looked at him the same way as he had been running out of the house to go and hang out with his friends. He had ignored it then and lived with that regret for the rest of his life.

"I need to follow up on these numbers and accounts and see if they lead us anywhere," he explained.

"Oh, yes of course." Julia looked down, crestfallen.

"Listen, I have some time later and I was planning to take out my boat and clear my mind a little. Maybe, if you like, you can join me and we can brainstorm a little out on the water."

Brody regretted the words as soon as they left his mouth, wondering what had gotten into him. It wasn't customary for a detective to take a suspect out for a ride on his boat. He knew he had stepped over the line and was preparing to apologize and withdraw the offer when the look on her face stopped him.

"Why yes, that would be wonderful. I would love to get out on the water for a bit. I haven't been on a boat in such a long time. Frank was afraid of the water."

Brody lifted one eyebrow, looking at her curiously. Hadn't she told him that she had planned a catamaran ride for their anniversary? It seemed he still had a lot to learn about Julia Masterson as well.

"I'll pick you up at three and we can head down to the dock together then," he said.

As he shut the satchel and headed for the door, he decided he would ask her about the anniversary trip later on.

CHAPTER 10

Julia stood on the dock, waiting for Brody to remove the cover off his boat and check the riggings. She held a cooler full of snacks and drinks. While preparing the cooler, she realized she really didn't know what Brody liked to eat and drink, so she had prepared a little of everything. The result was an overstuffed, very heavy cooler.

Brody walked over after his checks and prepared to help her onto the boat. He lifted the cooler with a grunt. "We're only going to be on the water for a few hours Julia," he said, grinning. "I assure you, we won't get lost at sea."

Julia smiled sheepishly. "It's better to be prepared."

She didn't want him to know she had spent the morning trying to anticipate what he liked and didn't like.

"I've never been this far out on the ocean and you never know. Didn't you watch Gilligan's Island when you were a kid?"

Brody laughed at that. In truth, he and his brother had spent many hours after school watching Gilligan's island and emulating the huts and hanging hammocks in their backyard.

Julia scrambled aboard, trying to get accustomed to the rocking of the boat. Brody directed her to sit up front next to the driver's seat. He released the moorings and expertly guided the boat out of its slip and into the harbor.

Julia watched in admiration. "You've done this a time or two, I see."

Brody just grinned down at her. "I grew up in the Keys. I wouldn't be a true native to the area if I didn't know how to handle a boat."

They were silent while Brody guided the boat out towards the open water, the waves splashing up more the further out they went. Julia relished the warm sun and the rocking of the boat, closing her eyes and hearing the waves splash against the sides; the seagulls screaming in the background.

As he guided the boat further out in the water, Brody glanced over at the woman sitting next to him from time to time.

With her head slightly leaned back, and her eyes closed and serene, Julia looked the furthest thing from a conniving wife. He tried to picture what it would be like if she were not a suspect in a missing person case he was working on. It had been a long time since he had taken anyone out on his boat. Normally, he reserved his time out on the water for himself, selfishly protecting this last bit of tranquility in his life.

Julia roused herself and settled in sideways, watching him maneuver the boat through the waves. "It's peaceful out here. I imagine you come out here often to unwind."

Brody looked up ahead, steering the boat into a wave and focusing on the buoy a little way out that they were headed towards. "I try to come out as often as I can. I'm a bit of a workaholic, so I guess it's not as often as it should be." He didn't mention to Julia that if he hadn't felt bad for her this morning, he would probably be working right now.

Julia had noticed some fishing gear as she had boarded the boat. "So, you fish also huh?" she asked. "Do your boys like to fish as well?"

Brody navigated another wave and glanced over at her. "They used to when they were younger. Now they are off at college and busy with sports. My oldest is studying engineering, and the middle son is busy playing college soccer at UNC Greensboro."

Julia looked duly impressed. "You must be very proud of them. Are you able to go and see any of your son's games?"

Brody shook his head regretfully. "Not very many. It's quite a trip to get there and the job doesn't really allow me to just take off for soccer games. Holly was the soccer mom while they were growing up." He didn't mention that his lack of attendance over the years had been a major source of contention between Holly and himself. "Becky likes to come out with me and fish sometimes," he added, smiling.

Julia gave him a curious look.

"Becky is my daughter." He explained. "She's a junior in high school. She's also into soccer and cheerleading in the off-season, but every once in a while, she'll come fishing with me."

"Sounds nice, father-daughter time is important." Julia thought back on her own childhood. Her parents had never been married and her father had taken off shortly after she was born. There had not been any father-daughter time in her life.

Brody nodded in agreement. "Yes, I don't think she really likes the fishing that much, but it gives us a chance to catch up."

Julia smiled a little, trying to imagine the serious detective listening to the chatter and drama of a high school cheerleader.

As if reading her thoughts, Brody smiled back at her. "Did you bring any bottled water in that massive cooler you brought?" he inquired.

"Of course, let me grab some."

Julia got up, headed towards the back of the boat and bent down, just as a huge wave slammed into the side of the boat. Flailing frantically, Julia felt herself get sucked over the side and into the ocean.

Julia held her breath as her body sank further and further down into the depths of the ocean. She opened her eyes and looked around in the murky water, picturing all the sea creatures that she knew were probably swimming around her. She felt strangely calm.

In comparison to the relentless pounding of the waves aboard the boat, the ocean seemed tranquil and quiet down here. She started to kick her feet and used her arms to propel herself to the surface of the water.

When she finally broke the surface of the water, she gasped for air, but her senses were immediately assaulted by the unrelenting waves, threatening to pull her under again. She struggled to tread water and looked around for Brody and the boat, marveling at the vastness of the ocean.

"Julia, Julia!" Brody finally saw Julia's head bobbing in the waves a few yards from the boat and frantically called out to her. "Hang on, I'll be right there!"

He expertly spun the boat and maneuvered it until he was only a few feet from where she was puddling to stay afloat. "Here, grab hold of this." He threw her a white rescue buoy attached to a rope.

Julia grabbed it and allowed herself to be pulled over to the side of the boat. Brody reached over the side and she felt strong arms grab and pull her into the boat.

"Are you alright? Did you swallow water?" Brody was eying her anxiously. "I'm so sorry Julia, that wave came out of nowhere. I should have been more careful!"

Julia looked up at him calmly, surprised at how anxious and worried he seemed.

"I'm fine Brody, don't worry." She grabbed the towel he held out to her and wrapped it around her, feeling the sun already warming her chilled skin.

Brody looked at her, astonished at her composure after having been swept into the ocean. Holly had fallen in once and it had terrified her so much she had never gotten on the boat again.

"Do you mind if I just take off the sundress? I do have a bathing suit on underneath," Julia asked, grinning.

"By all means… off with the soggy dress," Brody said, laughing, delighted and surprised that she didn't seem to be upset with him for pitching her into the ocean.

Julia slipped the wet dress over her head and secured it to the side of the boat, so the ocean breeze and the sun could dry it off. She flung the towel over her shoulders and headed over to the cooler.

"Now, however, I think I could use a wine cooler," she remarked.

She brought over her drink, and a bottle of water for Brody, and sat back down in the seat next to him. Brody had let the engine idle while he was pulling Julia over the side, and now, he started the engine again and headed towards his destination.

He looked at Julia, sitting next to him sipping her wine cooler, and wondered at her remarkable composure. She seemed completely at ease, sitting there and allowing the hot sun to dry and warm her skin.

When they reached their destination, Brody threw in the anchor and headed for the cooler himself.

"I guess I can allow myself a beer after that scare," he said, popping the can and settling into a seat in the middle of the boat where he could stretch his legs.

"You were scared?" Julia looked at him in amazement. It had not occurred to her to be scared.

Brody laughed at her. "Yes, I was scared! You fell into the ocean, Julia. You realize you could have drowned?"

She just shrugged her shoulders. "I can swim. I told you that when you asked if I wanted a life jacket, remember?"

Brody stared at her, amazed. "I didn't expect you to go overboard though. How is it you're not more shaken up?"

"I guess it never occurred to me I could drown," Julia answered truthfully. "Naturally, it was a shock falling into the cold water. But it just seemed so peaceful under the water, so vast and serene. It just never occurred to me to be afraid."

Brody thought back to the times he had been scuba diving, and could completely understand what Julia was describing.

"I take it you have never been scuba diving or snorkeling then?"

"No, I never have. Is that what it's like?" Julia asked. "I think I definitely want to try it."

"There are some great places in town to sign up. They'll take you to some of the nicest coral reefs we have around." Brody informed her before taking a sip of his beer.

Julia looked at him wistfully. "Oh, that would be nice. I've never experienced anywhere so peaceful and serene. Frank has never liked water much, so we didn't spend much time by the ocean."

As she spoke, Brody saw Julia's calm face become tense and sad again. It was as if she just now remembered the situation she was in.

"You've mentioned a few times that your husband didn't like the water…" He felt a bit like a cat pouncing on an unsuspecting mouse, but the detective in him was relentless. "I'm just curious why you booked a catamaran trip out on the ocean for your anniversary if he didn't like water." Brody studied her face carefully as she answered.

"Frank saw catamarans on one of our first days here. He seemed excited at the idea of getting into one, saying they seemed steady and secure. Frank has never shown any interest in going out on the ocean, so I jumped at the chance. I guess I hoped if he liked it, we could go out more in the future as well."

Brody couldn't see any signs of deception on her face, and the explanation seemed plausible enough. While Julia was looking down at the water, Brody took the opportunity to study her closely. Her tanned skin glistened in the sun, still slightly damp from the splash of the waves against the boat, and in Brody's opinion she had the most amazing body he had ever seen. He pictured her leaning against him, and how her warm skin would feel as he cradled her in his arms, her hair gently blowing against his face.

A sudden wave jolting the boat roused him out of his reverie. He chastised himself for allowing his mind to wander. Brody prided himself in his professionalism and he knew better than to allow himself to daydream about a potential suspect. He reasoned it had been way too long since he had spent any time with a woman.

To keep his wandering mind in check, he tried to make a mental note of all the evidence he had gathered so far and was frustrated at his lack of progress. The evidence neither completely pointed to Julia nor exonerated her. Though, watching her as she skimmed her hand lazily in the water, it was hard to believe she would be capable of any crime.

"How did you and the mother of Frank's children get along?" he asked, breaking the peaceful silence.

It seemed that Julia had been daydreaming as well, as Brody's sudden question jarred her upright and to attention.

"We didn't really meet that often," Julia answered, suddenly reminded again of the dire circumstances she found herself in. She had allowed herself to be lulled into a type of meditation by the rocking of the boat and the sound of the waves lapping on its hull. Brody's sudden question brought her back to the stark realization of her missing husband.

"I really only saw her on a few occasions when we went to pick up the girls, or if we met by chance. Frank made a point of picking his daughters up by himself most of the time."

And I prefer it that way, she thought to herself.

She had always felt like the interloper, or the "other woman" when it came to Jane Harper.

"And when you did meet, what was the interaction like?" Brody pressed on, not letting her off easy and wanting an answer to his question.

Julia thought back on the few occasions she had met Jane. The meetings had naturally been strained and awkward, but they had always been relatively cordial.

"I guess they went alright. It was awkward of course. I don't think either one of us really knew how to act, so we were polite and got the interactions over as quickly as possible."

Brody furrowed his brow.

Two women both interested in the same man, he thought to himself. He found it hard to believe that none of them had any hard feelings about their situation.

"There were never any bad feelings, or bad words exchanged? No accusations, nothing?" Brody pressed on, hoping she would remember something, anything that would help explain Frank's absence.

Julia just shook her head. "I'm sorry Brody, but we never spent more than a few minutes in each other's company, and even then, Frank did most of the talking for us both. We said the cursory *hi's* and *goodbye's* and *it was nice to see you again,* but that was it." Thinking back on those occasions now, something struck at Julia.

"To be honest, now that I think back on it, Frank seemed to be more uncomfortable and perplexed than either Jane or I. He did scramble a lot, and like I said, he did most of the talking. Maybe he was making sure that neither of us told the other anything." Julia frowned. "Who knows, maybe he was hiding things from both of us?"

Brody nodded his head, agreeing that was more than likely. "I'm really hoping that we can get an interview with Miss Harper soon. I'll be very interested to hear what she has to say about the father of her children and her take on his disappearance."

Julia looked at Brody curiously. "You know, I'm really starting to wonder about a lot of things that Frank told me over the years. Do you think I could go with you to that interview? I think I have a lot of questions for her myself."

Brody thought about it for a minute. It would be highly unusual for a suspect to be present at an interview with a witness, but as it was, both women could either be a suspect or a witness. Brody thought that he might glean more about Frank from how the two women interacted with each other within a controlled environment. Maybe he'd finally find the answers he has been looking for.

"No promises, but I'll see what I can do," he finally said. "For now, I still haven't been able to get her to agree to see me, and if she refuses to see you, there is nothing I can do."

Julia nodded in understanding. "Of course, but if it is possible, I think it will help clear up a lot of confusion and answer a few questions I am starting to have."

Brody again found himself admiring her composure and wondering how she kept it together. He wasn't sure how he would react if he were in her shoes, but he sure doubted he would be this calm and collected. In fact, he was pretty certain he would be cursing at the moon, stars and sun and anything or anyone else who would listen.

Julia heard Brody's stomach grumble and laughed at him. "I packed some sandwiches for us to munch on. Here, let me get them."

As she edged over to the cooler, this time staying low to the floor of the boat, Brody laughed at her, "Not quite ready for another swim yet?"

"Nope, one dunking a day is enough for me," she said and handed him a sandwich.

Brody gratefully grabbed the sandwich and the chips she handed him, taking a big bite and settling back into the seat, watching her get settled as he ate.

Julia smiled at him and started on her own sandwich, surprised at how hungry she was. "I guess the salty air makes you hungry," she commented, shoving some chips in her mouth to go with her ham sandwich.

Brody grinned back and agreed. She could certainly use a few extra pounds he thought, noting that although she had probably always been slender, he could see the outline of a few ribs showing.

Julia happily munched on her sandwich and looked out over the ocean, thinking there was no better view in the world, and marveling at how comfortable she felt with Brody. She had never been much of a flirt and had always felt rather shy and awkward around men. Even when Frank had brought home business associates, she had hidden in the kitchen or gravitated to the women in the group, never feeling comfortable conversing with the men. Right now though, she felt as if she had known Brody her whole life and didn't feel strange or awkward. She wondered if it was the intimacy of the boat or if it was the man himself.

"So tell me, Julia, how does one go from being an accounting major to a Reiki master? That seems like quite a stretch to me."

Julia took another bite of her sandwich, contemplating how to best answer the question, without opening up her heart or revealing her past too much.

"It wasn't really a sudden or spur of the moment decision," she said. "I think it was probably more of a process or even an evolution."

Brody took the last bite of his sandwich and listened to her intently.

"After Frank and I were married, Frank wanted me to quit working and

53

spend more time with him. He insisted that I could work with him at his firm, and it would be easier to sync our schedules. I hadn't really been at my firm very long, and I didn't want to quit so soon after starting there. I really liked the people I was working with, and I liked the feeling of independence it gave me."

Julia frowned, remembering the arguments they had had about her quitting her job.

"In the end, I guess he just wore me down and I gave in and quit. It seemed easier that way and caused less conflict. It made Frank happy, and it certainly gave me more time to spend on him."

"It sounds like you had quite a rough start to your marriage," Brody commented.

"I think all couples need some time to get used to each other and each other's habits," Julia said defensively.

Not wanting to offend her, Brody agreed. "I guess that's probably true. So how did you get into that Reiki stuff?"

"I worked with Frank for a while, but he was much too controlling, and I didn't enjoy it at all. I felt like I was always trying to read his mind, and he seemed to be upset with me a lot when I didn't do things exactly the way he would have done."

Brody was right, Julia thought, that had been a very tumultuous time in their marriage.

"I slowly drifted away from his business more and more until I became a full-time stay-at-home wife. I was in charge of our dinner parties and social events, and to be honest, I was miserable and tense most of the time."

Brody had seen firsthand how shy and reclusive Julia could be, so he could imagine hosting social events would not have been fun for her.

"One day, at one of our social events, I met a woman who could see how tense and unhappy I was. She suggested that I take up yoga and meditation. That was the start of a whole new life for me."

Julia thought back to her first yoga class and smiled. "I have to admit I was pretty awkward at first, but I had a great teacher who was patient with me, and I got the hang of it soon enough. While I was in class, I met another woman who was a Reiki master. After my first session with her, I was hooked."

"So, what exactly happens in a typical Reiki session?" asked Brody. "Do you chant or something?" He was trying to remember what he had read online.

Julia laughed. "No, no chanting. You don't really do anything but lie there. Sometimes there might be some soft music. The practitioner uses their energy to connect with yours and attempts to calm and heal your body. In my first session, she just barely ran her hands over my body. Afterward, I felt calmer than I ever had. I knew almost at once that I wanted to be able to help other people like I had been helped."

Brody looked at Julia doubtfully. "She just ran her hands over you without touching you and you felt it?" He shook his head. "It still sounds like a bunch of voodoo to me. It doesn't sound like anything a good, God-fearing person should be dabbling with."

Julia could feel herself getting angry at Brody's lack of understanding. She took a deep breath and attempted to gather herself. It was not the first time someone had compared her craft to witchcraft or voodoo, but for some reason, it bothered her more when Brody did it. In her opinion, yoga, meditation, and Reiki all blended together and had been a major catalyst in changing her life for the better.

"It's not at all like that," she explained. "Let me do a session with you once and you'll see."

"Uh uh, no way. I think I'll keep my energy to myself."

Julia was just about to protest some more when Brody's phone started to ring. The stormy look on his face when he answered it was enough to convince Julia to keep quiet.

CHAPTER 11

Brody hung up the phone abruptly and turned to Julia. "Sorry, Julia. I hate to cut this short, but I need to get back."

"Is everything alright? Did something happen?"

Brody hauled in the anchor and busied himself getting the boat ready to take off. "Sit back up here and hold on tight," he said without answering her, "We are going to be fast this time."

Julia did as she was told and clung tightly to the handles by the seat. The salty ocean spray hit her face and the boat jumped and slammed down on the waves as Brody sped along, heading for shore. She found the ride rather exhilarating and fun, but when she dared to take a quick glance over at Brody, she saw that his face was set in a grim and determined expression. Finally, they neared the harbor and Brody slowed the boat and eased it into its slip.

Brody efficiently moored the boat and threw its cover on as quickly as he could. Julia grabbed her cooler and hopped to shore, trying to stay out of the way, unsure of how to help. She stood to the side watching him and feeling a bit helpless.

When they were done, Brody took the cooler from Julia and headed towards the car, still quiet and grim. As they walked, Julia looked up at him, concern etched clearly on her face. Brody had always seemed so self-assured and in control, this new side of him worried her.

"Brody, what's wrong? What happened? Is there anything I can do to help?"

They had reached the car and Brody put her cooler in the trunk. As he opened the door for Julia, he paused for a moment looking at her, and then just shook his head.

He started the car and then finally looked over at Julia, anguish and frustration both defined in his eyes.

"It's Becky. She just got arrested for breaking and entering. I got a call from the precinct when they recognized her name."

Julia gasped. "Oh no, Brody, I'm so sorry. There must be some mistake."

Brody's eyes darkened and he looked thunderous. "For her sake, I certainly hope so."

He started the car and sped off. "I'll drop you off as quick as I can and head over to the precinct and see what's going on with her."

"Brody, no, the precinct and my house are in opposite directions. I'm fine. Go over to the station and check on your daughter."

Brody looked over at her. "Are you sure Julia? I have no idea how long this will take." But he was already turning onto the road heading towards the police station.

The fast boat ride had been exhilarating, but the car ride to the police station was absolutely terrifying. Julia grasped the sides of her seat in terror as Brody sped around corners and up the freeway at speeds Julia wouldn't have thought the car was capable of. Finally, they reached the station and Brody screeched into a parking spot and the car lurched to a stop. Julia found herself saying a prayer of thanks that they had made it safely.

Before Julia had a chance to unbuckle her seat belt, Brody had leaped out of the car and was at her door, grabbing her arm and hurrying her towards the entrance. He tore open the door and strode towards the front desk with long, determined steps.

"Daddy!"

Julia turned to where the voice came from and saw a young girl with a cute pixie cut struggling to get up with her hands cuffed to a bench.

"Becky!" Brody strode over to the bench where the girl was restrained and looked down at her, his face angry and concerned all at the same time.

"What the hell were you thinking?! Breaking into a building? Why aren't you at school? Where is your mother?" Brody towered over her, his fists clenched and wanting to ask a thousand questions all at once.

Becky cowered down at her father's wrath. "I'm sorry, Daddy. I didn't mean anything by it. It's just an abandoned building and all the kids were going. We were just having some fun."

"Fun?" Brody's face grew even more stormy. "You skip school, break into a building and start drinking for fun?!"

Becky looked at her father, scared and defiant all at the same time. "I didn't skip school! It's a teacher conference day so we had the afternoon off. Everyone always goes there to meet up, and I only had a sip or two of vodka. It's not that big a deal!"

Brody stared at his daughter in disbelief. "Not that big a deal?! Breaking and entering is not a big deal? Underage drinking is not a big deal? Illegal possession of alcohol is not a big deal? Getting arrested and handcuffed to the precinct bench is not a big deal?"

As Brody stood glaring at his daughter, a female officer walked over dangling a set of keys from her hands. Julia recognized her as the same officer who had been with Brody the first day he had come to her house, looking for Frank.

"Hey Brody," she said. "I guess I can release her to your custody now if you're ready to take her home." She looked at Brody with a slightly amused look on her face.

"Thanks, Kate, I appreciate you giving me a call."

Kate Klein gave him a quick nod and proceeded to uncuff the young girl. "I've been talking to the owner of the building and he is willing to drop the breaking and entering charges if the kids clean up the mess they left behind. Since Becky wasn't actually caught holding the bottle, we can probably reduce all of this to a misdemeanor ticket. I'll see what I can do."

Brody took Becky by the arm as she stood up and gave Kate a grim smile. "I really appreciate you intervening on her behalf Kate. I owe you one."

"Hey, I was young once too." She looked at Becky sternly. "Let this be a warning to you though. You may not always get off this easy young lady."

Becky looked down at her feet, ashamed and said, "Yes ma'am, I know. Thank you."

As Kate walked away, Brody held onto Becky's arm and steered her toward the door, looking back at Julia as he went. "Thanks for coming Julia. Let's get going then."

All three walked to the car in silence, Julia bringing up the rear. She could see from his taut shoulders that Brody was having a hard time holding in his anger. When they got to the car, Brody turned Becky around and looked her in the eye. He just stood for a minute staring down at her, clenching and unclenching his fists.

"You are the daughter of a cop, Becky. Of all the kids, you should know better. I thought I taught you better. Where is your mother anyway? Why weren't you home doing chores or something?"

"Mom is out of town for a few days. I'm staying with my friend Jen. Her mom said it was ok for us to go and hang out for a bit." Becky alternated between staring back at her father defiantly and looking down at her shoes nervously.

"What do you mean out of town? Why wasn't I told? You should have stayed with me. I wouldn't be letting you run wild around town!"

Becky snorted. "Yeah, right Dad, like you're ever there to watch me. You're always working, remember? It's not like it's the first time I've hung out at that building. It's just the first time I got caught." Becky looked at her dad triumphantly, as if she had won a sparring match with him.

Brody just looked angrier. "You think that makes it better Becky? I've told you before, as the daughter of a cop, you're set to higher standards. Your mother and I both expect better from you."

Becky looked like she couldn't decide if she should cry or argue.

"You and mom don't have time for me, let alone care about what I'm doing. At least Jen and my friends are there to listen to me and spend some time with me. You and mom are always running around busy with your own lives. Ever since the boys moved out, everyone is off doing their own thing and no one pays any attention to me. At least hanging out in that stupid old building gives me something to do; I get to hang out with my friends and people that care about me."

Brody looked stricken. "I thought you were ok with my work. You said you admired my job and were thinking of going into law enforcement yourself. And I thought you and your mom were spending a lot of time together? You were just telling me how great your relationship with your mom was, and how you were best friends? What is going on with you Becky?"

"Look Dad, a lot is going on ok. I don't want to get into it in front of a stranger if that's ok." She looked pointedly over at Julia. "Maybe we could talk later, just the two of us, without your "friend" around."

Brody looked at Julia apologetically. "I'm sorry to have dragged you into all of this Julia. Why don't I take you home now and we can talk tomorrow?" Then he looked at Becky. "You are being rude, Becky. This is Julia Masterson, and she was kind enough to let me drag her here so I could come and get you out of custody as quickly as possible."

Becky looked over at Julia and mumbled, "Sorry."

Julia smiled at Becky sympathetically and said, "Hi Becky. Don't be. It's no problem at all and it's nice to meet you."

Brody opened the back door to the car and told Becky to get in. Then he held the front door of the car for Julia, and as she climbed in, he said quietly, "I'm really sorry Julia. I don't know what's gotten into her lately."

Becky was staring sullenly out of the window as they drove, after a few minutes, she suddenly said, "Dad, where are you going? We just passed Jen's house!"

"You're not going back to Jen's house," Brody answered, looking at her through his rearview mirror. "I doubt you will go to Jen's house ever again. We'll pick up a few things at your mother's house since it's on the way, drop Julia off, and then you and I are going to my place for a long talk."

Becky moaned. "Dad, you live in a smelly, messy bachelor pad and you don't even have an extra bed there. Why can't I just go home or go to Jen's?"

"Because you've proven that you can't be trusted, that's why." Brody half-turned at the stop sign they were at, to look sternly at Becky. "I don't think you realize just how serious this is Becky. If the owner of that building had chosen to press charges or if any of the kids you were with had gotten drunk and seriously hurt, you could be facing felony charges. Even a few misdemeanors could mean the end of your scholarship, Becky."

"Ughhh, Dad. You are just a stickler. It was just a little bit of fun. You over exaggerate everything!"

Brody chose to ignore her and turned around to continue driving until they reached a simple little side street full of matching ranch houses. Julia looked around and thought the developer probably only splurged for one set of plans when he had bought the land for this subdivision. Even so, the houses all looked neat and kempt, and Julia could imagine it must have been a nice quiet street to raise kids on.

They turned into a neat, concrete driveway belonging to a nice little white ranch with black shutters on it. There was already a car sitting in the driveway with its trunk open. Becky called out gleefully from the back, "Mom's home!" and barreled out of the car before Brody had a chance to say anything.

"Mom, hey Mom!" Becky called out as she ran to the door. Julia got the impression Becky wanted to tell her mother her side of the story before Brody got a chance to talk.

A motherly figure came walking out of the door with a cute little pixie cut. She was wearing a t-shirt and Bermuda shorts, and Julia could imagine her running up and down the sidelines of a soccer game cheering on her kids.

"Becky! What are you doing here? I thought you were spending the night at Jen's?" Holly asked her daughter.

She glanced over at Brody who had gotten out of the car and was slowly approaching her. Julia got out as well, but she stayed by the side of the car, so the family could have some privacy.

"Hey Holly, how's it going? Becky said you would be out of town for a few days?"

Holly looked curiously from her daughter to Brody. "My trip got cut a little short. What's going on? Why is Becky with you, and why are you here?"

Brody walked over to the house and his ex-wife, and Julia could hear him telling Holly what had happened, how he was called to the police station to get Becky out, and how he was planning to take Becky to his house.

Holly frowned as she listened and looked sternly at her daughter. "Becky, I'm disappointed in you. You know better than to jeopardize your father's career or mine for that matter. This is a small town, and you know how people talk around here."

Brody looked at Holly, and Julia could see the shock and surprise on his face even from where she stood. "For heaven's sake Holly, this isn't about our careers! Becky could have been seriously hurt drinking with her friends in that old building. She could also have faced some serious charges if the arresting cop hadn't recognized her name and called me."

Holly looked at Brody and frowned. "It's a good thing the cop recognized your name then. I'm glad you have an established career and a reputation where people know you, but I just got my realtor's license and it's hard

60

breaking into the business. I can't afford to have anything tarnish my reputation right now."

Julia watched as Brody stepped back from Holly slightly and saw that his fists were again clenching and unclenching at his sides. On the surface, he looked cool and calm, but Julia could feel his energy all the way to the car, and she could sense he was about to explode.

"Anyway, thanks for bringing her home, Brody." Holly began to walk to her open trunk to retrieve some bags. She picked up a small suitcase and a heavy-looking tote and walked back over to her front door.

She looked over at Becky as she walked. "Becky, we'll need to have a long talk in the morning. I already have plans for tonight, thinking I would be home alone while you were at Jen's, so I need to hurry up and get going. For now, until we've had a chance to talk, you're grounded."

Brody looked at Holly dumbfounded. "She's grounded? That's it?" He took a step towards Holly. "She got arrested for breaking and entering, and underage drinking Holly. Those are some serious charges. If I weren't her father, she would probably even be spending the night in jail."

He looked at Becky and said, "Get some things together, you're spending the night at my house where I can keep an eye on you."

"Dad, no!" Becky groaned and looked beseechingly to her mother for help. "Mom! It's been a bad enough day, I don't want to spend the night at Dads!"

Holly deposited her bags just inside the door and turned to her daughter. "Go inside Becky and go to your room." Then she faced Brody with her hands on her hips, "First of all Brody Barker, you don't have a house to bring her to. You live in a one-room, ratty apartment above a diner. That's no place for Becky to spend the night after the fright she's had. Second of all, it's not your week. You don't have custody, so I'll decide where my daughter spends the night."

"Holly, you can't possibly think just giving her a pass on this and letting her spend the night here without supervision is the way to handle this?"

Holly turned a pair of angry eyes on Brody. "I'm not giving her a pass on anything. I will have a talk with her in the morning. And since when are you the expert in bringing up children? Seems to me I have done just fine without you up until now. We have two successful boys who both made it out of my home alive and well. Do you think this is the first trouble any of our kids have been in?" She took a step forward and pointed a finger at Brody. "Well, it's not. It just happens to be the first time you are around to witness it. You have hidden away from any responsibility for years, so you don't need to come creeping around now adding your two cents worth when it's not wanted or needed!"

With that, Holly turned around and shut the door in Brody's face. He stood rooted to the spot for a minute, staring at the closed front door to the house that had once been his home. Then, he turned around and walked back to the car and Julia.

"I'm really sorry you had to witness all that. I'm not sure what got into both of them tonight." Brody looked genuinely confused as he held the door open for her to slip back into the car.

Julia suspected that Holly's frustration had been brewing for quite some time and he just hadn't noticed it before, but for now, she thought it was probably prudent and not her business to say anything.

Brody sat quiet and sullen for most of the ride back to her house. When they got to her driveway, he got out to open the car door and Julia said, "You are welcome to come in for a drink if you like. I'm a good listener you know."

He looked at Julia with troubled eyes and nodded in acceptance. As they walked up to the front porch, Julia saw a huge planter filled with flowers sitting there.

"Oh my, those are beautiful." She looked at Brody in surprise. "I can't imagine who would have sent these?"

Brody bent down to retrieve the card taped to the planter and handed it to Julia. "Only one way to find out. Read the card."

As Julia opened the tiny envelope and looked at the writing, she gasped and paled visibly, handing the card to Brody with shaky hands. Curious at her reaction, Brody took the card and began to read. There were just a few short words.

To Julia. All My Love.
Frank.

CHAPTER 12

Julia's hands were shaking so bad that she couldn't even open the door. Brody took the keys from her and they both walked in. The first thing he did was check the house to see if it was secure, making sure no one was lurking around anywhere, and then, he returned to where he had left Julia, standing by the door.

"Sit down Julia," he commanded. "Where is your liquor cabinet?"

Julia sat down on the couch and pointed to a small little cabinet sitting in the corner of the room. Brody rummaged around a bit and emerged with a bottle of Jack Daniels and two whiskey glasses. He walked into the kitchen and filled the glasses with ice, then poured a generous splash of whiskey into each glass. He walked back over to Julia and handed her the glass.

"Here, drink this."

She took the glass with shaky hands and took a sip of the whiskey, coughing a bit as the strong liquid trickled down her throat. Brody took a generous gulp and waited impatiently for the familiar warm feeling in his gut as the whiskey made its way through his body. He finished his glass with one more swallow, poured himself another generous splash, and then sat opposite Julia, studying her intently.

"Feel a little better now?" he asked.

Julia nodded and took another sip of her drink, welcoming the warm, numbing feeling of the whiskey as it did its job.

"Yes, thank you. That was just such a shock. Why would Frank do that? Why wouldn't he just call or come home?" she asked quietly.

"I don't know. We don't know if those flowers are really from Frank yet Julia. I'll need to see if I can trace where they came from and see if we can find out who sent them."

"But if Frank didn't send them, who would? And why would they sign his name?"

Julia's eyes were wide, and she looked worried and confused. Brody shrugged. "I don't know that either yet. I'll take the calling card and see what I can find out in the morning. It's too late to do much about it tonight."

This case is becoming more and more complicated, he thought to himself. Could Frank still be alive? And if so, why hadn't they caught any movement on his cards or his phones since his disappearance? Had they maybe missed something, and he had more credit cards than they knew about? He certainly was a man full of surprises, and seemingly endless funds.

Brody thought about his own decrepit apartment and how hard it was for him to make ends meet and send Holly and the kids the money they all needed. How did an accountant make enough money to support so many people and still be able to stash away so much gold? Brody wondered if Julia had left the gold in the safe here at home, and for the first time since he had met her, he worried for her safety.

Julia seemed lost in her own thoughts when he said, "Listen, Julia, I know this is none of my business, but did you leave the gold we found here or did you move it to a safe deposit box?"

She looked up at him, surprised at the question. "I haven't touched it since the day we found it. It's Frank's gold, not mine."

"Besides you and I, who else knows about that gold and that it's here, Julia?"

"I haven't told anyone about it, but I have no idea if Frank told anyone else. He certainly never said a word to me about it. I'm finding out more and more that Frank had a lot of secrets from me. I guess he could have told many people or he could have kept it a secret from everyone, who knows. At this point, anything is possible."

"I don't want to scare you Julia, but we don't know what Frank was into or what kind of people he dealt with. I'm not sure it's safe for you to be here alone with all that gold. If those flowers came from Frank, then great. We'll find him. If not, then someone knows you're here alone and is trying to play some kind of mind game with you, and I don't like that."

Julia looked around the room suspiciously, as if she was expecting someone to jump out at her at any minute. "What do you think I should do, then?" she asked timidly.

"I think it would be best if you went to the bank tomorrow and rented a safe deposit box. I'll send a squad car over, and we'll move it there for safekeeping for now. I'll feel much more comfortable if you're not alone here with all that gold."

Julia nodded in agreement, but secretly, she thought it wasn't going to stop anyone from coming and looking for it if they thought it was here. She shivered slightly at the idea. Maybe she should post a sign on her door saying: *Gold has been moved to the bank for safekeeping.*

Brody saw her shivering and said, "It's ok, Julia. I'll stay with you for a while tonight until you feel safer."

She looked at Brody thankfully and downed the rest of her whiskey, feeling the warm liquid coursing through her veins and slowly starting to relax her. "I think I can see the benefits of drinking every night," she joked.

"Speaking from experience, that is not a good idea," Brody said bitterly.

Julia got up to refill both their glasses and as she carried them back, she felt emboldened by the alcohol already in her system and asked, "Is that what the outburst from your ex-wife was all about tonight?"

Brody grimaced. "Maybe in part," he admitted. "Honestly, I was shocked at what she said. I thought we had cleared up all of the hard feelings we had against each other a long time ago, but it seems that Holly still has a few."

Julia nodded sympathetically, but she wondered if Brody was not quite as composed as he let on, and maybe he had his own anger issues.

As if reading her thoughts, Brody continued, "I wasn't always the best husband and father I imagine, but I did the best I knew how. We were young when we got married and so sure we were meant for each other. We were high school sweethearts and when Holly got pregnant, it was the most natural thing for us to get married. I come from a long line of cops, and I learned to deal with my feelings from them. I thought Holly understood and accepted that. She never complained and seemed content enough with our life."

"What happened then?" Julia asked softly. "What changed?"

Brody shrugged his shoulders and looked at the glass in his hands. "I don't really know. Things got worse so gradually that I'm not sure what the final straw was for us. We both started having a few drinks at night to take the edge off when the kids went to bed. That was ok at first, and we both had a chance to relax together. Then, I got promoted and my schedule got erratic. I'd come home at all hours and drink alone to unwind, while Holly would be home alone, worried and waiting for me, so she would drink to unwind and keep herself occupied. When my schedule did allow us to get together in the evening, the alcohol had stopped relaxing us and it just fueled our fights."

Julia set her glass on the table, having lost her urge to take another sip.

"I guess she resented my career and me being away so much. I can't really blame her. She felt I had a whole other life away from her and the kids, and she was left holding the fort down all by herself. I resented the time that she had with the kids that I couldn't have. I always felt the pressure to solve more cases, get more promotions and take on extra hours so I could make more money and provide Holly and the kids the life I thought they deserved."

Julia got up and sat next to Brody, taking his hand in hers sympathetically. "I'm so sorry. I'm sure you both did the best you could."

"I guess we both did what we knew how to do. I spent more and more time with other cops, away from home. Only another cop can really understand the stress of the job, and what it's like to see the worst in people every day. I would try to explain it to Holly when I got home, but she had her own stresses with the kids that I couldn't understand. We found ourselves trying to shout over each other, both of us believing we were more stressed than the other. I guess when we couldn't find comfort or understand each other, we turned to the bottle, and that just fueled our resentment for each other even further."

Brody swirled the remaining alcohol in his glass around, watching the brown liquid sloshing in the glass and then downed it with one big gulp. "I wish I could say that when we both decided to stop drinking all our issues went away, but that's not what happened. We just realized that we couldn't blame the alcohol anymore and only had each other and ourselves to blame for our problems."

Julia looked at Brody, her heart breaking when she thought she saw tears glistening in his eyes.

"One day, I came home and my bags were packed. Holly asked me to leave and not come back. She had decided I wasn't worth the heartache and trouble anymore, and she wanted to continue her life without me."

He sat back and sighed. "So, we started the new chapter of our lives and called it co-parenting. To be honest, I think I made a better co-parent than I did a parent. Things were written down and I knew what was expected of me and when. Maybe if Holly and I had been able to communicate as openly and as honestly during our marriage as we did after, things could have turned out different."

Julia sat quietly listening, but thought to herself that things hadn't seemed all that hunky-dory or cohesive tonight when they had dropped off Becky. She wondered how much in denial both Brody and Holly still were, and how many unresolved issues still existed between them.

Brody stood up, subdued and sullen, and headed back over to the liquor cabinet. The memories of his marriage caused him to feel unsettled and he was starting to crave the numbness the bottle always afforded him.

Julia watched Brody walk over to the liquor cabinet, and looked past him and out at the moonlight bouncing off the ocean as the waves splashed noisily against the beach.

Brody felt a soft touch on his arm and looked down to see Julia gently holding it, stopping him from reaching for the whiskey bottle. He looked at her, puzzled and starting to feel a tinge of anger.

"Please walk with me on the beach?" Julia asked simply, her eyes imploring him to join her.

Brody reluctantly put the glass down and looked out the window. "Now? In the dark?"

Julia just smiled. "Yes, now. Haven't you ever taken a moonlight walk on the beach? I thought you grew up here?"

Brody thought back to all the times he had been on the beach at night. There were always parties, bonfires, or sneaking away to do some drinking or making out involved. He couldn't remember a single time he had been on the beach at night just for the sake of walking. The idea intrigued him.

"Ok," he agreed. "Let's go. But let me grab a flashlight or a headlamp just in case."

Julia retrieved a headlamp from the kitchen drawer and led the way down the well-worn path to the water's edge. Once there, she turned right, away from the direction of the pier and towards the break wall at the other end. Brody walked amicably next to her, his hands shoved in his pockets next to the headlamp he had stashed there.

"Do you do this very often?" he asked, looking sideways at Julia.

"Since we've moved here, yes. We obviously didn't live near an ocean or even a lake in Ohio, so I never had the chance there. I find the rhythm of the waves very calming when I am uneasy."

Brody chuckled, guessing she had sensed his restlessness earlier and suggested the walk for his benefit. They walked in silence for a few minutes, and Brody could feel the tension slowly easing out of his body. He looked over at Julia who was matching his steps stride for stride, breathing easily and rhythmically.

"So, is this your secret to staying so calm and cool?" he asked.

Julia nodded. "Walking is just one of the many ways I've learned to find peace over the years. The sound of the ocean adds a whole new level to it though. I think I've almost come to depend on its rhythm now."

"Where did you walk when you were in Ohio? Did you have a lot of paths around?" Brody wondered if maybe they had lived further out in the country than he had first thought.

"We had a bike path that wasn't too far away, but it became too dangerous to use after a few years." Julia shuddered at the memory of a particularly scary and dangerous encounter on that path. She had just barely escaped and only because she had been in training for a marathon at the time and could outrun the man. "We lived in the city, so I mainly ended up walking the city streets in the day or going to the gym."

"That doesn't sound all that relaxing," Brody commented.

Julia laughed. "Trust me it wasn't. That's where the meditation came in." She stopped and looked out over the water. "I've always wanted to live by the ocean. Frank used to say I was being silly and that I would get bored of it if we ever did move. He loved the city and the lights, with all its activities. He was wrong though. I haven't been bored for one minute since we moved here."

Julia breathed in the cool salty air. "Even when he started to leave for long periods of time again, I didn't notice it as much since we moved. I would just come out here and walk and feel such peace that it didn't bother me the way it did when we lived in Ohio."

She looked at Brody with a sudden realization. "Maybe that's the reason we got along so much better in the last few months? I thought it was because he felt better and loved it here just like I did, but maybe he was just happy that I wasn't always whining about him being gone."

The detective in Brody had to ask, "Just how often was he gone, Julia?"

She looked at him, the tears welling in her eyes as she thought of all the times Frank had abandoned her and all the nights and days she had spent alone, waiting for him. "A lot Brody, he was gone a lot. Even more than I realized."

CHAPTER 13

Julia woke up the next morning to see a dark and gloomy sky out her window, and her cell phone pinging with a message. Brody messaged that he had traced where the flowers had come from and asked if she had time for him to come over and discuss his findings. Julia typed in *yes* with a wistful smile on her lips. It seemed that she had all the time in the world these days.

She walked into the bathroom and turned on the shower, looking at her reflection in the mirror. The woman looking back at her seemed to be a stranger. After their walk last night and after Brody had left, Julia had sat on her back deck overlooking the ocean, thinking long and hard about her marriage to Frank. Brody's questions had made her realize just how fragile and shaky their relationship really was and how little time they had actually spent together.

Last night she had felt the first tinges of real anger again, a feeling she had not allowed herself to indulge in since the early years of their marriage. It had been safer and easier to suppress her feelings and go along with whatever Frank wanted.

She stared at herself, wondering where the real Julia, the young girl so full of hopes and dreams, had gone. Had she sold her out too cheaply for what she had believed was safety and security? She felt her eyes filling with tears again and turned away from the accusing stare of the woman in the mirror. Stepping into the hot and steamy shower, she tried to wash away the guilt and the frustration that had plagued her since last night.

Why did I give in so easily to Frank? Why did I not fight harder for my dignity? How did I not even realize how much angst I was living in? The questions piled on her mind.

As she turned the shower off, she heard knocking at her door and glanced at the time. Darn, she thought as she hurried. She had spent way too long in the shower and now she was late, and Brody was already here. She wrapped a warm robe around her and ran to the door to let him in.

Brody walked in holding two cups of coffee from the local coffee shop and frowned at her as he breezed past.

Seeing his displeasure and feeling guilty, Julia said, "I'm sorry I'm not dressed. I'll hurry and get ready in a sec. I took a little long in the shower I guess." She started to turn away, but Brody called her back.

"I don't care that you're running late and not dressed Julia. That's fine and you look great," he said, handing her the steaming coffee. "Here, sit down and drink your coffee."

He walked over to her kitchen table and looked out at the ocean, churning today with the wind. After Julia joined him at the table, sipping her coffee, he looked at her sternly. "I don't think it's a good idea for you to just open the door without checking who it is first, and especially not when you're not dressed."

Julia blushed slightly at his mention of her lack of clothing. "Sorry, but I knew you were coming so I didn't even think to check."

Brody frowned. "It could have been anyone at the door. Please promise me that you'll lock all your doors from now on and that you will check and see who is at the door before opening it."

"Yes, I promise. I'm sorry I was careless." Julia felt slightly ashamed, but also felt a flutter of excitement at the thought he was worried about her.

She took another sip of her coffee, savoring the rich strong taste. "Mmmm. This is good. Thank you for bringing it." Then, she set the cup down and looked at Brody inquisitively. "Did you find out where the flowers came from?"

"Well, yes and no," Brody said. "It's like I suspected. The flowers are from a large flower shop a few towns over that specializes in online sales, and they were purchased with a gift card. So, we're really no closer to knowing who actually sent the flowers. It could have been anybody and they could have ordered them from anywhere in the country."

Julia looked out the window, disappointed. "So, we don't know if it was Frank or someone else?" She looked at Brody concerned, "But if it wasn't Frank, why would someone else pretend to be Frank and send me flowers?"

Brody shrugged his shoulders. "I don't know Julia. But if it was someone else, they would probably know that Frank is missing, or else what would be the point of sending the flowers?"

Julia nodded slowly, trying to think who else knew that Frank had disappeared. "I don't know that many people. I haven't made any friends here yet, and I haven't told any old acquaintances back in Ohio about Frank. Frank's parents died a few years ago, so there's really only the girls and their mother who know. But why would they send flowers pretending they're from Frank?"

"I don't know Julia; that's what we'll need to find out," Brody answered, puzzled as well at the strange turn of events.

Julia found herself looking around the room fearfully. "Maybe Frank is not missing, and is around and only hiding out?"

Brody looked at her carefully. "It's possible Julia, anything is possible right now. But why would he do that?"

Julia sighed in frustration. "I don't know. I'm starting to think I don't know anything at all about the man I married 25 years ago."

Brody nodded but watched her doubtfully. He usually relied on his gut when it came to understanding suspects and their motivations, but with Julia Masterson, his gut felt both a mixture of concern and suspicion at that time. Even though there were still many things to be suspicious of, he wanted her to be innocent of any wrongdoing. Could she have sent herself the flowers in an effort to throw him off the trail?

Anything is possible, he thought.

"Have you thought about my suggestion of opening a safe deposit box?" he asked Julia, trying to avoid thinking about his nagging suspicions.

"Yes, I've thought about it, but I'm not sure. When Frank finds out, he will probably be very angry with me for moving his things." Julia shuddered at the thought of what might happen if she did.

"I understand that you don't want to touch his things Julia, but you are married and everything in this house is considered communal property. That means that what is in this house belongs to you as well as him. In fact, barring a document stating otherwise, everything of his is yours no matter where it is," Brody explained, thinking as well of all the offshore accounts they had discovered. He also wondered why Julia was so scared of upsetting her husband. Surely after 25 years they must have had their share of arguments and clearly their marriage had withstood them.

Seeing Julia's hesitation, Brody pressed further. "I don't think it's safe for you to have that much gold in the house with you Julia. We don't know who sent those flowers or why, but clearly someone knows you're here alone and we have no idea what else they know."

Julia shivered and rubbed her arms as she watched the angry ocean outside. The day was overcast, casting a gloomy glow over the ocean; its waves pelting angrily against the shore, giving the atmosphere an ominous feel.

"Alright, I'll call and get it set up today then. You're right. I don't feel comfortable with so many valuables in the house." She thought back to how upset Frank had been when she had absent-mindedly left the doors unlocked and finally understood why.

"Great." Brody stood up to leave. "Let me know when you set up everything and I'll send over a patrol car to get you there safely. The officer can help you carry the bars and take them in the bank for you."

Julia nodded, but couldn't help feeling disappointed that Brody would not be coming himself. She had started to feel a certain sense of comfort and safety when he was around. Chiding herself for being selfish, she walked him to the door and thanked him. He had been more than generous with his time and she knew he must have been extremely busy with other cases as well as hers.

Later that day, after she had dressed, set up the safe deposit box at the bank and sent Brody a text saying she was set whenever he wanted to send a car, she sat on her front porch and waited for the patrol car to show up. Absently, she looked around her neighborhood, taking in the smell of the impending storm and noticing how different the normally cheerful houses looked in the gloom and the raging wind.

Just down the road, she could make out a dark sedan that she had not seen before. She tried to see inside but the windows were tinted dark, and she couldn't tell if it was occupied or not. For some reason, the dark car looked out of place here in the coastal neighborhood. Her arms prickled with goosebumps, and she had the uncomfortable feeling that she was being watched.

She heard the car churning up the loose gravel before she saw it, and quickly turned towards the sound, seeing a patrol car pulling up at high speed. Kate Klein stepped out of the driver's seat with a huge grin on her face. Opening the passenger side door, a younger officer also stepped out, looking a little pale and shaky.

"I swear Kate, that's the last time I'm driving with you. Are you looking to get us both killed?" he said, glaring at Kate as he spoke.

"Oh stop whining. What's the fun of being a cop if you can't drive a little faster?" Kate was still wearing her mischievous grin as she turned to Julia.

"Good morning Mrs. Masterson. I brought Officer Jackson with me. Detective Barker said there might be some heavy lifting involved?"

Julia had stood up quickly when she heard the car speeding up, and now she turned to Officer Jackson. "Hello, thank you for coming to help with the heavy lifting." Then she smiled at Kate, "Hi Officer Klein, it's nice to see you again. Please come in." As she turned to go inside, she glanced over to where the dark sedan had been but only saw the empty street.

CHAPTER 14

That evening, Julia sat on the couch with her feet curled under her. She had wrapped a cozy blanket around her body and was watching the ocean battle with the storm winds. The ocean was sending its waves crashing against the rocks angrily while the wind was whipping the sparse trees around the shoreline in a frenzy. She could see a few lightning flashes further out and she shivered at the thought of facing a storm by herself tonight.

This wasn't the first storm she had braved alone, but today, she had not been able to shake the uneasy feeling she had carried with her since morning. She was grateful that she had listened to Brody and removed all the gold and valuable papers that Frank had hidden in the safe. Officers Klein and Jackson had been more than kind and helpful, but she had felt gloomy and guilty all day. She knew Frank would be very upset with her if he knew. When she came home, she had purposely left the closet door exposed and opened, with the safe also open and unlocked, hoping that if anyone did come in, they would see that anything of value was gone.

When the lights flickered, threatening to go off, Julia got up and grabbed a flashlight from the kitchen. Then, she put the kettle on the stove, thinking it might be better to make some tea and maybe warm up a bit of supper before she lost power. After she had the tea kettle going and some soup simmering, she gathered a few candles and lit them around her house, hoping to create a peaceful ambiance and chase away the gloom. As she sat down waiting for the kettle to boil and the soup to warm up, she remembered her promise to Brody to make sure her house was locked up tight.

Julia walked around and checked all the windows and doors. She discovered that she had indeed left the slider to the deck unlocked. She locked it and took the extra precaution of jamming a broom handle in the space where it slid open to make sure it couldn't be opened even if the lock broke. Then she walked to the front door, deciding she would lock the screen door as well as the door itself.

As she opened the door to lock the screen, Julia looked up the street to where the dark sedan from earlier in the day had been parked. It was so dark and gloomy that she could barely make out the house across the road.

She was just getting ready to pull her head back in and lock both doors when a flash of lightning illuminated the street. There, at the end of the street, in the same spot it had been this morning, sat the dark sedan, looking as foreboding as it had this morning.

Julia's heart jumped in her chest and started beating rapidly. She slammed the door shut and hurriedly locked both doors, shoving a chair against the handle for extra precaution. She raced back into the kitchen, checking the windows one more time. When she had decorated the house, she had left the windows without any window coverings, relishing in the views they afforded her. Now, she wished she could close some curtains and shut out the storm and any spying eyes.

The kettle on the stove started whistling loudly, and Julia pried her eyes away from the window and looked back at the stove, with her kettle and the soup bubbling away. She turned it off and covered the soup, no longer hungry, and banged loudly as she made her tea, hoping to drown out the sound of the wind and the storm outside. The lights flickered a few times, but as Julia carried her mug over to the couch, the power held.

She picked up a book and tried to read to distract her mind, but after a few minutes, she gave up and allowed her mind to wander. She found herself wondering what Brody was doing that night. She imagined him sitting in a stark and unkempt apartment, probably drinking a beer and looking over some papers. Shaking her head, she realized she had no reason to think he lived like that other than what his ex-wife had said in anger. For all she knew, he might live in a light and luxurious apartment.

In fact, he might not even be alone tonight, she thought.

Brody could be cuddled up with someone and they could be blissfully listening to the rain and the storm together.

The thought of Brody spending the night with someone bothered her more than she cared to admit, and she tried to put it out of her mind. Instead, she tried to imagine where Frank was spending the night. Was it storming and was he alone or hurt? Maybe he was with one of the many women whose names she had seen on that list? They had not yet been able to trace the women or find out where they were. Maybe he was hiding out with Jane and they were both just playing her for a fool? For the hundredth time since he had gone missing, Julia wondered why she had never asked more questions or followed up on his frequent disappearances.

Even now, Julia shuddered at the thought of questioning Frank too much, and deep down, she knew the answer to her own question. She had been afraid of Frank. As the lightning flashed and the wind howled, she finally admitted to herself that even now, she was still afraid of him.

Slowly over the years, he had worn her down to a cowardly sham of a woman, who was grateful when he wasn't angry and graced her with his presence. She had come to think the lull between his outbursts was the same as a happy marriage, and she accepted any attention from him, erroneously calling it love. She realized how on edge she had been for 25 years, always trying to appease him and avoid his temper.

As she thought back over the last 25 years, and the time that she would never get back, she could feel her stomach start to slowly clench in anger. Over the years, she had learned to suppress her feelings, but now that Frank was gone, she could feel them resurfacing.

She thought back to how Frank had coldly dismissed her pleas to have a child, and the agony she had felt at knowing she would never be a mother. How, after her initial pounding and crying in the early years, she had come to accept the "time out" room as something she deserved and needed to endure, as repentance for upsetting her husband.

Then, she remembered how shocked she had been when Frank had suddenly agreed to retire, leave Ohio and come to the Keys. She had been so happy and thought maybe she was finally deserving of his love. She marveled at the speed at which Frank had made it all happen. Now, she couldn't help but wonder if he had been running away from something.

She thought back to that night on vacation when she had finally reached her breaking point and told him she was thinking of filing for a divorce. He had begged her not to leave and promised her he would change. At that time, she had believed he truly loved her, or he wouldn't be so desperate for her to stay with him. Now, she wondered if maybe the threat of divorce lawyers examining his finances had more to do with his desperation than love.

Julia felt the knot in her stomach tighten and felt the tears that were threatening to spill out again. This time though, they were not tears of worry or sadness. Right now, when she thought of Frank, she only felt frustration and anger. What had he been up to all these years? And had he run off like a coward to leave her to deal with the aftermath of what he had done?

As the storm outside intensified, so did the anger inside Julia.

She got up and went back into his office, tearing out drawers and looking through papers with renewed vigor. She was determined to find out what he had been up to all these years, and wanted to find clues that would tell her what had happened to him. She vowed to herself, this time, she would not cower and grovel like a frightened child. This time he would need to explain himself.

Julia tore through the office, desperately looking for something that would point to Frank's whereabouts. Suddenly, the lights flickered and finally went out. Julia was left in darkness, the storm raging outside and only the faint flicker of the candles in the living room her only source of light.

Frustrated at the loss of momentum, she cautiously made her way back into the living room, where she had left her cell phone and the flashlight.

Julia looked around for a moment when she entered the living room, her body on full alert. Every shadow cast by the candles and the whipping wind sent her body reeling with nerves. Julia felt ridiculous, opting to draw in a few deep breaths to calm her nerves. She picked up her phone and the flashlight and lay them on the pillow before bending over to pick the slightly cold tea.

She was about to sit down and curl back up in her blanket to wait out the storm until the lights came back on, when she heard the sound of the front door lock being jiggled.

Slowly, her heart threatening to pound its way out of her chest, she crept toward the door, shining the flashlight at the lock with one hand and clutching her phone with the other. As she inched closer, she could only hear the loud rumbles of thunder and the fainter sound of the waves crashing violently against the surf.

"Frank? Is that you?" Julia called out, terrified, despite her earlier resolve. When there was no answer, she crept closer and with her heart in her throat, she looked out the peephole. All she could see was darkness and the occasional flash of lightning. Relieved, she slowly made her way back to the living room, shining the flashlight around as she went.

The loud crash and the sound of splintering glass in Frank's office caused Julia to jump in fright, dropping her phone and the flashlight. As Julia clumsily and desperately felt around for her phone, and the now extinguished flashlight, she could feel the wind and cold air coming from the office.

She finally put her hands on the flashlight, but when she tried to switch it on nothing happened. Desperate, Julia was down on her hands and knees, feeling around for her cell phone. Finally, at the next flash of lightning, she saw it lying a few feet away. Frantically, Julia dove for the phone and turned on its flashlight, shining it around her.

The faint glow of the light coming from her cell didn't reveal anything or anyone, so Julia crept towards the office where the wind and rain were blowing in. She held onto the flashlight with her other hand, brandishing it like a weapon, and did her best to shine the weak light from her cellphone around the room.

"Is anyone there?" she called out, her voice cracking with fright.

When she didn't hear anything, Julia walked further into the room. Shards of splintered glass from the broken window lay strewn all over the office. Wind and rain were blowing into the room, and the papers she had left out earlier were fluttering all around. She could see a huge rock, with what looked like a piece of paper wrapped around it, lying in the glass.

Julia gingerly picked her way through the glass to retrieve the rock, cutting her bare feet on some of the smaller shards. She grabbed the rock and hurriedly made her way back to the living room, away from the broken window, the rain and wind.

She sat down and started to unwrap the string securing a soggy piece of paper around the rock. When she finally loosened it, she shone her cellphone's light one more time around the room, assuring herself that she was alone. Then, she opened the paper and laid it flat on her coffee table shining the light from her phone on it. The words on the paper sent a chill up her spine.

I know what you did, Julia.
You won't get away with it.
I'm always watching you.

PART THREE

CHAPTER 15

Julia sat huddled on her couch as the storm raged on outside. Detective Brody Barker walked around the beach house, quietly overseeing and directing the officers mulling around her home. One officer was busy taping a piece of cardboard over the broken window while another swept up the glass shards that had strewn over the office floor. Brody had already taken the note from Julia and put it in a plastic bag so the forensics unit could examine it for fingerprints; though he doubted that the soggy paper would yield much.

Officer Kate Klein walked over and handed Julia a steaming mug of tea. "Here, drink this, it'll help warm you up."

Julia had not stopped shivering since she had read the ominous note attached to the rock someone had thrown through her window.

Had Frank been watching her while she moved his things? Or had the note been written by someone else? What could it mean?

Brody walked over and sat down beside her, both concern and suspicion vying for a position in his mind. He too wondered what the note meant. Was Julia involved in her husband's disappearance and someone knew about it? Was she being blackmailed? Or was Frank Masterson really lurking around watching, like Julia seemed to believe? This case was becoming more and more complicated, and Brody was getting increasingly impatient to solve it.

Julia rubbed her arms vigorously in an attempt to warm herself. "I'm scared, Brody. What is going on here?" She looked at him, her face clearly showing the shock and fright that she felt.

"I'm not sure, Julia." Brody felt that was the only answer he ever had for her. He vowed to double down his efforts and get to the bottom of this. This case needed to be solved; the sooner the better. Brody had solved quite a few missing person cases in his career, and he was sure none had ever had the unexpected twists and turns that this one did. He still wasn't even sure if he was looking for a person or a body.

"We're all wrapped up here sir," said a uniformed police officer, coming up to stand in front of Brody.

"Great, thanks everyone. Kate, could you take any bagged evidence and drop it at the station on your way home?"

Kate nodded in acquiescence and the officers all made their way to the door.

"Take a look and see if you can spot the dark sedan that Mrs. Masterson saw earlier," Brody called out as they opened the door to leave.

"All clear, detective," one of the officers called back, looking around and then hurriedly shutting the door, clearly eager to get home and back to his warm bed.

The power was still out, and the police-issued flashlights that the officers had used while cleaning up were now gone too. The only light left was from the flickering candles that Julia had lit earlier.

The thunder was still rumbling and with the next flash of lightning, Brody could see that Julia was huddled in the corner of the couch clasping onto her mug of tea, clearly distraught.

"I can take you to a hotel for tonight if you like, Julia," said Brody, walking over and sitting next to her.

Julia shook her head. "Oh, no. Thank you. I'll be ok. I don't think I'll be able to sleep tonight anyway. Most of the hotels are probably closed by now, too. Anyway, I shouldn't really leave the house with a broken window."

Brody nodded. Though he understood why she wanted to be at home, he did not like the idea of her being there alone. He made up his mind and settled back.

"I'll stay here on the couch then," he declared, wondering if he should take off his shoes.

"Brody! I couldn't ask you to do that." Julia shook her head. "It's enough that you rushed out here tonight. I'm sure you are as eager as everyone else to get home to bed."

Brody chuckled, thinking of his little one bedroom apartment above the noisy diner. The bedroom was so tiny, he could hardly fit his double bed in there. There was no door to the room and Brody could see the front door from where he lay in bed. Even if he had a door, he doubted he would have had the room to close it anyway. The couch divided the tiny kitchenette from the rest of the living area, and Brody slept there if he was lucky enough to convince one of the kids to stay with him. The smell of deep-fried food from the diner below permeated every bit of the apartment. His daughter, Becky, was right. It was a little dump of an apartment.

Brody looked around the beach house. Even with the ominous storm outside and the shattered window, Julia's house was much more inviting a place to spend the night.

"I'm used to sleeping on the couch. Trust me, I can sleep anywhere. And maybe you'll be able to get some sleep knowing you're not alone here."

Julia looked at him gratefully. She really hadn't wanted to stay alone tonight, but also didn't want to trek out in the storm in search of a hotel.

"I'll bring you some blankets and a pillow then. The couch is actually pretty comfortable. I've fallen asleep on it a few times myself." Julia rose to go to the bedroom to get the extra bedding.

Brody followed her, shining his big flashlight and illuminating her way to the bedroom.

The man really does think of everything, Julia thought as she gathered the bedding and went back out to the living room to make up the couch.

"Can I get you anything? Tea, a drink, some water?" Julia hovered around nervously, unsure what to do now that she had set Brody's bed set up, and somewhat reluctant to go alone to her room.

Brody was already yawning and removing his shoes and belt. Julia looked on wide-eyed as he took his chest gun holster off and laid it on the table next to the couch, after securing the safety.

"Wow, I never even noticed you carried that," she said, still looking at the imposing firearm laying on her coffee table.

Brody looked up at her surprised. "I'm a cop Julia. How do you think I catch bad guys? They don't always stop just because I ask them nicely."

Julia looked at him sheepishly. "No, I guess they wouldn't. I thought maybe because you're a detective you just solve mysteries and find people, not actually chase bad guys."

Brody just shrugged, nonchalant. "Not everyone wants to be found and there are a lot of people out there who don't want me to solve the mysteries they're covering up. It's just part of the job."

The gun looked big, imposing and out of place on her coffee table. "I think I can see why Holly would have been worried when you were out at work... I never really thought about the dangers you must face."

Brody sat back on the couch, holding the water Julia had brought him earlier. "Holly comes from a family of cops. She knew what she was getting into. Besides, it's not really that dangerous around here. It's a small town and we pretty much know our criminal element. Miami might be a different story, but around here, cops usually make it home safe at night."

"It's awfully big," said Julia, eying the firearm doubtfully.

Brody just smiled, leaning back against the couch even further, tired after the long day and his interrupted sleep. He wondered if Julia was really that curious about his gun or if she had other reasons for avoiding sleep.

Cautiously, he said, "I'm beat and I'm sure you must be exhausted too. If you think you'll be alright by yourself, we had better get some sleep."

"Yes, of course, I'm so sorry. You must be completely worn out. I'll head off to bed then. Please help yourself to anything you need."

As Julia was heading towards her room, she turned around and looked at Brody one more time.

"Thank you, Brody, for staying here with me tonight," she said, and went quickly into her room, shutting the door behind her.

CHAPTER 16

For most of the night, Julia had tossed and turned, unable to sleep. Now she found herself at the same beach she seemed to be on almost every night. The waves were once again pulling at her legs, trying their best to drag her under. Frank was walking ahead of her, oblivious to her calls.

"Frank, help me!" Julia cried out, but it was as if he couldn't hear a thing. Her ears rang in a roar of thunder as the waves crashed even more fiercely this time. Lightning flashed again, and she could see Frank look over his shoulder at her as the waves began sucking her in.

She reached out her arms, begging him to help her escape the unrelenting waves. They pulled her down until she was on her knees, the water now pounding all around her while she frantically gasped for breath.

Another flash of lightning followed, and Frank had turned his back to walk away from her. She wanted to scream, but her voice choked in her throat. Julia threw her arms about trying to get his attention. The harder she struggled, the further down she went.

"Julia, Julia, wake up." Brody gently shook Julia, trying to wake her from her nightmare without startling her too much.

Finally, she opened her eyes and looked at him, her face and body drenched in sweat and shaking uncontrollably. Brody eased her up to a sitting position and cradled her gently until her shaking subsided somewhat. She looked around her and tried to get her bearings.

"It's alright, you're here in your own house. You're safe. Nothing is going to happen to you." He gently looked into her face, waiting for some sign that she was waking up.

Julia shuddered, trying to shake off the memory of her recurring nightmare.

"Oh... right. Yes. I'm ok now. Thank you." She pulled slightly back from him, embarrassed that he had caught her in her nightmare. "I'm sorry I woke you."

"It's ok. I'm sorry I woke you too. I wasn't sure if I should, but you were thrashing about and I was worried you'd hurt yourself. You must have been having a nightmare. Can you remember it? What was it about?"

Julia slowly shook her head, trying to remember the dream. "I've been having the same one pretty much every night," she admitted. "It always begins with me walking in the ocean and the waves start to suck me in. I see Frank and I try to call out to him but I can never reach him. He always just turns away and disappears." Julia looked at Brody, stricken. "Do you think he's trying to tell me something?"

"I doubt that, Julia. It's probably just your subconscious trying to make sense of what's been going on in your life lately." Brody was not much of a believer in mystical signs. He preferred to deal with facts and real evidence.

"You're probably right. It just seems so real, and it's so similar every night. I can't help but think he might be trying to reach out to me for something." Julia leaned forward into Brody and buried her head, moaning slightly, "Oh Brody, what if Frank is dead? What if he is trying to reach out to me from the afterlife?"

Brody held Julia and gently patted her back, wondering if she really believed Frank had been alive this whole time. People who were still alive rarely just disappeared without a trace or any money.

"Julia... you have to start to think about that possibility," he said softly. "We haven't seen any signs of life from Frank since he disappeared. There is a strong likelihood that something has happened to him."

"What about the flowers, though? The note said it was from Frank. Maybe he sent them to give me a sign he was still alive. Maybe he just needs to hide out for a while?"

Brody looked at her doubtfully, "Anything is possible Julia. But there has been no movement in his accounts, his cell phone or any of his credit cards. He would have had to pay for the gift card somehow. He would also need money to hide out, and there is no evidence that he withdrew any large sums of money before he disappeared."

Julia knew that what Brody was telling her made sense, but she couldn't shake the feeling that Frank would pop back into her life at any moment, and if he did, she was sure he would be very angry with her.

"Lay back down and try to get some sleep, Julia. We'll look further into his accounts tomorrow. There's not much we can do tonight anyway. Listen, the storm sounds like it's calming down, so maybe you can relax and get some sleep now."

Julia lay back as told but looked around the room fearfully. Brody could see that she was shivering and reached over to cover her with the blankets.

"Brody... stay with me for a while please? Just lay next to me?" It embarrassed her to ask, but she was too shaken and terrified to care.

Brody looked at her curiously for a moment, but realized he was too tired to ask any questions. Taking her in his arms, he lay down beside her as gently as if she were a child.

"It's ok, I've got you. Try to get some rest now," he whispered as he made himself comfortable. He wasn't sure if he liked how cozy this arrangement felt, or if he should run back to his apartment as quickly as possible.

He could feel Julia's body slowly relax, and after a while, could sense she was breathing evenly, finally asleep. Brody had been exhausted just a moment ago, but now, holding Julia, sleep eluded him. He thought back over everything that had happened in the past weeks and all the evidence they had gathered.

Am I missing something? He thought.

People didn't just disappear like that. There had to be a trail somewhere and he needed to find it.

He looked down at Julia's peaceful face and felt an overwhelming tenderness he had not felt in a long time. Even though he knew she was a grown woman, she looked as helpless and innocent as a child. He had spent a great deal of time with her in the past weeks but still wondered how well he really knew her. Was she really the open book she seemed to be, or was she hiding some terrible secrets from him?

He had no doubt that the nightmare had been real. No one could fake the kind of terror he had seen in her. But the cynical part of him wondered why she had these nightmares. Was her subconscious just confused and trying to process the events happening to her, or were the nightmares a result of a guilty conscience? She had sounded convincing tonight when she had brought up the possibility of Frank's demise. Did she really believe he could still be alive and had sent her the flowers, or had she really sent them to herself in order to throw him off her trail?

As he watched her sleep, he finally felt himself grow drowsy as well, and nestled closer to her. Some of her hair tickled his face, and he could smell the sweet smell of her jasmine shampoo. He pulled her a little closer, as he pushed the last of his doubts aside for the night, and allowed himself to be lulled into an easy and restful sleep..

CHAPTER 17

Julia woke the next morning, looking directly at a muscular arm, attached to the man lying in her bed. Ashamed, she recalled last night's events and how she had asked Brody to stay in the same bed with her. He lay on top of the covers, but she was cradled in his arms in a very intimate way. She could tell by his even breathing that he was still sleeping soundly, and so she took advantage of the moment to secretly relish the warmth of his body, feeling more at ease than she had in a very long time. To her relief, she could see the sun shining in through the slats in her shades, letting her know that the storm had finally subsided.

After a few moments, she quietly slipped out of bed and hurried into the kitchen, hoping that the power had come back on by now. As she passed the closed door of the office, she shuddered, thinking about the rock that had been thrown through her window, and the note attached, wondering who would want to torment her like that. She turned back to the kitchen and was relieved to see the timer on her stove blinking, indicating that the power was back on. She busied herself preparing coffee and wondered absently how Brody liked his eggs for breakfast.

When she heard him step into the bathroom and turn on the shower, she started frying some bacon and scrambling some eggs, smiling at how blissful and normal it felt to prepare breakfast for two.

"Mmmmm, smells delicious," Brody said, as he entered the kitchen, his hair still damp and smelling fresh from the shower. "Thanks for making breakfast Julia, this sure beats diner food."

Julia smiled and handed him a cup of steaming coffee. "It's the least I can do after coercing you to spend the night here," she said. "Thanks again for staying. I don't think I would have slept a wink if you hadn't been here."

The truth was, with him here, she had slept better and more restfully than she had in a very long time.

"If there's breakfast like this involved, I could be coerced to spend every night," Brody teased, sitting down and pouring hot sauce on his eggs.

Julia sat opposite him and picked at her eggs, glancing nervously at the office door in her clear line of vision.

"I'll call someone to get that window fixed today, Julia. Don't worry. You won't need to spend another night with cardboard on your window. Kate dropped the note off at the station last night so hopefully we can lift some prints or get a vague idea where it came from later today," Brody said, hoping he could alleviate some of her fears.

"Thanks, Brody, I really do appreciate all your help. I'm not sure I would even know who to call to fix the window." Julia sighed, regretting that she had not made more of an attempt at getting to know her new town in the last few months. "I'll be home all day cleaning up, so just tell them to come anytime."

Brody finished the last of his eggs and bacon, sat back in his chair cradling his coffee and noting the melancholic look on Julia's face. "Maybe you should get out of the house later when the window is fixed," he said. "There's a great little coffee shop in town you can visit... They sell books you might be interested in. Or even the little art shop on Main Street. I'll keep looking into Frank's papers but there's not much you can do, for now anyway. I think maybe you could use a distraction for a day."

Julia nodded her head in agreement. "I think you may be right. I don't think I realized how the constant stress is getting to me until last night." She looked at Brody. "As long as you promise to update me as soon as you hear anything, no matter how small."

"I promise I'll fill you in daily with any details," Brody said. "Now I better get going. It's going to be another busy day today. If it's ok with you, I'll give the window guy your number and tell him to call you with a time."

Julia nodded and stood up with Brody, walking him to the door. As she opened it, she looked up the street again, but no mysterious-looking sedan was in sight. She only saw bright sunshine and the comings and goings of a peaceful coastal neighborhood.

"I'll keep you posted, Julia," Brody said, and then walked over to his car and got in, giving her a quick wave before he took off.

Julia walked back inside and began to listlessly clear away the breakfast dishes. After all the excitement from the night before she felt drained and lost.

She hadn't heard anything from Frank in weeks and the constant uncertainty was definitely playing with her nerves. She hadn't even been able to meditate in the past few weeks and could feel the old emotions she had fought so hard to suppress coming to the surface. Julia wasn't sure she was ready to face them quite yet, but she suspected she would need to sometime soon. Although she feared that once they were out, she would have a hard time shoving them back in.

She put the last of the dishes away and walked over to her desk, picking up her notepad. Maybe it was time to schedule some Reiki appointments. People had been calling her since she and Frank had moved here, but she had been putting them off, not wanting to work. She had begged Frank to retire so that they could spend some time together. But now that he was gone, she felt that throwing herself back into the work she loved might be just what she needed to do to help clear her mind.

A few hours later, Julia had a few Reiki sessions scheduled for the following week and even more scheduled in the coming weeks. She was excited to be working again and meeting and helping new people. She had not realized how much she missed talking with people and helping them. She decided that even when Frank came back, she would continue working and not sacrifice so much of her life for him.

As she shut her computer, she heard a knock on the front door and went to answer it. She went to the door and swung it open it with a welcoming smile.

Brody stood at the door with a paper bag and a frown on his face.

"Didn't I tell you not to open the door without checking who was there first?" He walked in and deposited the bag on the kitchen table before giving her a stern look.

"Oh, sorry, I just assumed that it was the window guy that you said was coming." Julia looked at him innocently.

"Really? Did you even look outside to see if there was a van with a window repair sign on it? Or maybe even a man carrying a window? It could have been anyone standing there Julia. Until we find out who threw a rock through your window, you need to be more careful."

This time, Julia did look a bit more chastised. "Yes, you're right of course. I will be more careful and look before I open the door next time. I really am sorry."

Her eyes instantly brightened when she spotted Brody's bag and realized she hadn't eaten since breakfast.

"So, what's in the bag? Food I'm hoping."

Brody smiled, already forgetting his frustration with her. "Yes food. I thought I would bring us both some lunch and be here when the repair company comes over. They should be here any minute now."

"Thank you. I'm starved. I was so busy this morning setting up appointments, I forgot to eat lunch. Let me get some plates." Julia bustled over to the kitchen cabinet to retrieve plates and napkins.

"I'm beginning to think that keeping you safe and fed is going to be a full-time job," Brody teased. "What are you setting up appointments for?"

Julia walked over and started to unpack the deli sandwiches and steaming coffee that Brody had brought. She looked at him excitedly. "I've decided to start working again. I have several Reiki sessions scheduled, and more in the coming weeks. It looks like there are quite a few people in this town who are very interested after all."

Brody sat down at the table and opened the lids on the coffees for them. He was still skeptical, but couldn't help feeling her excitement and didn't want to say anything to squelch it. "That's great, I'm really happy for you. It should help you meet some new people as well. I have to admit I'm surprised you could line up so many sessions. Maybe the people in this town are more enlightened than I am. I honestly never heard of Reiki before I met you."

"Yes, there is quite a bit of interest actually. Frank had said he doubted that anyone in a small town would be interested and I shouldn't waste my time, but apparently he was wrong."

Julia watched Brody take a big bite from his sandwich, and asked, "So, have you heard anything new? Either about Frank, or the stone that was thrown through my window? Or maybe even the dark sedan?"

"No, no, and no." Brody shook his head. He took a sip from his coffee. "I guess I sound like a pretty lousy detective, don't I? This case just has me baffled. None of it makes any sense. I keep thinking that I must be missing something."

Julia nodded her head in agreement. "It doesn't make any sense to me either," she admitted. "For years, I thought Frank and I just lived an ordinary life. Now I'm wondering if it was ever really that ordinary, or if I just gotten used to it over the years."

Brody furrowed his brows. "Julia, was Frank ever... abusive to you in all the years you were together?"'

Julia swallowed hard, almost choking on her sandwich. She looked at Brody, shocked at the question. However, before she could answer the question, they heard a knock at the door, and a deep voice called out, "One Day Window Replacement here! Anyone home?"

Brody stood up, headed to the door to open it and then proceeded to guide two repairmen on where to go. By the time they had assessed the situation and started on the repair, Julia had gotten over some of her shock in response to Brody's question.

As she contemplated his question, she watched as Brody confidently directed the men on where to go and what was expected of them. Had Frank been abusive?

She finished her meal and stood to clean up their lunch dishes as Brody came back into the kitchen. "Let's go for a walk while they are working. We can talk while we walk." He took her by the arm and guided her to the door.

They walked along the beach in silence for a while, until finally Brody looked down at Julia. "I don't want to pry into your personal life but if we are ever going to figure out what happened to your husband, I need an answer to my earlier question. Whatever you tell me could help me find him."

Julia nodded but continued to walk on in silence for a while. Finally, she spotted some driftwood, sat down and started talking. "I never thought of Frank as abusive. Of course, there were definitely times he could be cold and condescending, but for the most part, he was pleasant and just went about his business and allowed me to go about mine."

Brody had sat down next to her and now looked at her with his brows furrowed. "You seemed to be awfully afraid of making him angry Julia. Why? What did he do when he was angry?"

Despite the warm sun, Julia shuddered a little. "All husbands get angry at their wives sometimes, don't they? I'm sure that you were angry with your wife too on occasion?"

Brody sighed. "Don't avoid the question, Julia. Of course, I got angry at Holly sometimes, and she got angry with me. In fact, we had some real blowouts at times. But I don't think either one of us was ever visibly shaking at the thought of making the other one angry. You seem to be terrified of Frank, Julia. Why?"

Julia looked down at her hands. The thought of talking to someone about Frank and his moods seemed like a betrayal, and one that would cost her if he ever found out. Still, maybe Brody was right. Maybe whatever she told him would help the case. This unknown limbo was starting to get to her. It was better to find him and face his wrath than this constant unknown.

"Frank never hurt me or anything like that," she began. "He never left marks, so he told me it wasn't wrong. He said I needed to learn my place in the relationship, and once I did, he wouldn't need to correct me anymore. Even so, I probably shouldn't have made him so angry… and I liked it even less when he put me into timeout. That was the worst."

Brody was shocked at what he heard, but his voice remained emotionless as he asked, "What exactly did he do to put you into *timeout*?"

Julia shrugged, now feeling embarrassed to go on after her brave start. "Maybe I'm overreacting. Timeout is just in the spare bedroom. He would lock me in there if he was really angry with me and leave me there until he cooled down. Sometimes, if I seemed sorry enough for what I had done, he would bring me something to eat. But other times, if he felt I was not repenting enough for what I had done, he would leave me in there for a day or two."

Brody looked at Julia, stunned that the articulate and seemingly assured woman sitting next to him would allow herself to be locked into a room for days. "What kinds of things would set him off?" he asked.

Julia looked up at him as if she were confused by the question. "What do you mean? I wasn't a bad person if that's what you're asking. I didn't make him angry on purpose. Sometimes I was just late because of a client, or I forgot to pick something up for him at the store. He wasn't always angry when that happened, just sometimes. I know I should have tried harder, but often, I just didn't think I was being so bad." Julia looked out at the water. "Frank said that was my problem, I never realized when I was bad, and I needed to learn."

Brody just stared at Julia's emotionless face as she talked. It seemed like she had learned to shut down when she needed to. A part of him wanted to tell her it was ok, and she didn't need to tell him more, but another part of him needed to know all the details, so he let her continue.

"The last few years of our marriage have been better. I think I finally figured out how to be good and not make him angry. He even agreed to move here with me and didn't punish me for threatening to divorce him." She looked at Brody. "That proves that he loves me, doesn't it?"

It sounded to Brody as if she were trying to convince herself as much as him, and he just shook his head, incredulous at her reasoning. It must have taken years of psychological abuse to get Julia to blame herself for Frank's own lack of control.

"It was not your fault when Frank locked you in the spare bedroom, Julia. No one deserves to be locked away."

Julia looked at Brody slightly embarrassed. "Frank said that when his kids were little and misbehaved, they needed to go into their room and stay there. And if they really misbehaved, they needed to go without supper. If I behaved like an unruly child, then I needed to be treated like one."

As she spoke, she wrapped her arms around herself and continued, "He blamed my mother for not scolding me enough when I was a child. If she had taught me to be a better person, he wouldn't need to teach me now. He said I was lucky that he did not believe in hitting women and children, and it proved he was a good husband."

Brody shook his head in disbelief. "No Julia, that's not normal or right. Real men do not treat their wives like children just because they are angry. It's also not right for a man to lock his wife away. Guest rooms should be for guests, not *timeout*."

"Maybe cops are different than the men that Frank hung out with… sometimes when a woman didn't show up for a dinner party, the husband would say she was not feeling well and had stayed home to rest. Later, Frank would tell me it was because the wife had misbehaved and was left alone at home to think about what she had done."

Brody was beginning to wonder what kind of business associates Frank had been dealing with if spousal abuse was that normal for them. Brody had seen a lot of abuse in his time as a detective. Depending on the circle of men and who they hung out with, abuse could definitely be more common in some groups. Still, abuse was often more prevalent in the less educated or gang-like groups. He had not heard it happen that often or openly in the upper class.

"It is not normal or acceptable for a man to hit his wife or lock her away Julia. There is never an excuse for that no matter what Frank told you. When he married you, he should have accepted you for who you were and not tried to change you or manipulate you into being any different than who you are."

Julia looked at him again, trying to comprehend what he was saying. Did Brody believe she had been abused? She had sometimes wondered that herself, but Frank had always managed to convince her that it was only for her own good, and he hated having to put her in timeouts, but she forced him to do it by misbehaving.

"How did you punish your children when they misbehaved Brody? Didn't you ever send them to timeout when they were younger?"

Julia herself had never gotten into any real trouble when she had been a child. She and her mother had been very close, and she had rarely needed to be scolded. Unfortunately, Julia's mother had been diagnosed with cancer when Julia was in high school. Julia had never gone through a rebellious stage because she had been busy taking care of her mother and going to school.

Brody sighed, exasperated, "Yes we sent the kids to their rooms if they were misbehaving Julia. But they always got supper and they were not locked away like some kind of prisoner. It was only for a short while until we could go and talk to them and discuss whatever needed to be corrected. It's not the same as locking your wife away for days at a time. And no, we never spanked the kids. Neither Holly nor I ever believed that we should resort to physically punishing our kids, ever."

Julia nodded her head, happy they finally had some common ground. She thought back on how happy she had been as a child growing up with her mother. Her mother had been young, but she had always made Julia feel loved and safe despite not having much money.

"I agree with that, Brody. If I had been lucky enough to have had a child, I definitely would have never spanked them. I don't believe I would ever have sent them to bed without supper or locked them away. I would always have wanted my child to feel loved and wanted!" As she was speaking, Julia stood up and was emphasizing her words with her arms.

Brody had been watching Julia when suddenly, from his left, a familiar voice said, "My, my, Brody. What are you two discussing that's got the young lady so heated?"

He turned and looked into the smirking face of Krystle Davis, a local reporter who was notorious for her sensationalistic writing. She was looking at Julia like a spider eying up the fly it had just caught in its web.

CHAPTER 18

Brody appraised the woman standing next to him in the sand. She was wearing a tight pencil skirt with a smart-looking jacket in her hands, while holding a pair of heels.

"It doesn't look like you're dressed for a day at the beach Krystle. What brings you here?"

Krystle gave him a sly smile. "I came to the pier to grab a quick sandwich and take a break, and I thought I spotted you down here. You were having quite the discussion it seems. Since you've been avoiding my calls, I decided to come on down and see what gives." She looked over at Julia with a slight sneer. "I guess I can see what was keeping you so busy now."

Julia watched the newcomer with curiosity. Sensing the evident tension between the two of them, she walked over to Krystle, holding out her hand ready to shake Krystle's. "Hi, I'm Julia Masterson, how are you? Detective Barker is helping me find out what happened to my husband."

Krystle gave Julia her own hand in a limp, halfhearted handshake, and with an appraising look said, "Yes, I've heard. Your husband disappeared without a trace a few weeks ago, didn't he?"

Julia's cheeks reddened slightly, partly from embarrassment, but also with annoyance. There was something in Krystle's tone of voice that warned her to be on alert around this woman.

"Yes, sadly he did. I'm hoping that the detective can find out where he is soon though. I wasn't aware that my husband's disappearance was public knowledge?"

"This is a small town and people talk. Everything is public knowledge around here, isn't that true Brody?" Krystle looked pointedly at Brody.

"Besides, it's my business to know what's going on around here," she continued, looking back at Julia. "Not much happens without me knowing it."

Brody stepped up to Julia's side. "Julia, meet Krystle Davis, Longboat Key Island's most infamous reporter."

Julia raised her eyebrows slightly at this news. "Oh, you're a reporter? I see. Well, I guess there's not that much of a story here. A man walking out on his wife certainly isn't all that exciting unless you're the wife that's involved. And I'm sure that when we find him, there will be a perfectly logical and probably mundane reason for him having left so suddenly."

"Well, it's true a man going on a short little vacation may not be much of a story," said Krystle, "But a man just disappearing under mysterious circumstances never to be heard from again... well, that might be an extremely interesting story. Especially when he leaves behind an attractive wife who just moved into the area."

Shocked, Julia just stared at Krystle, not knowing what to say to the implied accusation. "We don't know that my husband left under mysterious circumstances and I certainly do expect to hear from him again soon. Detective Barker is just helping to locate him in case he needs help in some way."

Krystle gave her a cold smile. "Well, if that's the case, who knows, maybe the public could be of help in locating him. If you would agree to an interview, we could get the story out in the open and maybe find out what happened to your husband and where he is."

Brody stepped in between Krystle and Julia. "I know exactly how your interviews and stories turn out Krystle, and Mrs. Masterson is interested in finding her husband, not being fodder for your next sensationalized story. I'm afraid you're going to need to look somewhere else for your next victim. Now, if you don't mind, we were in the middle of a conversation when you interrupted." As he spoke, Brody motioned for Krystle to move back towards the pier.

"I am sorry to have interrupted such an animated conversation, but the beach does seem like a strange place to interview a woman about her missing husband, doesn't it?" said Krystle. She stayed rooted to the spot and looked suspiciously at Julia, wondering if there might be a story here for her after all.

After a moment of silence from both Brody and Julia, Krystle gave Brody a suggestive and provocative look. "Maybe you could give me a call tonight and we can clear up any misconceptions over a drink? I've been trying to reach you for days now; you don't have anything to hide, do you, Brody?"

"I'm busy tonight," Brody said tersely. "Why don't you get going now and find a real story out there somewhere. I'm afraid I can't help you, Krystle."

Krystle started to leave, but as she turned towards the pier, she looked back at Julia. "Nice meeting you Mrs. Masterson. I'm sure I'll be seeing you again; it's a small town, like I said. And don't forget, I'm always available if you ever feel you want to clear something off your conscience."

As she turned away and walked up the beach, Krystle smiled to herself.

Julia watched her go and turned to Brody. "She's not a very pleasant woman, is she?"

"No, she's not. More snake than human to be honest." Brody looked in the direction of Julia's house. "I guess we better get back. Hopefully your window will be fixed by now, and I also want to see if forensics found anything unusual or helpful on the note we found."

As they walked back, Julia wondered what kind of relationship Brody had with Krystle Davis. It was clear that there was more going on between the two of them. Krystle seemed possessive when she looked at Brody, and Julia wondered if their relationship was much more personal than Brody admitted. Julia just hoped that she would not be running into Krystle Davis again anytime soon. The woman made her feel very uncomfortable, and she wondered again what Brody possibly saw in her.

CHAPTER 19

Julia and Brody walked into the house just as the repairmen were packing up their tools and getting ready to leave.

"You're all set Mrs. Masterson, the window is as good as new. You'll be getting the bill in the mail in a few days. Unfortunately, we had to add some charges for an emergency call, but I'm pretty sure that if you submit it to your homeowner's insurance, it should be covered." The man looked at Julia, trying to be helpful, and looking truly regretful at having to charge extra after the trauma of having her window broken in the middle of the night.

"Thank you so much, I understand, and I really appreciate how quickly you came. Thank you for the advice as well, I'll be sure to do that." In truth, Julia did not know if she even had homeowner's insurance, or any insurance for that matter. She realized again how much she had left for Frank to handle.

After they left, Julia sat wearily on her couch and sighed. "I guess I'll have to look through all the paperwork again, this time to see if there are any insurance papers."

Brody looked at Julia sympathetically. "Do you have a personal lawyer or accountant that you use? Someone that can help you sort through all the paperwork like insurances, house deeds, mortgages and things like that?"

"Yes, Frank does have a lawyer he would call for help with planning some of his assets. His name is James Carson. I think I gave you his name when we first looked through Frank's papers. I met him shortly after Frank and I were engaged. He's always been a very pleasant man. You're right, he may be able to help me sort through some of this. I'll look for his number again and give him a call."

Brody remembered calling James Carson at the beginning of the investigation. The man had seemed very pleasant, but unfortunately had not turned out to be very helpful. Frank had apparently been very secretive even with the lawyer, only giving him the bare minimum of information and paperwork needed to complete whatever Frank needed. Brody wondered if by now, the lawyer might have more information than he had been willing to share during their first phone call. He nodded to Julia.

"I think that's a great idea. The longer Frank is gone, the more you are likely to have to take care of some things yourself. If you don't mind, I would like to sit in on that meeting. I'm wondering if the lawyer really told me everything he knew. Maybe now that Frank has been missing for a while, he might be willing to share some more information with us."

"I'll give him a call right away then. If he agrees, you can certainly listen in on the conversation. I'm sure he would have told you everything he knows, but if you think talking to him again will help find Frank, then you are more than welcome to join in."

Julia went into Frank's office and retrieved his address book, looking for James Carson's number. As soon as she found the number, she dialed it and asked to speak to him. Brody could hear her talking to who he assumed was the receptionist and while he waited, he walked over to the repaired window to examine it, making sure it was as safe and secure as it needed to be.

"He is in meetings all day, but his secretary said he has an opening tomorrow at 9 am and could speak with me then," said Julia, hanging up the phone. She looked at Brody, inquisitively. "Will that time work out for you as well?"

"It's as good a time as any." Brody walked over to the desk and absently shuffled through the address book again. "I know I already took pictures of all the numbers in here, but do you mind if I take it for the rest of the day to look through the actual book? I'll bring it back in the morning when I come for the meeting. I can't shake the feeling that I'm missing something, and I'd like to take another look at the book itself."

"If you think it will help, be my guest." Julia sighed. "At this point, I'm willing to turn the whole house upside down to see if we can find anything."

Brody smiled encouragingly at Julia. "I don't think we need to tear the house down yet, but if you do think of anything, it doesn't hurt to look." As an afterthought, he asked, "Have you really looked through the house since he left? I mean, did you look specifically to see if there is anything here that Frank would normally take with him? Or maybe, something is missing that he wouldn't have bothered to take with him? Anything out of place really."

Julia thought about what he had just said. She thought back to the weeks since Frank had been gone, and realized, other than Brody looking through his office, she had not really ever looked through his clothes or belongings to see if there was something unusual.

"No, I guess I haven't looked very carefully. I mean, I didn't notice anything unusual when he first left, but I also didn't really look. The duffle he usually took was gone and so was his briefcase. I didn't see his wallet, so I assumed he took that with him as well. He always had his passport in his briefcase and his license on him anyway, so I never thought to look and see if they were still here somewhere."

"Well, it might be a good idea to look around tonight and see if anything is odd or out of place. It might give us a clue as to whether he left voluntarily or not, or if he intended to stay away longer this time." Brody headed for the door. "I'll see you in the morning then. If you find anything, give me a call."

After he left, Julia decided to take a look around the bedroom. She normally did not look through Frank's nightstand, but now, she timidly approached his side of the bed and slowly opened the drawer. She saw the book he had been reading, a bunch of loose change, and a pad and paper with some numbers scribbled on it. She also found various cords, probably belonging to his cell phone and iPad, but couldn't find either of them.

As she opened the bottom drawer, she saw a strange-looking case she didn't recognize. She picked it up and set it on the bed. She could see that it had a combination lock on it, but it looked like the lock had been left open.

Just how many secret little safes and boxes does that man have around here? She thought as she opened the box with some apprehension, somewhat afraid of what she would find inside and gasped at what she saw.

Inside, there was a neat little compartment that was in the shape of a handgun, and a spot for extra bullets. The gun compartment was clearly empty, but Julia saw that there were still some bullets in the box. She had never seen the case before and had certainly never seen Frank carrying a gun. In fact, he and his friends had been to several anti-gun rallies and Julia had always thought he did not believe private citizens should carry weapons. She was starting to wonder whether she knew her husband at all.

Carefully, she carried the gun case to Frank's office and placed it on the desk. She contemplated calling Brody right away and letting him know about her discovery, but decided to wait and keep looking around the bedroom to see if there was anything more she could find. She went back into her bedroom and decided to look through Frank's side of the closet.

Here there were no surprises. She had always taken care of the laundry and put away Frank's clothes. She looked through everything but didn't see anything that caught her eyes as missing. He had apparently taken a few shirts and pants, mostly normal business attire. She did see that his favorite pair of khakis were gone and two of his polo shirts. The trip was clearly not strictly for business. Even that was not odd, as Frank often took a few casual shirts and pants. She did notice one strange thing however. He had left behind his favorite leather jacket. Normally, he took that with him whenever he planned to be gone for more than a few days. It was odd for him to plan to be gone as long as he was and to leave that jacket behind. She made a mental note to let Brody know in the morning when he came over for the phone call with the lawyer. She was curious if Brody would find it odd as well.

When she was done taking inventory, and finding nothing else out of the ordinary, she went back to the living room and sat down with a sigh. She wondered yet again where Frank might be and if he was in some kind of trouble. Was he hiding from something or was he being held against his will somewhere? Wherever he was, she certainly had a lot of questions for him when he came back.

CHAPTER 20

The next morning, promptly at 8:45, Brody showed up at Julia's door bearing the customary steaming coffee he always brought with him.

"Oh yes, thank you. I think I really need coffee this morning." Julia had not slept well last night and was eager to show Brody the gun case she had found.

"Let's go into Frank's office, I have something I want to show you." She led the way and pointed to the gun case sitting on the desk. "I found this in his nightstand drawer last night. I have never seen it before, and I certainly would never have thought that Frank would carry a gun with him."

Brody set his coffee down on the desk and carefully looked at the gun case, examining the lock and the exterior before opening it and looking inside. "It definitely looks like there was a gun in here. I wonder if he took it with him and if that means he was anticipating some kind of trouble? You say that the lock was still open? Maybe that means he was in a hurry and took it as an afterthought."

Julia thought about what Brody was saying. She wondered if Frank had received a call from someone while she was out on her run. He had not warned her that he was going away before she had left for the run, and his text had said he had needed to leave suddenly. Who could he have gone to meet on such short notice, and why would he feel he needed to take a gun with him?

"I had no idea Frank even knew how to shoot a gun. Is there any way to see how long he has had it? I am just wondering if he has always had one, or if it was acquired recently since we moved here."

"We did run his name through our system when he disappeared and nothing showed he had a license to carry, but we also didn't look for that in particular. I'll have them check again for a gun license both here in Florida and Ohio and see if anything comes up now that we know. Unfortunately, we don't have the serial number to see where it was purchased. Once we find out where he applied for a license, maybe we can check some of the surrounding gun dealers."

Julia nodded, wishing they could get answers sooner. "I just don't understand any of this. Frank was never the kind of man to carry a gun."

Brody looked at Julia contemplatively, wondering what else Julia did not know about her husband. "Did you find anything else while you were looking around?" he asked.

"No, not really. He seemed to have taken enough clothes for 4 or 5 days and one pair of casual pants and shirts, so he must have planned to spend at least a little leisure time somewhere." Julia took a sip of her coffee and looked at Brody. "That's not really unusual though. What does strike me as a bit odd is he didn't take his favorite leather jacket. He always took that if he planned to be gone for longer than a few days. It was definitely his go-to jacket wherever he went."

Brody thought about what Julia had said. "It is summer though, and he may have thought he didn't need it, especially if he was staying here in Florida. It stays awfully warm here even at night." He gestured towards the gun. "But the fact that the gun case was left unlocked could indicate he was in a hurry, so he might have just overlooked it in his haste to pack his bags."

"Yes, that is possible of course," Julia agreed.

"How long do you think he had from the time you left for your run until you came back?" Brody asked.

"I'm not sure. Maybe an hour and a half to two hours. I just remember that I took a longer route and then walked a bit, to enjoy the scenery. I also stopped and did some yoga out by the cliffs. It always helps to clear my mind."

Brody thought about it. "That is enough time to receive a call, pack and grab an Uber I guess. But if he wasn't planning on leaving, he must have received the call right after you left."

Brody glanced at his watch. "We'll run all this through the system after we take the call from Frank's lawyer. It's almost 9:00 and time to give him a call soon."

The two of them settled in their chairs with their coffees and waited for 9:00 when Julia could call James Carson for their meeting.

"Did you find anything new or interesting in Frank's address book?" Julia inquired, glancing at the address book that Brody had handed back to her.

"I might have. I have someone cross-referencing some of the numbers with the numbers that were in the second phone we found. None of the names match, but we might get a match with the actual numbers. It's worth a try anyway. I feel like some of the names in the book are eerily similar to some of the names we saw in both his phones actually."

Julia looked at Brody with interest. "Really? That's something then. Can we call the numbers and see who answers?"

Brody nodded. "If we find any matches, we'll start with those. But even if we don't find any, I think it's time to start calling all the numbers in his book." He looked at Julia sympathetically. "Until we find some evidence to the contrary, we have to assume that Frank is still alive and protect his privacy and his rights to a certain extent."

Julia nodded, but looked at her hands guiltily. How much of Frank's privacy had she already violated?

"Honestly though Julia," Brody continued, "The longer we don't hear from Frank or see any evidence of life, the more I am convinced that something may have happened to him." Brody steered clear of using the actual word deceased, and when he saw how vehemently Julia was shaking her head, he was glad he had.

"No, no Brody. I just can't believe that. I think after 20 years of being married I would know if he wasn't alive. I would feel something, don't you think? He's out there somewhere, I'm sure of it!"

Brody looked at Julia sympathetically.

She took a sip of coffee and continued, "Maybe he got himself into some kind of trouble and is hiding out somewhere until he feels it's safe to come out. Someone in that address book may know where he is, and we need to find him as soon as possible, so we will call every number in there, privacy or privacy rights aside. We need to find him."

Brody nodded in agreement. As long as Julia continued to allow him free access to any of Frank's belongings and papers, he did not need to worry about violating any of Frank's rights, even if they did find him alive. Although Brody was starting to believe that it was highly unlikely at this point.

Julia's phone rang, and as she looked at the caller ID she said to Brody, "It's James Carson."

"Hello, Julia? It's James Carson here. I decided to call you a few minutes early if that's alright. I've got a busy day ahead and wouldn't mind getting a jump on things, if you know what I mean?" The cheerful and energetic voice of Frank's long-time lawyer rang out over the speaker.

"No, that's fine. I was just about to call you anyway," Julia answered. She glanced over at Brody. "I have Detective Brody Barker here with me and he was hoping he might be able to speak with you as well, so if you don't mind, I'll keep you on speaker so we can all hear."

"Not at all, fine with me if that's what you want, Julia." James Carson had always called Julia by her first name. The familiarity he had always treated her with had endeared the lawyer to Julia from the time she had first met him. "I gather that you still haven't heard anything from Frank as the detective is still with you?"

"No, I haven't heard anything. I was hoping that maybe he would have tried to contact you?" Julia asked, her hopes of the lawyer knowing something quickly dwindling.

"No, I'm afraid I haven't Julia. This is all very strange. Frank has always stayed in fairly close touch with me, you know. He relied on me to handle a lot of his business dealings and some of his personal dealings."

"That's where we were hoping you might be able to help us out," Brody interjected. "I think it might be time to take a closer look at some of those business and personal dealings. There might be some leads there that could help us find Mr. Masterson."

James Carson remained silent for a few seconds before answering carefully, "You know that my business with Frank is protected by lawyer-client confidentiality clause?"

Brody tried to use his most convincing voice. "Yes of course. But if Mr. Masterson is in some kind of trouble, I'm sure you would want to do whatever you could to help him, wouldn't you? I know you've been working with him for a lot of years and I'm sure it would weigh heavily on you if something happened to Frank and you could have done something to help."

The lawyer remained silent for some time. *At least he's thinking it over and not just dismissing me outright,* Brody thought.

"Please Mr. Carson, if you can help us with any information that might lead us to Frank, please help. I'm desperate to find my husband." Julia was pleading now, convinced that the lawyer had some information that would be helpful.

"Ok, I think I have some information that you would find potentially helpful, etective. But I want to talk here in my office and not on the phone. Also, I want Julia to be here as well. You are my client as well Julia, and I will not be breaching any confidentiality if I am giving you the information."

"You want us to come to Ohio?" Julia asked. She looked at Brody. "Are you allowed to travel out of state?"

Brody nodded. "Yes of course, it's not that unusual to follow up on a lead in a different state," he said to Julia. Then, he turned his attention back to the phone. "I'll run it by the chief, Mr. Carson, but I'm sure we can get there in the next few days. I'll be in touch."

"Excellent, I look forward to hearing from you, detective. I think I might have some very interesting information for you both. Oh, and Julia, I will be emailing you the copies of your insurance documents so you can deal with the claims you told my receptionist about yesterday."

"Thank you, Mr. Carson, I appreciate your help. I guess we'll be seeing you soon then."

After the final goodbyes, Julia set down her phone and looked at Brody. "That was a bit unexpected. Why do you think it is so important that we go back to Ohio instead of him just sharing the information on the phone?"

"I'm not sure yet, but I'm assuming whatever he wants to share with you might be of a sensitive nature and he feels it's best if it is delivered to you in person."

Seeing Julia's worried look, Brody was quick to reassure her, "Don't worry Julia, no matter what it is, I'll be right there with you and help you deal with it. This might be the lead we've been waiting for to find out where your husband went."

Julia didn't look quite convinced but nodded her head anyway.

"As long as we're up there, I think we should try and see Jane Harper and Frank's daughters also, if I can get them to agree." Brody looked at Julia, curious what her reaction would be to his suggestion.

Julia looked even more worried now. "I don't know if that's such a good idea. I don't think that Jane or the girls will want to see me. Especially now."

"Let's not jump to any conclusions right now. I will call all three today again and see if I can set up some interviews with them. Who knows, they may have some helpful information they are not even aware they have. Since you'll be in Ohio anyway it might be helpful to have you there. You are probably a better judge than me as to whether they are being truthful or not."

Julia nodded noncommittedly. "I'm not sure that's true, but I'll think about it. I do want to find out if they know something about Frank or where he is."

Brody looked at Julia and tried to set her mind at ease. "Don't worry Julia, someone somewhere has to know something. We'll find him."

Or his body, thought Brody cynically.

CHAPTER 21

A few days later, Julia was once again toting an oversized cooler down the dock towards Brody's boat.

"I thought you learned last time that you didn't need to feed us for a week?" said Brody, laughing as he lifted the cooler onto his boat and helped Julia climb on board.

"I guess I might have overdone it a little bit," admitted Julia. "What a beautiful day to be on the water. Thank you for asking me to come."

"Thank you for coming," Brody said. "I wanted to share the news I received today in person, but since it's my day off, I was already down here cleaning the boat and getting ready to take her out. I appreciate you making the trip. I haven't had a chance to take her out lately."

Julia looked down, feeling guilty. "I guess that's my fault. I know the case with my husband has been keeping you very busy."

"It's not your fault. The chief has been on everyone lately and we are all overloaded. I guess he feels a lot of pressure to solve any open cases and the pressure then trickles down to the rest of us."

Julia nodded and sat next to him in front of the boat, admiring again the expertise to which he maneuvered the boat out of its slip and towards the open water. Brody had called her a few hours earlier and said he had received some news he wanted to share with her and asked her if she could join him at the dock. She was curious about what he had to say, but decided to wait until they were out on the water and Brody had steered them well away from the other boats leaving the dock.

When they were finally out on the open water, Brody slowed the boat and drove at a comfortable speed so that he could talk. Julia looked over at him expectantly and he glanced over and then looked back out over the water, as if trying to decide how best to start.

"I don't want you to get your hopes up too much Julia, but we got a report of a possible sighting of your husband."

Julia gasped audibly. "Oh my, where is he? Is he alright?"

"The sighting wasn't current, so I don't know the answers to your questions. He was sighted around the time that he went missing, and it might give us some clues as to where he might have gone after he left here."

Julia looked out over the water, trying to hide her disappointment. It seemed every time they found something it just led to more questions and no answers.

"Where was he seen? What was he doing?"

Brody gave her an odd look before he answered her. "You said that your husband was afraid of water, right?"

Julia nodded. "Yes, it was definitely not something he loved. Why?"

"Well, it turns out that a man matching your husband's description tried to rent a boat at a small marina in Miami, with cash. When the owner refused to rent to him without any ID, the man got quite irate and stormed off."

Julia looked at Brody, confused. "That can't have been Frank. Why would he want to rent a boat? Why would the boat owner think it was Frank, anyway? Did he know him?"

Brody shook his head. "No, I don't think he knew him, but he thought it was very odd behavior. Frank needed to show some ID especially since he was renting an expensive boat. The boat owner happened to be a retired cop and decided a few days ago to stop by his old precinct to report the incident. He thought maybe the man might be involved with a smuggling scheme of some sort."

Brody maneuvered the boat around a large wake that had been created by a speed boat passing them and waited till the water calmed before continuing.

"While he was talking to one of his old buddies, he glanced down at his desk and saw your husband's picture. We have forwarded it to all the surrounding precincts and asked them to keep an eye out, in case he's spotted anywhere in Florida. As soon as he saw the picture, he recognized him straight away."

"He has to be mistaken," Julia said perplexed. "Why would Frank rent a boat? He hated being out on the water. I wasn't even sure he'd be up for the catamaran on our anniversary. How can we be sure it's really Frank that he saw?"

Brody kept his eye on the boat cutting in a bit close to them and shrugged his shoulders. "We don't know for sure I guess, but the guy was a cop. Cops are trained to notice certain things, and if a cop ID's someone, I tend to believe them."

"It just doesn't make any sense. If he wanted to go out on the water, why didn't he just come home and go on the catamaran with me? And why the secrecy?" A sudden realization seemed to hit Julia, and Brody saw her pale slightly under her tan. "Was he alone? Did the cop see if anyone was with him?"

Brody had been waiting for the question, and now he tried to answer carefully. "Frank walked back over to a car parked quite a distance away and entered the passenger side. That means someone else had to be driving. Unfortunately, it was too far for the cop to see the driver or the make of the car. All he could tell was it appeared to be a dark sedan of some kind."

Julia paled even more as she remembered the mysterious dark sedan that had been parked on her street the night of the storm. The very same night that someone had thrown a rock through her window with an ominous note.

"So, what now?" Julia asked, trying to sound brave in spite of the sudden chill she felt.

"We keep looking at other boat rental places around Miami to see if he tried somewhere else. Unfortunately, there are hundreds of places to rent a boat in Miami, and he could have gone to any of the surrounding areas to rent one as well. If he was that determined, I'm fairly sure he would have found someone willing to rent to him."

Julia sighed and sat back. "So more unanswered questions and more mysteries."

"I'm afraid so, but in a few days, we are going to see his lawyer, and hopefully we'll get a chance to talk to his children and Jane Harper. We'll see if we can draw any connections to Miami from any of them." He looked over at Julia questioningly. "You wouldn't know why he would be in Miami, would you?"

Julia just shook her head, discouraged. "No, as far as I know, all his business dealings were up North or overseas. I never heard him mention having to go to Florida, let alone Miami."

"We didn't find much on the gun your husband had either, unfortunately. We ran his name through the registries in both Florida and Ohio but came up with nothing. The gun was not legally registered under Frank's name in either of those states."

Julia looked perplexed. "So, does that mean if he had a gun, it was illegal? He could go to jail for that, couldn't he?"

"Yes, he could. But remember, we didn't actually see the gun. We only found a gun case and it's not illegal to own that. In theory, he could just have gotten the case without a gun in it. We only assumed he must have taken the gun belonging to the case with him, but we don't know that for a fact." Brody maneuvered around another wake and headed toward the same buoy they had anchored at before.

"That doesn't make any sense. Why would he have a gun case and bullets if he didn't have the gun?" Julia looked at Brody hoping he had an answer.

He just shook his head, not knowing what to tell her as he continued towards the buoy.

Julia sat quiet and pensive, staring out over the ocean as Brody drove to their destination. Brody took the time to mull things over in his own head as well. Julia was right when she had remarked they had even more questions than answers yet again. He had not been able to get hold of Jane or either of her two daughters, and even after leaving several messages, they had not yet returned his calls. Brody thought it odd that they seemed to be avoiding him when it was them that had reported their father missing. There seemed to be so much about this case that was strange.

He dropped anchor next to a buoy marker and walked back to the cooler Julia had packed. Just like last time, there was an assortment of drinks and food. He took out a beer and offered Julia a wine cooler, which she absently accepted. They sat and sipped their drinks in silence for a while, each lost in their own thoughts.

"Why did you name this boat *The Partner*?" Julia asked suddenly, looking up at Brody curiously.

Brody was slightly taken aback at the sudden and unexpected question, not sure if he was ready to give her a complete answer. It had been years since the incident, and he had never talked to anyone about it.

"I bought the boat years ago with my old partner. We never got to finish it and get it seaworthy before he died. I guess it only seemed fitting to somehow pay him tribute." Brody took a long drink from his beer can and hoped she would be satisfied with the answer without asking any more questions.

"Oh my, how sad." Julia looked at him compassionately. "How did he die?"

"He was killed in the process of serving a warrant on a fugitive," Brody said, not elaborating and hoping desperately she would drop the questions.

"That's just awful. His poor family. How tragic. You must have been devastated." Julia looked at him in shock, expecting to see some sign of outward emotion, but she only saw his face set in stony silence.

She could tell he didn't want to talk about it, but she asked anyway, "Was your partner married? Have you been able to stay in touch with his family?"

Brody had never been able to speak about his partner's death to anyone, not even with Holly, his ex-wife, but for some reason, he felt himself finally wanting to let out all the pain, bitterness and guilt he had been bottling up all these years.

"No, I haven't stayed in touch with his wife," he said curtly. "It was my fault that he was killed. We were there as backup to serve a warrant. It should have been no big deal, just a low-life drug dealer who had missed his court appearance. We were watching the back door, while the primary officers were at the front door to issue the arrest warrant. Suddenly, the back door opened, and we saw a young girl run out, carrying a baby. She was screaming and crying, and Jack ran over to her to grab her and the baby. I walked over to help him, but before either of us knew what was happening, the perp we were looking for came out shooting. He shot Jack in the head, just barely missing the girl, and got me in the chest. Luckily, I was wearing my bulletproof vest and I was ok, other than some major bruising in the ribs. Jack wasn't so lucky. He never regained consciousness and was taken off life support at the hospital later that night."

Julia gasped at the story, "Oh Brody, I'm so sorry. That's horrible, but it wasn't your fault that your partner was killed. No one could have known that man would try and kill you."

Brody just shook his head sadly. "It's my job to know that could happen. That's why we were there as backup. I should have been watching the back door, covering for Jack and I should have seen the guy come out with a gun. Instead, I let my emotions get the better of me and ran to the girl. It's what the drug dealer counted on, and it cost my partner his life."

Brody walked over to the cooler and took out another beer, cracking it open. "Jack was the best person I have ever met in my life. We could talk about everything, and we were so close we could have been brothers. He would have gladly taken a bullet for me and my family. He was the most heroic person I ever met. But instead of a long and successful partnership, I lost him to some two-bit drug dealer all because I let my emotions take over common sense. I swore to him that day, while he was still on life support, that I would never make that same mistake again."

Julia just looked at him sadly. "I'm so sorry for your loss Brody. I can't even imagine how hard that must have been for you."

Brody looked at Julia curiously, surprised that she wasn't giving him the usual, *you need to stop blaming yourself, get over it and move on with life* spiel that he got from most people. In fact, that's why he had stopped talking about it. He wasn't ready to just get over it and move on, and he wasn't sure that he ever would be.

"I imagine that Holly must have been extremely worried about you after that happened," said Julia.

Again, Brody looked at her, surprised at her insight. He took another long drink and said, "Yeah, she was. She wanted me to apply for a desk job right then and there. It became a major source of contention between us, and you could say it might have even been the beginning of the end. She couldn't understand why I couldn't just transfer, and I couldn't understand why she didn't understand my reasons behind staying."

"And why couldn't you?" Julia asked simply. Brody opened and shut his mouth, stunned. In all the years and all the arguments he and Holly had had over this very subject, she had never once asked him why he couldn't just move to a safer position.

"I just couldn't. I owed it to Jack to keep going. I just needed to finish the job that Jack and I started," Brody finally said.

Julia shook her head, not accepting his answer. "I don't buy that. The truth is you didn't want to quit, isn't it? You thought you could make it up to him by risking your own life, and it was easier for you to forgive yourself for making a mistake that way, wasn't it?"

Brody could feel the familiar tightness in his gut and the uncontrollable anger start to well up in him in response to her statement.

Who is she to make a statement like that anyway? He thought.

Julia didn't know anything about him or Jack, or what they had shared, and he wanted to lash out at her to mind her own business and stop playing second-hand shrink. When he looked over at her though, she was watching him with such a look of genuine compassion and understanding that his anger melted away. He realized she wasn't judging him. In fact, she was right, he didn't want a desk job and he had sought out the riskier assignments, almost daring someone to come after him, thinking if he got killed, he would be making it up to Jack.

He nodded at her. "You're right. I volunteered for the riskier assignments, and I did it without regard for how it affected Holly or the kids. I felt I deserved to die just like Jack, but I couldn't tell Holly that. I came up with feeble reasons and excuses; we both started to drink and just stopped communicating with each other. I guess she probably knew the real reason, and I guess I just didn't really care if she knew."

Brody raked his hands through his hair. "Man, I sound like such a selfish schmuck when I look at it truthfully. No wonder she threw me out."

Julia moved over close to him and took his hand. "You're not a shmuck and you're probably not the only one to blame for your marriage not working. I'm so sorry you lost your partner that way. No one who hasn't been through that would know how they would react either. But if the situation had been reversed, and you had been killed instead of Jack, would you have forgiven him and wanted him to go on and live a happy life?"

Brody nodded vehemently. "Of course, I would. Jack was a great cop. I wouldn't want him to waste his life feeling guilty for one mistake. We all make mistakes. Thank God most of them don't turn out deadly."

"Then why don't you honor him and learn to forgive yourself as well?"

Brody was silent while he thought about what Julia had said. She wasn't trying to convince him it wasn't his fault like everyone else had. He knew it was his fault and she simply accepted his conclusion. No one had ever done that, so no one had ever been able to tell him it was ok to forgive himself. That simple revelation – that he could permit himself to forgive himself for a mistake – gave Brody a feeling of hope that he had not had since Jack had died.

Julia could see that Brody was wrestling with his thoughts, and she hoped she had not overstepped her boundaries. Ever since she had met him, she had sensed that Brody had been carrying a heavy burden and a deep anger. It was a relief to finally find out what it was that had been triggering him, but now, she wondered if she had gone too far in her advice.

Hoping to change the subject, she said, "So, that reporter Krystle Davis has left me a few messages. She wants to do an interview and write a column about my missing husband. She claims that her report may cause someone to remember something if they have any information or have seen anything. I don't really like her, but what do you think I should do? If it helps find Frank, I'd be willing to do almost anything."

CHAPTER 22

Krystle had been leaving Brody almost daily messages as well. But the messages she was leaving Brody were of a completely different nature.

What exactly is that woman up to now? Brody wondered.

"I don't trust Krystle and I wouldn't give her an interview if I were you. Her reporting is sensationalistic, not helpful. She is always looking for that next big story. We've been able to feed her some information at times to help flush someone out, but I'm guessing she doesn't intend to be of help to you. I'd advise you to steer clear." Brody decided it was best not to mention he knew Krystle a little more intimately than he let on.

Julia nodded. "That was my impression as well, so I guess I'll just ignore her calls for now. Thanks. Now let's watch the sunset and dig into the sandwiches I brought."

*

A few miles away, onshore, Krystle Davis looked up from her computer and also looked out at the sunset. She sighed contentedly. It had been a very busy few days for her, and she leaned back in her chair, looking out at the magnificent red glow, content in the view and the day's work.

You really shouldn't ignore me Brody Barker. I'm sure we could be of great use to each other, she thought as she pulled up the article she had been working on and looked it over one more time. She was disappointed she had not been able to get an interview with Julia Masterson. A few well-placed quotes would have been a powerful addition to her exposé. As it was, she had had to resort to some strategic photos that she had been able to sneak in. A little minor photoshopping and she hoped they would be just as effective as any quotes she might have gotten. She had also hoped to get some pillow-talk information from Brody, but he had been avoiding her recently. She smiled to herself, thinking it served him right if he were just as shocked as Julia Masterson when he saw the headlines in the morning. She was fairly certain after he saw them, he would be calling her soon enough, and smiled delightedly.

Sitting back in her chair, she looked at the picture she had of Julia Masterson. She had taken a lot of pictures and waited patiently for just the right shot. It showed Julia in a bikini, half in and half out of the water, skin glistening while she seductively pulled a shirt over her head. Granted, Julia had actually been out of the water and pulling the shirt on to cover herself, but Krystle liked her photoshopped version better. She looked at the headlines accompanying the pictures and laughed out loud.

I might even have to give Brody some credit for this one, she thought.

There in bold lettering, right above the very seductive picture of Julia, Krystle read:

Innocent Victim or Black Widow Killer? What Really Happened to Frank Masterson?

PART FOUR

CHAPTER 23

Julia watched as the clouds slowly closed around the rising airplane. After a few minutes of climbing, they broke through the clouds and bright sunshine filled the plane, causing several passengers to close their blinds against the blinding light. As they gradually rose, Julia could feel some of the tension from the past few days fall away, as if to finally give her some well-deserved peace.

She looked over at Brody sitting next to her. He was studying some papers he had retrieved from the well-worn satchel he seemed to always carry with him. She thought back on the last few days with a shudder and wondered if she should even return to her home on Longboat Key Florida or just stay in Ohio.

The unexpected disappearance of her husband had recently shattered the bliss and tranquility she had believed she had found by the ocean. Not to mention the inflammatory report written by a local reporter, Krystle Davis, all but blaming her for Frank's disappearance and alluding strongly that she might have murdered him.

As the plane finally hit its cruising altitude, the fastened seat belt light went out and Julia could see the stewardesses getting ready to take drink orders. Julia was not much of a drinker, but she was tempted to order a double of anything at this point. The stewardesses approached, and Brody shoved the papers he was looking at back into the satchel. He looked over at her and smiled reassuringly.

"Everything all right?" he asked.

"I guess as alright as it can be… considering the circumstances." Julia started to contemplate what it would be like to spend the rest of the flight in a welcome stupor and how much she would need to actually drink to get to that point.

As if reading her mind, Brody grinned and remarked, "I guess since it's so early and we have a long day ahead, we better stick to coffee and tomato juice."

Julia nodded, but was already regretting the lost opportunity to drown her feelings.. "You're right, but some liquid courage would sure go a long way right now."

She was thinking of the meeting they had set up for later that afternoon with Frank's children and their mother.

When Brody had first discussed setting up a meeting with Jane Harper, the mother of Frank's girls, Julia had been eager to join in, hoping she might learn some information about Frank's whereabouts or his nefarious business dealings. But as the time had gone by, and Jane had seemed more and more reticent and hostile, Julia had started to fear facing the woman in person. Then, after reading the inflammatory article that Krystle Davis had published about her a few days earlier, she had lost any bit of remaining courage and just wanted to run and hide.

"Two coffees and two cups of tomato juice please," Brody said to the stewardess with a smile, taking the liberty of ordering for Julia as well. He looked at Julia.

"Relax, everything will be fine. Hopefully, this time, these two interviews will actually yield some real information and we will have a better idea of where to look for Frank or what might have happened."

"Yes, I hope you're right. I really want to just get this nightmare over with, once and for all."

Before their meeting with Jane Harper, they were meeting with Frank's long-time lawyer James Carson. Julia had called him a few days earlier looking for some insurance information and he had asked to meet them in person to share some information with them.

"So… how are things going with Becky lately?" Julia asked Brody before taking a sip of her warm coffee, hoping the change the subject for a few minutes.

Brody grimaced. "If I'm honest, not great. I've been swamped at work lately and haven't really followed up on that much-needed conversation since I picked her up at the station last week. Which only proves her point that I am a lousy father who doesn't give her any attention."

"Don't be so hard on yourself Brody. If I remember being a teenager correctly, she has probably been doing everything in her power to avoid you until enough time has passed and it's safe to see you without a lecture." Julia had been a good kid for the most part, but no teenage girl wanted a lecture from their parents.

Brody shrugged. "You could be right, but it doesn't change the fact that I am neglecting my duties as a father. And it proves Holly's point. I am not around when it comes to the tough love of being a parent." He sighed. "I just can't seem to get it right. I keep thinking things will get easier between us but it just gets more complicated."

"So maybe you could give up on the tough love part and just be a dad for a while?" Julia suggested. "When was the last time you took her out on your boat? You know, just to have a good time; no lectures and no hidden agendas. Just fishing and some bonding time between father and daughter."

Brody thought about it for a while, sipping his coffee and staring at the cup. Julia was afraid she might have overstepped her bounds and insulted him when he finally looked at her with a smile. "You know, you might have something there. I think I may have been avoiding her myself, dreading that stern talk with her as much as she dreads hearing it. It might be really fun to just skip the lectures and lessons and spend some time enjoying being with her."

Julia smiled in agreement. Despite the circumstances under which they had met, she had had a good impression of the teenager.

"She's a good kid Brody, just going through some growing pains. I think some time to reconnect on a fun level and not always an authoritarian level will do you both some good."

Brody smiled at her, and Julia could see some of the tension had left his face. "I'm going to text her as soon as we get off the plane and suggest a date. Thanks for the advice. This is the first time in a long time I'm actually looking forward to spending some time with my daughter."

Julia settled back in her seat, happy that Brody was taking her advice. It had been clear as day to her that poor Becky had just been crying out for some attention, and Julia was happy to have mediated on her behalf so that she could spend the time she clearly craved with her father.

If only it had been that easy with Frank's girls, she thought.

*

The plane touched down at Cleveland airport and Julia and Brody fought the crowds to get to the car rental area. They only had a short time to get to the lawyer's office and Brody was anxious to hear what Frank's lawyer had to say.

As he shouldered his way through the crowd, he assumed Julia was right behind him when he heard her scream in panic and yell out.

"Hey stop that! Leave me alone, that's mine!" Julia's heart was pounding, and she was struggling mightily to get out of the grip of a very unkempt man, who was fighting to take her purse off her shoulder and was dragging her off in the process. She had crossed it over her body for safety, and now it was stuck, causing her to be hauled along with the man who was trying desperately to run off with it.

Brody turned around quickly at the sound of her voice and saw Julia shoving against the disheveled man who was tugging at Julia's purse and dragging her off into the crowd.

He quickly ran through the sea of people to Julia and pulled her to safety behind him. At the same time, raising his fist and punching the man squarely in the face, sending him sprawling into the crowd. As he turned around to see if Julia was hurt, he could see the man out of the corner of his eye scrambling up and making his escape, disappearing into the throng of people.

"Are you alright? Did he hurt you at all?" Brody was looking at her, searching for any signs of injuries. He couldn't see any, but Julia was wide-eyed and shaking.

Cowering behind him and desperately clutching at his arm when she answered, "I don't know...I don't think so. Oh, thank goodness you were here Brody! I couldn't get away from him! I was screaming, and no one is even stopping to see what happened! No one cares."

Sure enough, the crowd of people had just continued on their way, with only a few people giving them a curious look, and no one stopping to offer any assistance.

Brody put a big protective arm around Julia and guided her over to the car rental terminal. Still shaking from her frightening encounter, Julia stayed very close to Brody while he took care of the paperwork and was very grateful that he kept his arm around her as they walked over to the rental car. She didn't relax until Brody had safely put her in her seat and started to drive out of the airport.

"Now I remember why I wanted to leave the city so badly," she said trying to breathe deeply to regain some composure. "Did you notice, no one even stopped to look or help? It's like they are all oblivious to what's going on around them."

"Yeah, it does seem that way," said Brody, shaking his head in disbelief. "Hopefully the law firm is in a better part of town. But stay close to me from now on, just in case."

Julia leaned back in her seat and looked at Brody's broad shoulders and strong physique, thankful he was here in the city with her.

I'm sticking as close to you as I can possibly get! She thought to herself.

CHAPTER 24

By the time they had pulled into the lawyer's office, which turned out to be in a very posh and safe part of the city, Julia had regained some of her composure.

"Okay then, let's see what Mr. James Carson has to tell us." Brody walked over to her car door, opened it, and gathered her protectively close as they walked to the entrance. Julia was not afraid anymore, but she stayed quiet and secretly enjoyed the warm feel of Brody's strong arm on her shoulders.

They were greeted by a friendly receptionist who led them into a large and opulent office. The desk was huge and the surface was relatively empty, except for a few folders that were piled neatly in front of a very large and rotund man. James Carson rose from his seat and took Julia's hand in his relatively large beefy one, shaking it and then covering it with his other hand.

"Julia, it's so nice to see you again. I'm sorry for the circumstances. I would much rather have met you again at your beautiful mansion at one of your famous dinner parties."

Julia smiled weakly, not sure how to answer, and nodded instead to Brody. "It's nice to see you again as well, Mr. Carson. This is Detective Brody Barker. He is here to help me with Frank's disappearance."

The lawyer gave Brody a hearty handshake and asked them both to take a seat in two of the biggest chairs Julia had ever seen. "Would you like some coffee, tea or water? I can have Sarah bring us some."

Julia and Brody both declined, each of them anxious to hear what the lawyer had to say.

"So, you said you had some information you wanted to share with me?" Julia began.

"Yes, I think in light of the situation, there are some things you should know. I consider you my client as well Julia, and I'm here to look out for your best interests as well as Frank's." He smiled at Julia and then looked over at Brody.

"Some of what I have to say may be of a confidential nature. Are you sure you want to have the detective involved?" He looked questioningly over at Julia.

Julia hesitated slightly. She had no idea what the lawyer was about to tell her. She knew she had never broken any laws or knowingly done anything illegal, but she had no idea what Frank had been up to, and to what extent he could have involved her without her knowledge.

"Don't worry Julia." Brody gave her arm a reassuring squeeze. "Anything I hear here will remain strictly confidential. I won't use any of the information against you or Frank. I just want to find out if we can get a lead to follow and figure out where he is or what happened to him."

"Okay then." She looked back at the lawyer, "You can speak freely. We're at a dead-end right now with more questions than answers and I'm worried what will happen to Frank if we don't find him soon." She motioned for the lawyer to continue.

James Carson glanced at Brody as if trying to decide what to do, and then just shrugged his shoulders and sat back down behind his massive desk. He pulled over the neatly stacked folders and opened the one at the top.

"As you may or may not know, one of the tasks I have been performing for Frank has been the disbursement of some of his funds to various people."

Julia nodded. She knew that Frank had instructed the lawyer to send regular payments to an account he had set up for her, and he had told her he had similar accounts and trusts set up for his children and for Jane.

"I also make sure that insurance payments are made, mortgages are paid, and tuitions and other incidentals are taken care of."

Julia nodded again, remaining quiet, but a bit surprised that Frank, being an accountant, had left so many tasks to his lawyer. She wondered what he had been working on all those nights when he had claimed to be doing the necessary payments and paperwork.

"You seem to do quite a bit for Frank Masterson," Brody commented.

Carson nodded. "Yes, that's true. Frank trusted me with a great deal. I was a fairly young lawyer when Frank decided to give me a chance and sent me my first bit of business. Up until then, he had been using the same law firm his parents had been using and I was somewhat surprised when he approached me one night at a fundraiser, proposing we do business." He paused, remembering vividly the first encounter he had ever had with the very charismatic and persuasive Frank Masterson.

"Anyway," he continued, "It wasn't really strange that a young man would want to hire a law firm other than the one his family was dealing with. Many family members have interests they like to keep secret from their families, but I was young and fairly inexperienced. Frank Masterson came from a very well-connected family and could have hired any law firm in town. I asked him why me?"

Brody looked extremely interested in James Carson's story. "Yes, why did he choose you, Mr. Carson?"

"To be honest, I think he wanted to groom me into his personal keeper of his secrets. I was young and eager to do whatever he wanted without asking too many questions myself. It's a cutthroat business and, once you get out of law school, you find yourself competing with hundreds of other hungry wanna-be's, all vying for the same job. I was more than willing to keep a few secrets if it helped me break into the business. Frank has always been shrewd and knew how to charmingly manipulate people to do his bidding."

Julia could only agree wholeheartedly with the lawyer's assessment of Frank. She knew all too well how manipulative Frank could be.

"Don't get me wrong," the lawyer continued. "I like to think that Frank and I became good friends over the years, and I did become his confidant of sorts. I just believe that his reasons for choosing me to represent him in the early days may have been because he believed he could have more influence over me than a more experienced lawyer."

"So, why did he need his own lawyer, Mr. Carson?" Julia asked, wishing he would get to the point, becoming increasingly curious about what information the lawyer had on the matter.

"It turns out that Frank had quite a few separate business dealings bringing in quite a bit of money that he didn't necessarily want the rest of the family to know about. That was also about the time he had met a girl named Jane Harper."

Brody and Julia both sat up higher in their chairs, eager to hear what the lawyer had to say about the early days with the mother of Frank's children.

"It seems that Miss Harper became pregnant and Frank was not quite ready to be a father yet. My first task was supposed to be to offer Miss Harper some money to take care of the pregnancy and send her on a nice long cruise."

Julia audibly gasped. Frank was a devout Christian and she couldn't fathom that he would even consider abortion as an alternative.

"He seemed convinced that Miss Harper would have no problem agreeing to his solution. Unfortunately for him, she made it abundantly clear that she would never get an abortion. Frank was not convinced the child was even his, but Jane Harper insisted it was and if he didn't step up, she would go to his parents and ask them for help."

Julia had never heard this part of the story. Frank had always been very close-lipped about how he had met Jane and the circumstances under which the kids were born. He had always just said that he loved his children and was more than happy to take care of them, but marrying Jane had been impossible.

The lawyer continued his story, "In the end, Jane agreed to keep their relationship and the child a secret, as long as he continued to provide for them. Apparently, that arrangement worked well enough for her, because a few years later, another child was born, and I was instructed to set up a trust and provide for her as well."

Julia sat silently, trying to absorb this bit of history from her husband's past. This was not at all the story that Frank had told her, and it would help explain why Jane had been so hostile towards her on the few occasions they had met.

The lawyer looked down at the folder he had opened. "You and Jane Harper were two of the accounts I was instructed to take care of, as I am sure you are aware. What you may not be aware of, however, is that I was instructed to take care of the accounts of four separate families." He looked at Julia as he spoke. "Yours and Jane Harper's of course. But he also had accounts set up for Charlotte Taylor and her child, and Maria Martinez with her son."

CHAPTER 25

James Carson paused and waited to see how Julia was reacting to the news. She sat stone still in her seat, her face pale and her hands clasped together, as if trying to keep herself from falling apart with the sheer force of her clasped hands.

Brody leaned over and took Julia's clasped hands in his own, not sure what to say to her. "We knew this was a possibility, Julia. We saw the names on the lists we found in his office. Maybe now at least we can find out if any of these women have any information we can use."

Julia nodded, but continued to stare down at her hands without moving. Her body and mind felt numb, and Brody's voice seemed to come from a far-away place, making it hard for her to register his words. She knew that Brody had suspected something like this since finding the lists of names in Frank's papers, but until now, Julia had not allowed herself to believe it could be true. She had known Frank was taking care of Jane financially, but she had been convinced that he was doing so because of his girls. Even after the girls were grown and had left their mother's house, Julia had believed he only felt a sense of responsibility because Jane had born him his children.

She finally roused herself and looked at Carson with tormented eyes. "The Frank I know is not the man that you are describing," she said, the accusation in her voice apparent.

"Do you really believe that Julia?" The lawyer responded gently. "Out of all the women I have taken care of for Frank, you have always been the one I worried about the most. Partly because you were the one that Frank actually married and seemed to have the most control over."

Julia just stared at him. "What are you saying? What do you mean worried about?"

"Julia," James said kindly, "Think back on your relationship. You had to have felt that something was strange, or at least a little odd."

Julia just shook her head, still not comprehending. Frank had loved her. She knew that was true. He had told her that often enough. If he hadn't loved her, he wouldn't have felt the need to control so much of what she did. It was only because he couldn't bear the thought of losing her. If he hadn't loved her, and only her, he would have let her divorce him, and not moved to Florida when she had insisted.

"Jane Harper was the first woman I was instructed to take care of, but you were not the second woman, Julia. Charlotte Taylor was." The lawyer spoke softly, as if trying to lessen the blow by keeping his voice low.

The bile started to rise from Julia's stomach to her throat and she felt as if she had been sucker punched. Even when she had listened to Brody when he found the papers listing the other women's names, or now as the lawyer had said Frank was taking care of two women other than her and Jane, she had believed the other women had to have been affairs that came after her.

We've been married for 25 years, just how long has this betrayal been going on? She thought, panicked.

She shook her head, looking at the lawyer. "No, that's not possible. We've been married for 25 years. He fell in love with me after Jane. There can't have been anyone in between. I would have known."

James looked at Julia sadly. "The truth is, Frank met you right around the time that tragedy struck the family. I'm sure you remember Frank's sister?"

Julia nodded. She had only met Frank's sister a handful of times but had found her to be extremely warm and friendly. Frank's parents had seemed pleased to welcome her into the family, but Francine had seemed like the only member of the family who had been genuine, and Julia had truly enjoyed spending time with her.

Unfortunately, shortly after they were married, Francine had been in a car accident and her brain had been damaged. Francine had been shuffled off to stay in an adult care center and Julia had never seen her again. She had asked to go and see her, but Frank had insisted it was much too painful for him to visit with her.

Carson's voice broke Julia out of her memory, "Frank and I had a habit of having a few drinks at the club together back then. One day he seemed upset and drank more than usual. He confided to me that his parents had found out about Jane and Charlotte and were far from pleased. They had always promised Frank that he would inherit the business, but now they were so upset with him and his lifestyle choice. They threatened to give it all to Francine if he didn't straighten up, marry someone they approved of and start becoming the upstanding citizen they expected him to be." James paused again, waiting to see if Julia was following his story.

"Francine was engaged to a delightful young man at that time. He was younger, but he seemed to make her happy and Frank's parents decided to let Francine and her soon to be husband run the business, as they had lost trust in Frank's judgment."

Julia looked at the lawyer, wide eyed, dreading the words that she knew were coming next.

"A short time later, Frank invited me and a few of our other business associates over to his home to introduce us to his new fiancé. I believe you might recall that particular get together?" James asked.

Julia did remember that evening. It was only a few days after she had accepted his proposal, and Frank had insisted on the party to introduce her to everyone.

When they had first met, she was so smitten. Frank was the older, charming, mature guy and when she was with him, she the envy of all her friends. She had hoped they would someday get married but expected they would have more time to get to know one another before they actually got married. She had been surprised when Frank had suddenly proposed, but was so flattered that she had quickly accepted.

It had been a whirlwind from the day she had agreed to marry him. Frank was already making wedding plans and setting a date. There had been many parties and engagements she had to attend; it had all gone so fast that Julia had never had any opportunity to reconsider what she was doing.

"You're saying he only married me to please his parents? So they would give him the family business?" she asked in shock.

"I'm afraid it goes further than that. By then, Frank's parents had started to see their son for the manipulator he really was. It was stipulated in their will that the company would belong equally to Frank and Francine, until and unless he was to get divorced. If that were to happen, the entirety of the company would go to Francine."

Julia was slowly starting to comprehend the reason Frank had been so adamant about not getting a divorce. He would have lost the company to his sister.

"But Frank had more than enough money to live comfortably without his parent's business. He certainly doesn't need it anymore." Julia was still trying to comprehend what the lawyer was trying to tell her. "And why me? Why not marry Jane or the Charlotte woman if they just wanted Frank to get married?"

"At the time, Frank's parents were still hoping they could bring their son back from his sinful ways and back into the folds of their church. Neither Jane nor Charlotte were Christian, and both of them had children out of wedlock. They just didn't pass muster as far as Frank's parents were concerned. Apparently, you did."

"But they were Frank's children!" Brody interjected. He had been listening quietly, taking notes throughout the lawyer's dialogue, but now he found himself unable to hold back.

Carson just shook his head. "You would have had to meet the two of them to understand, detective. Frank's parents were every bit as controlling as Frank. His children were born out of wedlock and therefore they did not consider them to be part of their family. Before they would agree to reinstate Frank into the business, they had to approve of who he was going to marry."

"I still don't get it," said Brody, remembering the stacks of gold that had been stored in the safe in Frank's office. "He didn't need the money, why play their game?"

"Well for one, he didn't have the money he has now back then. He needed the money from his parents to leverage some of the business ventures he was into. But even if he had enough money, there was no way his ego was going to lose the family business to Francine and some young punk, as he liked to call Francine's fiancé."

Julia could believe that Frank would not have been happy losing his business to anyone. It had always been clear to her that money wasn't the only thing that drove her husband to work so hard. He relished the power and the control it gave him, and she could see why he would not have handed it over easily.

"Poor Francine," said Julia, "It's so unfortunate she had such a terrible accident. They say she almost died. Do you know whatever happened to her fiancé?" she inquired.

Carson gave her a funny look, but then answered her, "I never actually met the fellow. I was Frank's lawyer, so I only met the rest of the family occasionally and I never had the pleasure of meeting Francine's betrothed. From what I heard, he stuck around by her side at the hospital for a few weeks, and then just suddenly disappeared. No one really knows where he ended up."

Brody scowled. "He probably saw his chance at any money dry up and took off," he remarked.

"I wouldn't be so quick to judge, detective. We never know what's truly in someone's heart, and from what I understood, he really loved Francine."

Brody looked at the lawyer quizzically, wondering if there was more that the lawyer wasn't telling them.

"You're sure there were only four families you were taking care of?" Brody asked, thinking of the fifth name on the ledgers that Frank had kept.

"Those are all the families I knew of. Julia can have the folders and all the information in them if she wants, and it will be up to her if she wants to share

126

it with the police. As his legal wife, the money is technically hers as well, and in the absence of Frank, she can decide what she wants to do with it." The lawyer glanced at his watch, indicating the meeting was over, and stood up, handing the neat stack of folders to Julia.

"Thank you, Mr. Carson. I only have one more question. Where was Frank getting all the money from to fund these women?" asked Julia, accepting the stacks of folders.

Carson looked at Julia with tired eyes. "I'm sorry Julia, I'm sure I don't know the full answer to your question anyway, but if I did, that part of Frank's business is privileged, and I wouldn't be able to disclose it to you without his consent."

Brody could see that they had gotten all the information they were going to get from James Carson and stood up as well, thanking him for his time, and steering Julia out to the car.

He settled her in and started driving towards town. He remembered seeing a little coffee shop on the way to the lawyer's office and figured that Julia would need a few minutes to process and regroup before they met with Jane Harper and her girls.

Brody brought two cups of strong coffee over the little table Julia was at and sat across from her. He looked at her concerned.

"How are you feeling right now? That is an awful lot to take in."

"Yes, it is. Part of me still can't really believe Frank would have done all that, and another part of me feels like I should have known what he has been doing all these years. It definitely explains all the long absences."

"Don't be too hard on yourself Julia. There's no way you could have known all of that." He was thinking how naïve and innocent Julia now seemed to him. She must have been the perfect candidate for Frank Masterson's manipulations. He found it hard to believe he had ever thought she could be responsible for his disappearance.

"At least now we have some names and addresses to follow up with. Maybe one of the women on that list has some information about Frank or some kind of connection to Miami. They'd be able to explain why he was there." Brody planned to call in and turn the names over to his precinct later that evening. Maybe they would even have some information for them by the time they got home tomorrow.

Julia nodded in agreement. It had been a challenging morning and she wasn't sure if she was ready to handle the impending conversation with Jane and Frank's daughters. She felt completely emotionally drained at this point.

Brody could see how exhausted she looked. "Don't worry about the interview with Jane and the girls. I can do most of the talking and ask the questions. You can just sit and listen. You don't need to talk at all if you don't want to."

127

Julia sighed, thinking back to the confrontational phone call she had had with the girls a few weeks ago when she had informed them of Frank's disappearance.

"I really hope the conversation goes better than last time, I don't think I can take too much more today. Hopefully Jane can shed some light on some of the information we just learned. I wonder how much she knows or if she was kept in the dark as well."

Brody nodded. He hoped that Jane would be able to fill in some of the holes that the lawyer had left. *Who knows, maybe she or the girls have some kind of connection to Miami,* he thought. Aloud he said, "I am really eager to hear what Jane and the girls know about Frank's affairs and business dealings. It wouldn't be that unusual if he had recruited Jane or one of his daughters for help, or even let them be part of some of his businesses."

"Even if they know anything, they may not be that eager to share it with you or me." Julia had not had many interactions with Jane, but the few she had, had not been overly friendly, and lately, the girls had also given her the cold shoulder.

"I'm sure if they really want to find him, they will be willing to share any information that might lead to him or to find out what happened to him."

Julia shook her head somewhat doubtfully but said, "I hope you're right."

Glancing down at his watch, Brody stood up and gathered the cups to return to the counter.

"I guess we better get going if we want to be on time. I'd like to be there early if we can, and watch them as they come in. I find you can learn a lot from how people act when they don't realize you are watching."

Julia slowly stood up as well and did her best to look ready. The truth was, the last thing she wanted today was to find out even more secrets that her husband had been keeping from her.

CHAPTER 26

Julia and Brody sat at a long table they had secured on the outdoor patio of the local tavern where they had agreed to meet Jane and the girls. Julia absently watched the other patrons coming and going, and Brody's eyes rarely left the only entrance to the patio, waiting impatiently for them. When they finally arrived, Cynthia led the way, with Jane next, looking around furtively for the detective. Mary followed a few steps behind, looking much more timid than either her mother or sister.

Brody stood up and gave a small wave in their direction. Upon seeing him, the three women headed over. Brody shook hands with all three ladies, introducing himself as Detective Barker and sat down again. When the waitress arrived to take their drink orders, Cynthia promptly asked that their order be added to Julia's tab. "You are the one in control of my father's purse strings, at least for now, aren't you?" she remarked snidely.

"There's no need to be rude, Cynthia," her mother chided. But Jane gave her order to the waitress without saying anything about paying her own way and looked at Julia with disdain as the waitress bustled away.

She then looked over at Brody, "Has there been any news on Frank's disappearance yet detective? I feel certain if he had vanished up here in Ohio, we would probably know something by now. It seems you southern boys tend to take your time getting down to business."

Brody did not rise to her challenge immediately and just gave her a cool look, deciding to ignore her remark for now. "Thank you for agreeing to meet with me today. I am hoping to learn some information from you that might help to find him. I'm sure if we could have met sooner, we might have been a little further in our search, but I'm happy we are meeting now and I'm confident it will help my investigation."

Jane gave him a cold stare without saying anything, but Cynthia said, "I doubt that we have any information that will help you, detective. If we knew where he was, we would have already let the local authorities know. Maybe if his disappearance had been reported in a timelier fashion, we would know his whereabouts by now." She looked at Julia pointedly.

"I am curious why it took so long for any of you to return my phone calls. I would have thought you were more concerned with your father's disappearance and would be anxious to help in any way possible," Brody remarked, looking at Cynthia intensely.

Mary had the decency to at least squirm uncomfortably in her seat, but Cynthia and her mother just stared coldly back at Brody.

"Honestly, I'm not even certain why we are here wasting our time. If it weren't for Mary nagging us to come, I don't think I would have agreed to meet you. You haven't been much use yet, so I doubt answering your questions will be very helpful either. I'm beginning to think we are going to have to go and physically search by ourselves." Cynthia crossed her arms over her chest and looked at Brody insolently, clearly pleased with herself and her speech.

Brody was about to snap back a retort, when the dialogue was interrupted by the waitress bringing over the drinks. Julia was surprised to see that both Cynthia and Jane had ordered Manhattan's. To Julia it seemed like a strange drink to order, considering the circumstances, but she secretly hoped it might help to loosen them up and make them less confrontational. Mary had been content to order a Sprite on the rocks.

Brody also noted the strange choice of drink, and vowed to keep their glasses full, also hoping that the alcohol would keep them talking. He decided to let Cynthia have her little sparring victory for now and start with the basic questions slowly, hoping to give the liquor a chance to work.

Raising his glass of Coke, he said, "Cheers, and I appreciate you agreeing to come today. I'm sure we can all figure out what happened to Frank if we work together."

"So, Miss Harper, maybe you could tell me, when was the last time you spoke to Frank?" Brody wished he could take notes but had decided it would be better to keep it more casual and he hoped he could rely on Julia's memory as well as his own.

"There are three Miss Harpers here, detective, perhaps you would like to specify who you are addressing," Cynthia looked at Brody with scorn as she took a sip of her drink.

Julia was beginning to wonder if they were ever going to get any answers from any of the women, or if Cynthia was just going to try and pick a fight at every turn. She was surprised when Mary timidly spoke up from her spot at the end of the table.

"Please, detective, just call me Mary and I'm sure that Cynthia won't mind you using her first name either, just to simplify matters," she spoke softly, all the while glancing from Cynthia to the detective and then back to her mother with an appeasing look.

Brody gave her a kind smile and said again, "Now that we've cleared that up, maybe you could tell me the last time you spoke to Frank, Miss Harper," he looked directly at Jane and ignored Cynthia as he spoke.

Jane took a long drink from her glass before answering. "I spoke to Frank about a month or so ago. It was probably a few days before Julia says he went missing. He called to ask about the girls and how the weather in Ohio was. I think he complained a bit about the heat and the sand in Florida and said he was looking forward to coming up North for a few days very shortly." Jane kept her eyes on Julia as she spoke.

"How often did you and Frank talk? Was it normal for him to call and ask about the girls?" Brody asked, clocking how Jane didn't look at him even though he was the one asking the questions.

Jane looked smugly at Julia. "Yes, we spoke every few weeks or so, sometimes more if he wanted to bounce some ideas off me or if he just wanted to vent. Of course, he was always interested in what the girls were up to."

Julia took in this bit of news with surprise but managed to keep her demeanor calm and emotionless.

"Wouldn't he have just called the girls themselves to find out what they were up to? They are after all adults now." Brody was having a hard time gauging if Jane was being truthful about the frequency of Frank's calls or if she was just trying to torment Julia.

"You'll have to ask them how often he called. That was their business. I only know how often he called me." Jane took another long drink, almost emptying her glass, and Brody couldn't help wondering if she was drinking because she was uncomfortable about something.

He signaled the waitress to bring another round, just as Cynthia spoke up again.

"He called me every few days actually. I truly miss hearing from him. I've had to make quite a few business decisions by myself, but I'm sure he wouldn't mind. He always said he had complete trust in me." Cynthia had also finished her drink, and she looked around the table triumphantly, clearly enjoying the surprised looks she was getting from the other women.

Brody gladly took the bait and turned his attention to Cynthia. "So, you were in business together with your father then? How nice for you to be able to work with him, I bet he was so proud of you." Brody tactfully fed her ego, hoping she would open up more.

Jane looked at her daughter doubtfully. "You worked together with your father? I never heard that before. He never said a word to me about it. I know how secretive he has always been about his business. Frankly, Cynthia, I find that hard to believe."

The drinks had arrived, and Cynthia took one and drank half the glass in one gulp. "He asked me not to say anything to you because he wanted to make sure you didn't try to influence me in any way. Frankly, mother, Daddy did not trust you completely. He has been letting me help with his business transactions for several years now." She again gave her mother a superior look, and this time, took a very measured sip of her drink, waiting to see what her mother would say.

Jane's face was slightly red, and Brody could see that she was having a hard time not lashing out at her daughter. "It seems that your father was quite the keeper of secrets then, doesn't it? He always told me if he were to go into business with either of you two, it would be with Mary, because she has a much more mathematical brain than you do."

Cynthia was about to say something when Mary softly spoke up again from her end of the table.

"Actually, I was helping Daddy a bit with some of his books. He had quite a few foreign transactions going on, and he asked me to help keep track of the ins and outs with the payments and such."

Now it was Cynthia's turn to stare at her sister in surprise. It was clear to Brody, that Frank Masterson had been playing all the women in his life, and he doubted he had been completely truthful with any of them.

Ordering yet another round of drinks, Brody addressed both girls, "I'm wondering if it would be at all possible to look at some of the business dealings you helped your father with? Do you think that any of his associates may have held a grudge or had hard feelings towards your father? Someone who might have wished him harm?"

Mary looked shyly at Brody. "I'm afraid I wouldn't know any of that. I helped him track money going in or out. I only dealt with numbers and amounts and I never saw any names or knew where any of the money actually came from. It was all just transfers from one bank to another, often foreign banks. I'm afraid that information would not be that helpful to you."

Cynthia was once again looking smugly at her sister. "It figures he would only trust you with a bunch of numbers. I actually had to make a few of the deals myself if he was busy." She took a smaller sip this time, but it was clear she felt she had trumped her sister when it came to their father's trust.

Brody turned his full attention back to Cynthia. "Then you would probably know if there is anyone out there with a grudge against your father. We should probably take a look at some of the people you were dealing with and see if there is anyone questionable among them."

Cynthia looked down and tried to gather her thoughts. "Well, I'm not really that sure if I can help with those kinds of names," she finally admitted.

"I mean, I actually only took a few calls from some men and relayed to them account numbers where they could transfer money too. I don't really know who they were, of course. It was all very confidential and stuff. That's why Daddy trusted me with it, I'm sure."

Jane gave a harrumph from where she sat and took a sip of her drink. "So you didn't really help with your father's business after all. You just gave some messages to some unknown voice on the other end of a phone." She laughed loudly. "We all have done that Cynthia. Frank was always asking someone or another to relay a message to someone else. I could never understand why that man couldn't just relay his own messages."

Brody suspected he knew the answer already but asked anyway. "Did you make any notes of account numbers or what it was you were relaying? Maybe you even have a record of the calls somewhere?"

Jane laughed again and looked at her daughter, who sat silent for once. "Well Cynthia, do you have any records? No?" She looked at Brody and he could see she was having a difficult time focusing well after all the drinks she had had. "There won't be any records or phone numbers to trace. Any calls were made or received from burners." She again looked at her daughter. "Isn't that right Cynthia dear?"

Cynthia nodded silently and took a smaller sip of her drink this time, while Jane looked at her daughter, clearly triumphant at having called her bluff.

Disappointed, Brody felt they were once again at a dead end. "Do any of you know what it was that your father did exactly to warrant all these money transfers he seemed to be getting?"

Jane mumbled under her breath, "Nothing good I'm sure," but Cynthia just looked at her drink and stayed silent.

"There weren't just transfers in, detective," Mary volunteered. "I also had to make several outgoing transfers, so I'm sure whatever Daddy was doing was perfectly legitimate."

Brody doubted that, but asked, "Did you keep a record of any of the transfers you made by any chance?"

Mary shook her head. "No, Daddy said it was of the utmost importance that we protect our associates' accounts from hackers. Everything was coded and protected. I only had a few hours each time to make the transfers and then I was locked out."

Even though Brody hadn't really expected that Mary would have any workable information, he was disappointed nonetheless.

"Well, it seems like we've come to another dead end there, so let's just concentrate on what any of you might know about his whereabouts." Brody looked back over at Jane. "You said that the last time you talked to Frank he said he planned to come up North in the near future. Did he give you any details about that trip?"

Jane leaned back and motioned the waitress to bring another round of drinks. Brody could see she was quite inebriated by this time and hoped they had not yet crossed the fine line of her passing out.

"Of course, he didn't give me any details. Frank Masterson never gives details. He just pops in and out whenever he wants, and then expects you to just drop everything for him." Jane was not looking at Julia this time as she spoke, and her voice was filled with bitterness and resentment.

"Now Mom, that's not entirely true. Daddy would let us know plenty of times if he was coming." It was clear that Cynthia could see her mother was drunk and it seemed she wanted to stop her from talking too much.

"I imagine that you will want to know when Mary and I saw our father the last time as well. I haven't personally seen him in at least two to three months. I've been quite busy traveling out of town on business, so even if he wanted to pop in, I wouldn't have been here." She looked at Mary. "I have no idea when my little sister saw him last. It seems the two of them had their little secrets from the rest of the family. Do tell us Mary, have you seen or heard from our dear Daddy since he went missing?" She gave Mary a malicious smile and sat back to sip her fresh drink as well.

"Of course, I haven't!" Mary blushed and looked down at the Sprite she was drinking, then she looked at Brody, ignoring her sister completely. "I spoke to my father around the week before Julia says he went missing. He asked me to make a few more transfers from one account to another and this time he sounded like it was urgent, and insisted I needed to do it right away. I was a little upset with him because I had planned to go to dinner with some friends and I was going to be late." Mary looked like she was about to cry. "I asked him if it could wait until the next day or even until I got home, and when he said no that I needed to do it straight away, I called him selfish and hung up on him."

"Did you end up doing the transactions for him?" Brody asked.

"Yes, of course. I always do what he asks me to do. And I was late for dinner with my friends because of it. He tried to call me later that night, but I ignored his call because I was still upset about putting my plans on hold. He didn't call back again, and I really didn't think that was strange, because he usually only calls me when he needs something, and I assumed he could see I had made the transfers." Mary buried her face into her hands. "I can't believe that the last words I might have said to my dad were so mean! I hung up on him without telling him I loved him like I usually did. Now I may never get the chance!"

Julia's heart melted for the poor girl, and she got up and went over to put her arm around the visibly upset young woman. "It's alright Mary, you couldn't have known he would disappear. Don't give up hope, we can still find him."

Mary turned to Julia and buried her head into Julia's shoulder, sobbing quietly. "Oh Julia, do you really think he is still out there somewhere? I just can't stop thinking that something awful has happened to him and I'll just never see him again."

"Well maybe you shouldn't have been so nasty to him when you talked to him," Cynthia remarked. "Maybe it's all your fault that he disappeared? Maybe he needed help when he called you and you didn't give it to him and now he's gone forever."

Julia looked up from patting Mary's shoulder, shocked that Cynthia could say something so cruel to her sister, who was clearly already upset. But before she could say anything, Jane snorted, and in a very slurred voice said, "Or maybe Francine and her fiancé are finally having the last laugh on dear old Frank."

CHAPTER 27

Brody and Julia both just stared over at Jane, who was sitting in her chair gazing off into the distance, as if she could see something no one else could see.

"What could Francine have to do with Frank's disappearance?" asked Julia. "The poor girl has been languishing in an institute for years now."

Jane just smiled sadly. "Ah yes, poor dear Francine. So very bright and smart. Daddy's little darling. That turned out to be her downfall though, didn't it?"

"What are you talking about Jane? Her father didn't have anything to do with her accident. He wasn't even in town when it happened." Julia still sat with her arm around Mary, but her attention was now fully on Jane.

"If her dear Daddy had just left her out of the family business, she might be living her best life right now with her loving husband. Maybe if she had just been a bit dumber, he would never even have considered handing the business over to her, but she was such a shining star, so much intelligence inside such a pretty little head. Don't you agree Julia?" Jane looked over at Julia, waiting for her affirmation.

Julia just nodded her head in agreement. She had never had the chance to fully get to know Francine, but Jane was right. From what she had seen, Francine had been just as bright as she had been kind and beautiful.

Jane seemed satisfied with Julia's acquiescence and continued, "We had a good thing going, me and Charlotte. Frank split his time between us, and he was a good dad to my girls and his son. He always promised me that when he was ready, he would marry me over her, because I had been his first love and the first mother of his children." Jane gave a somewhat cynical smile.

"Of course, who knows what he told her."

Jane now had the full attention of all four of the others at the table. Mary and Julia both sat ramrod straight in their seats, staring at Jane, Julia with her hands clenched together in her lap. Brody had secretly turned on the record button on his phone, and Cynthia just stared at her mother, her hands around the drink in front of her.

"If Francine had just left with her fiancé like they had originally planned, it would have all been alright for all of us. Frank was just waiting for his parents to relinquish control of the business to him, and then we could all just have continued on with our lives. But then, for some reason, Frank decided to tell Francine about us, and Francine had to go and blab to his parents."

Jane shook her head absently as if she was still confused even after all these years.

"Why he felt the need to confide in Francine I'll never know. They weren't even that close. The two of them were about as different as any two siblings could be." Jane looked over at her own daughters and mumbled. "I guess it runs in the family."

"So what happened when Daddy's parents found out about us? What did they say?" Cynthia was leaning slightly forward in her chair as she spoke, hands still clutching her drink.

"They weren't pleased, that's for sure. Those two holier than thou hypocrites decided that Frank was now too soiled to run their precious business for them, and they decided to recruit Francine to run it. They intended to officially make her fiancé the CEO after he and Francine were married, and shut Frank out of the business altogether."

"Didn't they even want to meet us?" asked Mary quietly from the far corner of the table.

Jane laughed bitterly. "As far as they were concerned, you two should not even have existed. According to their warped minds, I was a Jezebel who had turned their son away from God and into a sinner. The only way Frank could get back into their good graces was to repent and make amends. That's when he promised them he would never see me or Charlotte again and would marry a good Christian woman who would help him stay on God's path."

Julia had visibly paled and was staring at Jane intently.

"That's right dearest Julia. That's where you come into the picture. You were the figurehead wife that Frank needed to get back into his parent's good graces. It worked too. They loved everything about you and so did Francine. Of course, Frank swore to me that his marriage to you would only be for a little while, only long enough to get control of the business again."

Jane threw Julia a triumphant smile as she said, "I made him promise to not have any more children, especially not with you. I certainly didn't want any more setbacks or complications for our future."

Brody gave her a look of disbelief. "He agreed to that?"

Jane looked over at Brody with bloodshot eyes, the alcohol clearly blurring her sight a bit. "I'm not completely dumb, detective. I told him if I ever found out he was having a child with her, I would go to his parents and let them know that me and Charlotte were still in his life, and that he had lied to them about cutting us out and repenting for his lifestyle. Losing his parents' trust again was not something that Frank was willing to risk."

Brody knew some of what the next part of the story was but wanted to hear Jane's version. "So, if all was forgiven with the parents, what happened? Why did he stay married to Julia all these years?"

Jane looked off into the distance sadly, clearly lamenting the life she felt she should have had and missed out on.

Jane continued, "It was too late. The damage had already been done. Frank's father was no longer willing to give Frank sole control of the company and insisted that Francine take an active part in running it. At first, she refused, knowing how much the company meant to her brother and not wanting to cross him, but her father would not take no for an answer. He said if she didn't take control of her half at least, he would sell it all. Francine finally relented, believing it was better for Frank to run half the company than to lose it all."

"Poor Daddy," said Mary. "He has always worked so hard for the company."

"It's not like he didn't get paid for it. Daddy made a pretty good penny with that company, and it's not like he was giving us that much of it, so he was clearly cashing in." Cynthia's voice held a hint of resentment. "I wouldn't say Daddy was a poor Daddy."

Jane continued on, ignoring her daughters. "Frank was furious when he found out of course. He did not intend to share the company with anyone, let alone Francine. They definitely had different ideas as to what direction to take the company, and Frank *did not* like to compromise."

Jane took the last sip from her drink and frowned slightly. "He came over one night ranting and raving about how it was impossible to work with her and how even her fiancé was now starting to add in his opinion. He said he had spoken with his parents, but they remained steadfast that he needed to learn to work with his sister. That's when he said that he would need to take matters into his own hands and solve the problem himself. Less than a week later, Francine had a car accident that nearly killed her. Apparently, the brakes on her little sports car failed and she drove right over a cliff. They said that if it had been any other car except a Mercedes, she would have probably not survived."

Julia gasped. Was Jane really insinuating that Frank had anything to do with Francine's accident? Frank might have been cold and calculating sometimes, but he wasn't a killer. Besides, he loved his sister. Julia

138

remembered how devastated he had been after her accident.

Brody finally said what the others were all thinking. "You think that Frank had something to do with Francine's accident?"

Jane just shrugged her shoulders. "Who knows. I have no proof of course. But no one could ever figure out what she was doing up in the Bluffs that night anyway and, with her traumatic brain injury, she was never able to tell us why she was there, or what exactly happened to her."

Julia and Brody had both noticed Jane's demeanor change to what now looked like a very sad and defeated person.

"I do know that he never denied being involved to me, and after that, I stopped pushing him to marry me. I figured if he could arrange to have his own sister *removed* he certainly wouldn't hesitate to get rid of me if I became too much of a burden." She looked sadly at her children. "I couldn't bear the thought of the two of you not having me there to raise you, so I just gladly excepted whatever money he gave us and did the best that I could."

Julia shook her head in denial. She wasn't ready yet to accept the fact that her husband of 25 years could have had anything to do with his sister's accident. "He couldn't have had anything to do with it. The Frank that I knew was not a violent man. What about her fiancé? He disappeared shortly after her accident, didn't he? Maybe he met her up in the Bluffs and they had an argument or something. She could have been driving too fast and brakes do fail, even on a Mercedes. It may have had nothing to do with Frank."

Jane looked at Julia as if she were a fool in denial. "Francine's fiancé wasn't even in town when it happened. I doubt she would have ever gone up there if he had been here with her. That poor man was devastated. He spent every moment he could with her, trying to get her to recognize him."

"So why do you think he left and never came back?" asked Brody.

"Honestly, I think Frank threatened him somehow. He was annoyed at how much time he spent with Francine, and he was worried his parents would somehow let them still get married despite Francine's brain injury. One day he was just gone without a trace. No note, no goodbye, nothing. He just disappeared. I think either Frank paid him off, threatened him with something, or he just made him disappear like he tried to do with Francine. He always told me he had connections."

Julia just stared at Jane in shock. None of this could be true. This was not the Frank she had known or what she remembered from that time. Julia remembered how he had come home one day so upset that Francine's fiancé had just up and left without saying anything. Frank had told Julia that he must have been a true coward to have done that and was probably pursuing someone else for their money now. For a few months after the accident, he had even hired a driver for Julia because he said he was so worried about her driving and having an accident herself. The Frank she knew just couldn't be the same Frank that Jane was describing.

"But I don't understand Mom. If his sister and her fiancé weren't in the picture anymore and Daddy had control of the company again, why didn't he just ditch her and marry you like he promised?" As she spoke, Cynthia gave Julia a disdainful look.

Jane gave a sardonic laugh. "Yes, that's the irony of it all isn't it. It all worked out the way Frank needed it to, but despite that, he didn't get what he wanted. His parents always seemed to be a step ahead of him it seemed. They gave him sole control of the company, but with the stipulation that if he ever got a divorce, the company would be completely liquidated, and half put into a trust for Francine and the rest to charity."

She looked over at Julia bitterly. "Part of me thinks that Frank was actually quite content with the arrangement. My guess is you were much easier to manipulate than I had ever been."

Julia's head was spinning with the shock of everything she was hearing about the man she thought she had known for the last 25 years of her life. She was sure she would have many questions for Jane later, but right now, she was having a difficult time comprehending what she had already been told.

"So what happened with Charlotte after she found out that Frank would need to stay married to Julia? Was she bitter or upset? Could she have anything to do with his disappearance, or could he maybe be hiding out with her?" Brody was not done questioning Jane quite yet.

"Of course Charlotte was upset. Neither one of us was thrilled that another woman was in the picture, but Charlotte was always much more pragmatic than I was. She went and found herself a live-in boyfriend and made a new life for herself and her son. She told Frank that as long as he continued to support their son, she would stay out of his life and not tell his parents he had continued his involvement with her. Frank seemed to keep his word, and Charlotte seemed content with the arrangement. Her son was younger than the girls at the time, and I think she raised him to believe that the man she was living with was his father. Still might be raising him that way actually."

"Did you stay in touch with Charlotte?" asked Brody.

"For a while we did. The accident with Francine had us both a bit spooked and we promised we would keep an eye out for each other. But after a few years, the calls and texts gradually reduced, fewer and fewer each month, until we just lost touch."

"Do you still have a way to get in touch with her? Even if you just have her last known address or phone number it would help. I would really like to ask her some questions as well." Brody finally took out his notebook, ready to jot down an address or number.

"I think she moved down to Florida, and the last time I contacted her, she still had the same number. I'll look it up and text it over to you later. No reason she should get out of the same grilling that I have to go through." Jane was staring at her empty glass, twirling around the ice cubes that were slowly melting in the heat.

Brody's ears perked up at the news she lived in Florida. Was this the Miami connection they had been looking for? "Do you know if she happened to move to Miami?"

Cynthia had been silent while her mother had recounted her story, but now she looked over at Brody with interest. "Why would you want to know if she moved to Miami?"

Before he could answer, Jane said, "No I don't think that's where she went. I think she moved to Orlando at the time. But that was many years ago, but she may have moved again for all I know. You'll just have to ask her yourself when you find her."

Brody looked at all three of the women. "While we're on the subject, have any of you been traveling to Florida recently?"

Mary's face turned slightly red, and she looked down at her hands while Cynthia and Jane looked at Brody belligerently. "What if we have? Is there a law against traveling that we are not aware of?" asked Cynthia.

Brody was a bit taken aback, but continued. "No, I'm not aware of any laws against traveling. I'm just gathering potentially useful information. Exactly when were you down there and where did you go?"

"We decided to take a sightseeing tour to reconnect as a family," said Jane. "We traveled all over, spending a few days here and a few days there. Of course we avoided Longboat Key, for obvious reasons." She looked at Julia as she said that. "I don't have the exact dates and I have no desire to go over our entire itinerary with you, detective. It was a vacation, and we went wherever the mood took us."

Brody wondered if Jane was trying to hide something from him, or if she was just being difficult. He decided he would try and call Mary later, to see if she would be more willing to provide him with dates and locations once she was away from the influence of her mother and sister.

Jane stretched and yawned a bit, clearly getting tired after all the alcohol she had consumed and all the talking she had done. "Well, detective, I think I have given you quite a bit of information for one day. Now it's time for you to get to work and look for Frank. The girls are missing their father."

"Yes of course, you've been more than informative, thank you. Before we go though, I was wondering if you know where I might find Maria Martinez?"

Now, it was Jane's turn to look puzzled. "Who? I've never heard of her before. Why would I know who she is?"

"You seem to have been privy to much more of Frank's private life than even his wife. I just thought you would know why he was also providing for a fourth woman?" Brody asked, keeping to himself the possibility of a fifth woman. The lawyer hadn't been much help with that and Brody was playing this close to his chest, giving as much information without giving too much away, in the hopes of getting a lead to Frank's whereabouts.

"What do you mean? What are you talking about? There was only Charlotte and I until Julia came along." Jane seemed truly surprised and shocked at this piece of information.

"No, it turns out that there was actually at least one more woman in the picture." He gave Jane a slightly sardonic smile as he and Julia stood to leave. He was convinced that Jane was truly surprised at this piece of news but couldn't help leaving her with one parting shot.

"It looks like Frank still had a few extra secrets up his sleeve, even when it comes to you, Miss Harper."

CHAPTER 28

Julia sat back in the comfortable easy chair located in the hotel lounge she and Brody had booked for the night, before they flew back to Florida in the morning. She gratefully sipped some of the herbal tea that Brody had brought to her in the Styrofoam cup also provided by the hotel. The lounge was located in clear view of the hotel's restaurant, which was bustling with dinner guests at this time of the evening.

Brody had ordered himself a scotch on the rocks from the bar and sat across from Julia in a matching chair, absently watching the other guests coming and going. His stomach grumbled and he glanced at his watch impatiently. The restaurant had been full when they had returned from the interview with Jane Harper and her girls, and they had been told it would be a least an hour wait.

He had called into the precinct and given them the names, addresses and numbers of all the women they had gotten from James Carson and now he sat back, listening to his stomach complain about the lack of food and contemplating what Jane Harper and James Carson had told them. He looked over at Julia, who had been extremely quiet since they had left the meeting and wondered what she was thinking. It was clear to him that Frank Masterson was not the man that Julia had believed him to be, and he was curious as to what her thoughts were now. He wanted to ask her about it, but he also wanted to give her enough time to process the information she had received.

He took another sip of the scotch, and felt it move down his throat and into his gut, easing some of the tension and fatigue he felt. Brody was starting to believe that Frank had been involved in a much more sinister business than he originally had thought, and concerned he might be in over his head.

For the hundredth time since his partner Jack had been killed, he wished he could talk to him and get his opinion on what they had learned and what direction he should take now. If Frank Masterson was truly involved with the mob, he might need to call in some higher guns.

Brody looked up and saw the hostess waving them over to the restaurant. He stood up and took Julia by the arm, steering her over. As they sat down, Julia sighed wearily and picked up the menu half-heartedly.

"You must be exhausted after today," said Brody, ordering them both some ice waters. "That was a lot to take in all at once."

"Yes, it certainly was." Julia placed her menu back on the table. "I'm not even sure I can eat anything. I'm just too exhausted."

Brody himself was starving after a long day of eating hardly anything and couldn't relate to Julia's lack of appetite at all. "I really think you need to eat something. We haven't eaten all day and you still need to keep up your energy." He glanced at his own menu. "How about I order you some soup and a salad?"

Julia just nodded wearily and sipped on her water. She was still trying to process and comprehend everything she had learned about her husband today. She felt like she didn't know her husband at all anymore.

Looking over at Brody she said, "I feel like such a fool. I didn't think we had the best relationship, what with Frank being gone all the time, but I truly never imagined he was cheating in our marriage. He always talked about how wonderful his parents' marriage had been and how he wanted to have the same kind of relationship."

Julia was silent while the waitress refilled their glasses. After she had thanked her, she continued, "His parents died within a few months of each other, and Frank thought that was just so touching. He told me he had always admired how close his parents were and how they sometimes seemed to finish each other's thoughts. He said we needed to strive to build a relationship where each of us was so intertwined with the other that we couldn't live without the other."

Julia looked off in the distance and sighed. "I liked the idea too, of course. It was why I quit working and tried to spend as much time with Frank as I could. I never planned much because I never knew when he would be home and I didn't want to miss being there for him when he was." Tears started to fill her eyes. "I was such a fool. I don't think he ever loved me or intended for our marriage to be like his parents. It was all just a sham. He was just using me this whole time."

Brody silently agreed with what she was saying but didn't think this was the right time to tell her that. She needed time to work things out in her own mind without any input from him or anyone else. Thankfully, their meal came before he had to say anything.

"Eat something now Julia, then we'll go up and you can get some sleep. I think you will need some time to think all this through, and we still need to follow up on all the leads that we found today. We still need to find Frank after all."

Julia took a few half-hearted bites of her soup before putting her spoon down. "To be honest Brody, I don't think I want to find him anymore. What will I even say to him? Things can never go back to normal now, and I'm not sure what he will do if he finds out I know about all his secrets."

Brody took a big bite of his steak, savoring every bite he took, despite feeling bad for Julia. "Let's focus on finding him first, and after that, I promise I will be with you every step of the way when it is time to confront him."

If Frank is even still alive, he thought.

If Frank was really involved in the mob scene, Brody knew the police would have a number of questions for him too. Although he was starting to increasingly suspect that Frank may have finally crossed someone one too many times and paid the ultimate price.

Brody's phone pinged, and he looked at it to see a message.

I'm sorry it's so late but I have some information I think you need to hear and see. If possible, please meet me tonight. I didn't want to say anything in front of my sister or mother but I think we should meet tonight, before you fly out.

The message came from Mary's phone number.

Brody took the last bite of his steak and looked over at Julia who had barely touched her dinner. "If you are done Julia, maybe I could take you up to your room to rest now. I have some business I still need to take care of tonight before we head out in the morning."

Julia pushed back her plate and stood up, more than eager to get up to her room and lie down. Her head was starting to pound and that familiar feeling of nausea started to make its way into her stomach again. "That sounds great, I'm exhausted and I just want to lie down for a while."

Brody smiled at her.

He decided not to tell her about Mary's message for now. She had enough to process tonight and he didn't want her to worry about anything else.

As they walked out of the hotel restaurant towards the elevators, neither one of them noticed the man sitting at the bar, staring intently at them as they walked by.

CHAPTER 29

Brody exited the Uber he had taken to the address Mary had sent him and walked up the sidewalk to a nice, older looking Victorian home. He knocked on the door and waited for Mary to come and answer. When she finally came to the door, she looked just as prim and proper as she had this afternoon.

"Come in, detective. Thank you for coming on such short notice, but I wanted to speak with you in person before you flew back in the morning. I think I have some information that might be important."

Brody walked in, looking around at the old architecture as he entered the home. "Of course, it's no problem at all. I am very interested in what you have to say."

"Please come this way," said Mary, leading the way to the living room. "Can I get you anything? Some tea, coffee or water?" She looked at him apologetically. "I'm sorry I can't offer you anything stronger, but I don't drink so I don't have any alcohol in the house."

Brody followed her in and sat in the chair she gestured to. The living room was tastefully furnished and Brody wondered if it was due to the money Frank provided, or if Mary made a good living on her own. He just said, "No thank you, I just came from dinner and I am all set. Maybe we can get to what you wanted to tell me?"

Mary looked at Brody nervously. "It's not so much what I need to tell you as it is something I think you should see."

She stood up and walked over to a little writing table sitting in the corner of the living room, and picked up a small, leather-bound ledger and some sheets of printed out paper.

"That last day that Daddy asked me to make transfers for him, I actually did print a screenshot with all the accounts on them, thinking that I would do them later in the evening or even in the morning. As I had said, the accounts were only accessible for a short time, so I figured if I took screenshots of them, I might still be able to access them later."

Mary handed him the printed-out sheets. "Here they are. I lost the courage to wait and do them later though, thinking I would probably not be able to access the information I needed, and like I already told you, I ended up being late for dinner. I'm not sure if you can do anything with them, but I thought you might want to look."

Brody looked at the sheets that Mary had handed him; they were instructions with sums of money and the accounts they were to be transferred to. He would run the accounts through the system, but he doubted they would yield much. If Frank had truly been involved with the mob, these account numbers would be long obsolete.

"Thank you, Mary. I'll look into these and see if we can find any leads that might point to what happened to your father." He didn't have the heart to tell her that it would probably not be much help at this point, and he also didn't want to say anything about her father's possible mob connection. Mary clearly adored her father and Brody doubted she would accept that he may have been involved in illegal activities.

"There's more, detective." She looked at the ledger in her hand as if she were undecided whether she should hand it over or not. "My father gave me this ledger a few months ago. He told me to hide it, keep it safe and a secret from anyone else. When I asked him what it was, he said it was his little insurance policy."

Brody's ears perked up at this news and he listened to Mary intently as she continued. "He heard about the trip that the three of us were planning to Florida, and said when we got there, I was supposed to contact Julia and give her the ledger. He said I was to tell her to hide it somewhere and keep it safe until he asked her for it." Mary handed Brody the ledger.

He opened it and saw it contained recorded transactions. The names were coded, but it showed a clear record of transactions that had taken place over the last few years. Brody was unsure if his department would be sophisticated enough to decipher any of it, but he was sure that anyone who knew the codes would be very interested in this little book.

"This seems like a lot of cloak and dagger for no reason," Brody said. "Why didn't he just give it to her himself and tell her to hide it?"

Mary looked at Brody intently. "I asked him that same question. He told me that he had just obtained the ledger, and he didn't feel safe taking it to Florida by himself. He was apparently meeting some associates before he went back, and he didn't think he should be carrying it on his person at the meeting." Mary stood up and walked to the window, drawing the curtains even tighter.

"Daddy was always so secretive about everything, but even I thought it was a bit strange he didn't just take it with him, if it were that important."

Brody took the ledger and the printed papers and folded them into his coat pocket. "So, what changed your mind? Why didn't you give it to Julia when you were in Florida like he asked you to?"

Mary shrugged sadly. "I just never got the chance really. It was all so awkward. Mom and Cynthia were always hovering around, and I couldn't convince them to go anywhere near the Keys, so I couldn't figure out a way to sneak away from them to go to Julia. I was afraid to call her and ask her to meet me somewhere else because I hadn't talked to her in years, and I thought she would probably just refuse to see me. It all just seemed so stupid to me at the time, and I resented Daddy for putting me in a difficult situation. I was also still mad at him for making me late for dinner with my friends, and I really just wanted to enjoy my vacation with mom and Cynthia. I figured I would just give it back to him next time I saw him and tell him to take it to her himself."

Mary walked back over to the couch and sat down. "After everything Mom said today though, I'm really worried. What if Daddy is connected to some bad people somehow? Maybe he needed the ledger, and when he didn't have it, they hurt him or even killed him? It could be all my fault if anything happened to Daddy!" Mary put her head in her hands and sobbed quietly.

Brody got up and walked over to her, awkwardly patting her shoulder. He didn't know what to tell her to console her. After everything they had heard today, he thought it was a very likely scenario.

"Please calm down Mary. We don't know who or what your father was involved in at this point, and whatever it was, it may have absolutely nothing to do with this ledger. There's no sense in blaming yourself for your father's disappearance. We will find out what happened to him, I promise."

Mary retrieved a tissue and wiped her eyes and nose, nodding sadly. "Thank you, detective. I really do appreciate everything you are doing to help find my father. I also want to apologize for my family's rudeness. I guess we are all harboring our own little secrets and we all carry some bitterness. I found out a number of things I was unaware of at today's meeting. I think there is a lot we all need to process and figure out at this point."

Brody walked to the door, thanking Mary again for sharing the information she had and reminding her to call him if she heard anything new about her father, also reassuring her he would keep in touch with any updates.

Before he got to the door, Mary gently took his arm. "Please tell Julia I'm sorry that I never contacted her in all these years. She has always been very kind to me, and maybe you could ask her if, after all this is done, she would mind if I contacted her?"

Brody smiled at her, nodding his head. "I'm sure she would like that, Mary." With a last handshake and thank you, Brody headed to the waiting Uber, noticing that it had started to rain. He pondered what information the ledger contained, hoping it would turn out to be useful.

At the hotel, Julia was tossing and turning in her bed. She had gone to bed completely exhausted, but now that she had laid her head down, sleep seemed to elude her. Finally, she decided she may as well get up and head to the lobby and see if she could get some herbal tea to calm her mind.

The restaurant was closing when she got there, but the hostess kindly directed her to the bar, assuring her the bartender would be more than happy to accommodate her with some herbal tea. The barkeep smiled at her when he heard her request.

"Having a hard time sleeping tonight, huh? You sit right here, and I'll be right back with a glass of some nice warm chamomile." Then, he disappeared into a doorway that Julia assumed led to the kitchen.

"Can I buy you a drink?" Julia looked to her left and saw that the voice belonged to a good looking, dark haired man in a very elegant and expensive-looking suit.

She smiled politely at him while shaking her head. "Thank you, but the bartender is already getting my drink." Just then, the barkeep returned with her tea, giving the man an appraising stare and setting it in front of her.

"You just let me know if you need anything else. I'll keep my eye out for you if you need anything." He shot the man a warning look and went to wait on a patron at the other end of the bar.

The good-looking man eyed her tea, surprised at her choice of drink for the night. "I'd be happy to buy you something a little stronger if you'd like?"

"That's very nice of you, but I'm happy to just drink my tea for tonight. I have a lot on my mind and I'm sure this will help calm me down."

Julia didn't want to be rude, but she was really in no mood for small talk tonight and hoped that the man would take the hint. She just wanted to think things through by herself for a while.

"I hope that nothing is wrong? I am a very good listener if you need someone to talk to." He smiled a charming smile. Clearly the man did not intend to give up that easily.

Julia sighed. It seemed she would need to be more direct, or engage in some small talk, hoping the man would get bored and just go away.

"Thank you for your concern, you're very kind, but I'm fine. It's just been a very busy day." She took a sip from her tea and hoped that the man would get the hint and she would not need to get even more direct.

The man stood, but instead of walking away, he took her arm and tried to gently pull her to her feet.

"Please join me over here at one of the tables. It's much more comfortable and maybe we can discuss whatever is troubling you. I don't feel right leaving a woman sitting at a bar unattended. It doesn't seem safe."

Julia smiled and was once again about to politely decline, when she looked up and saw Brody walk through the door. Relieved, she smiled at him and waved him over.

She watched as he approached and saw that his hair was slightly damp.

"Has it started to rain again? It always seems to rain here in Ohio," she remarked.

"Yes, it just started. I have to agree, I prefer our weather down south to this. Who were you talking to?" he asked as he looked over her shoulder.

Julia glanced over to her left, but the man had disappeared. "Oh, no one. Just a nice man wanting to buy me a drink. Maybe I'm not that old after all," Julia said smiling.

Brody just raised his eyebrows at her. "How about we should head up to the room? We have an early flight and you should really try and get some sleep. There are some things I want to talk to you about in the morning." With that, he picked up Julia's tea with one hand and, nodding to the bartender, he steered her out the door to the elevators with the other.

The handsome man standing in the shadows at the end of the room watched them walk out. He cursed under his breath at the sudden appearance of the detective and his missed opportunity.

Grant should have been able to nab her this morning at the airport, he thought. *I can't believe the fool let her slip through his fingers.*

The dark haired man had no sympathy for the fact that Grant was now sporting a black eye from his encounter with Brody this morning. He considered trying to grab her again at the airport the next morning but dismissed the idea quickly. The detective would still be with her, and the airport would not be very crowded at that time of day. Also, two encounters with a mugger at the same airport would be too suspicious.

He sighed tiredly. He would just need to follow her to Florida and grab her when she was alone. He watched her as she smiled at the detective before getting into the elevator.

Such a shame, he thought. *She seems like such a nice lady.*

PART FIVE

CHAPTER 30

The hot Florida sun beat relentlessly down on the sandy beach, while the ocean pounded angrily onto the shore. Sailing high above it all, seagulls screeched out with defiance, circling over the tumultuous ocean and the hot sand.

Inside her newly renovated beach house, Julia stood and stared around her in shock and dismay.

Just yesterday morning, she had left her peaceful haven to fly to Ohio, hoping to get answers as to why, or where her missing husband might have disappeared to. What she and detective Brody Barker had discovered, however, had left her mind and heart in shambles; chaos that was mirrored in the mess she and the detective found in her home when they had returned.

Brody picked his way around the upturned furniture and the slashed-up pillows in Julia's living room to make his way over to her, talking to a patrolman as he moved through the mess. When he reached her, he attempted to right an overturned chair and indicated that Julia should sit down on it. She sat down numbly and looked up at him, her clear blue eyes showing a mixture of fear and confusion.

"I don't understand." She whispered as she scanned the room, noticing her favorite wedding photo was shattered on the floor. "Who would do something like this?"

Brody glanced over at his police chief, who was surveying the damage with some of the other officers. Then he looked down at Julia and tried to put on a reassuring face despite the chaos all around them.

"It looks like whoever did this was looking for something, and they were convinced it was hidden somewhere in this house. There is not an inch of this place that hasn't been turned upside down."

Julia looked at Brody even more frightened than before. "But what on earth could they have been looking for? I don't have anything of value here anymore. Nothing that would warrant this kind of destruction anyway." She thought back to the bars of gold that she and Brody had found in the secret safe that Frank, her husband, had hidden in a closet. "Do you think they were looking for the gold we found? I left the safe wide open so anyone could see it was empty."

Brody was doubtful that was what they had been searching for, but he nodded his head at Julia anyway. "It's possible of course. I guess we need to figure out who would have known or suspected that Frank was hoarding that much gold in the house."

The police chief marched purposefully over to where Brody and Julia were talking. He was a tall, military-style man with a no-nonsense look about him. It was clear to anyone watching that he was a man who was accustomed to getting his way, and right now, he did not look happy.

"Hello, Mrs. Masterson. I'm Daniel Wilson, Chief of Police for the Longboat Key area. I don't believe we have formally met yet?" As he spoke, he held out his hand to Julia. When she put out her hand to shake it, it was grasped immediately, followed by a brief, firm shake, before quickly releasing it back to her.

He looked around the room, surveying all the damage, and then looked back at Julia. His question was direct and to the point. "Do you have any idea what someone might have been looking for here, Mrs. Masterson?"

Julia got the impression from his tone that he expected her to know the answer to his question and tell him what he wanted to know immediately.

"I'm sorry, but I really don't know." She looked up at Brody. "Detective Barker and I discovered some gold and a little cash that my husband had stashed in a safe, but on his advice, I moved that to a safe deposit box weeks ago. I can't think of anything else that anyone could possibly have been looking for."

The Chief looked at the destruction around the house. Every pillow had been slashed and every cupboard opened with the contents strewn about. The couches and chairs had been turned upside down and the bottoms had been cut open in a clear attempt to find out if anything had been hidden in them. The books were strewn all over and it appeared that every one of them had been meticulously searched, as if looking for any hidden compartments.

It was clear from the expression on his face that he did not believe that all this damage was caused by looking for a stash of gold.

He looked at Julia sternly. "I'm going to be perfectly straight with you Mrs. Masterson. This looks to me like someone was looking for a stash of drugs. Are you sure that maybe you or your husband didn't have something like that hidden here?"

Julia gasped at the police chief's question. "I assure you, sir, neither Frank nor I would have ever been involved in anything like that. I have no idea why someone would destroy my home, but I am certain that there were no drugs hidden here anywhere."

The Chief looked down at Julia coldly. "Hm. Unfortunately Mrs. Masterson, from the reports I have received so far, it seems that you are not in a position to vouch for your husband. According to Detective Barker, Frank Masterson has kept many secrets from you and it is probable that he might have stashed drugs here without your knowledge. Unless of course, you are not as clueless to your husband's activities as you have been telling us?"

Daniel Wilson was getting extremely impatient with Julia with this whole case of her missing husband, and it was starting to show.

The Mayor was up for election in a few months, and it looked like he stood a good chance of being re-elected if nothing big went wrong before then. He did not need an unsolved missing persons case muddying up his chances, and he was on the Chief's case to get it solved. Now that the Chief was convinced that Frank Masterson was more than likely involved in drug dealing, he wanted this case solved even more than the Mayor.

Local reporter Krystle Davis had also just published an expose accusing Julia of being responsible for her husband's disappearance or possibly even, his demise, and the Mayor was getting a lot of heat from the public. In turn, the Mayor gave the Chief of Police pressure about not having made an arrest yet, especially if Julia was as guilty as the reporter claimed. The Chief did not doubt that as soon as Krystle Davis got wind of the break-in at Mrs. Masterson's home, there would be a new article in the press.

He turned away from Julia and looked Brody directly in the eyes. "I expect you to solve this within the week. If we have drug activity in our small town, I expect the perps to be caught and jailed. Our citizens need to feel they are safe, and that they do not need to fear any break-ins in their own homes." With that, he gave a curt nod to Julia and walked out the front door, heading back to his unmarked car.

Brody smiled at Julia apologetically. "Ah, sorry about that. He is not always the most charming man… especially when he is under a lot of pressure to solve a case."

Julia stood up from the chair she had been rigidly sitting in and walked over to her kitchen window, looking out at the pounding surf.

"He really believes that Frank was dealing drugs, doesn't he?" She looked up at Brody. "Do you think that Frank was involved in drugs? I can't believe he would have been. But the Chief was probably right when he said I don't really have any idea what Frank was up to."

Brody thought about the ledger that he still had tucked away in his pocket and was wondering to himself what Frank had really been up to. He was starting to believe that Frank Masterson had been involved in far more than just dealing drugs.

He had intended to talk to Julia about what Frank's youngest daughter, Mary, had told him the night before about the ledger that she was supposed to deliver to Julia. However when they arrived at the beach house, they had been met with utter chaos and destruction and he had not had a chance to talk to her yet.

Brody had immediately called the break-in into the precinct, and before long, the house had been swarming with officers taking pictures, notes and inventory. Brody had been shocked to see even the police chief had shown up to survey the house.

He silently cursed Krystle Davis. Her inflammatory article must have had a lot to do with the pressure the Chief was feeling.

Detective Kate Klein walked over to where Brody and Julia stood, and this time, her normally cynical look was replaced with a look of true sympathy and concern. "I think we are pretty much done here, detective." She looked at Julia gently. "If you do notice anything missing that you haven't seen yet Mrs. Masterson, please call me directly on my cell and I'll make a note of it." She handed Julia a card with her name and cell phone number written on it then looked at Brody and continued. "It looks like this wasn't our usual burglary sir. The only thing we can tell was stolen was the computer and Mrs. Masterson's iPad. Jewelry, paintings and anything else of value seems to have been left behind."

Brody nodded to Kate Klein and couldn't help but let out an exhausted sigh. He had not slept much last night, mulling over all the information they had learned about Frank Masterson on their short trip to Ohio. Now, coming home to the destruction in Julia's home, he was more convinced than ever that Frank had been involved in some kind of mob activity.

"Thanks, Kate." He looked around at the dusting powder on the furniture from the fingerprint technicians and said, "Let me know immediately if they come up with anything useful."

Kate nodded and left, and slowly, the rest of the officers shuffled out after her. When it was finally quiet, Brody looked over at Julia, who had stayed sullen by the window, watching the officers walking out of her house. He contemplated telling her about his meeting with Mary and the ledger, but decided to wait. She had enough to worry about for now.

"We'll have to look for a cleaning company to fix this mess up," he said, walking over to her slowly. Julia just nodded absently, without really looking at him. He glanced around at the slashed cushions, couches and chairs.

It's going to take a lot more than a cleaning company to clean up this mess, he thought. It was clear that Julia would need to replace a great deal of the furniture that had been destroyed.

"How long do you think they were in here, going through all my things?" Julia asked quietly. "It must have taken them hours to do all this damage."

Brody looked around and tried to survey the scene through Julia's eyes. He could imagine her feeling violated from her privacy being invaded. "It probably didn't take that long Julia." He could see the torment in her eyes and he reached out and pulled her in close to him. "They were clearly looking for something. I don't think they were here to look through your private things. I'm sure they left right after they were done and didn't linger around."

"I just..." Julia sobbed. "I don't feel safe here anymore."

Brody held her tightly as she sobbed, but he had to agree with her. Until they found out who had broken in and why, he did not feel she would be safe here in this house alone.

Someone must have known that Julia would be out of town, at least for the night, he thought. He shuddered involuntarily as another thought hit him. What if they hadn't known that Julia was gone? What if her presence didn't matter, and they would have broken in anyway?

He knew then that Julia was not safe until they found out what was going on with Frank. "I need to get to work and go over a few of things that we discovered on our trip to Ohio. Do you know anyone here that you could stay with until we get this mess cleaned up?"

Julia shook her head. "I haven't had a chance to make any friends yet. We haven't lived here long, and I never really reached out to meet my neighbors. I was busy setting up our house and taking care of Frank."

"Then it's settled. I'll take you over to the Oceanside Palace. It's a nice hotel on the beach, and you can stay there until things are back in order here."

Julia looked around at the disaster in her home and agreed. She couldn't stay here, and right now, she was so tired and worn out that all she wanted was to lay down for a few minutes and gather her thoughts.

Brody took her arm and led her back to her bedroom. The room was as much of a mess as the rest of the house. Her bedding had been stripped away and her mattress was tipped over and slashed in several places. All the drawers from her dresser had been taken out and most of her lingerie had been strewn about on the floor. The clothes from her closet had also been thrown about, but thankfully, most of her clothes did still seem to be intact.

"Just take a few things now and we can come back and get more later if you need to."

Julia nodded and began to gather a few things into her overnight bag. She was nauseated at the thought that someone had gone through and touched all her personal items.

When she had gathered what she needed, she turned to Brody. "I guess that will do for now. I will need to come back and wash most of my things though. I can't bear to think of wearing what someone else has rifled through."

"I understand Julia. I can only imagine how violated you must feel right now. Take a few days to rest and then we'll come back and sort through this mess. In the meantime, I'll look for a cleaning crew to help you put it all back together again. We should have everything back to a livable condition in no time."

Julia looked around her, sadly. "I'm not sure that I can ever come back here, Brody. I think I might need to move back to Ohio. I moved here with such hope and excitement. This was the beginning of a new and happier chapter for me and Frank. Now, it is all turning into a nightmare!"

Brody took her bag and steered her out of the ruined room and towards the front door. He found himself disheartened at the idea of Julia moving away, "Don't give up on this place yet Julia. It can still be everything you imagined. You should take some time and think things over." He hoped she wouldn't make any rash decisions. He shut the door behind him and steered her to his car. "Come on, let me get you to the hotel where you can relax a little."

As they walked to his car and he placed her bag in the trunk, he looked up and down the street, checking for any suspicious vehicles.

What he failed to see was the dark-haired man that was crouched low in the driveway of the house across the street, about two doors down. The owners of the house were out of town for a few days, so they wouldn't have noticed the white jeep with tinted windows that was parked in their driveway. In fact, the jeep looked just like any other vehicle on the street. The man with the dark hair prided himself on his ability to blend into the background.

He watched as Brody pulled out and waited a few minutes before also slowly pulling out and following him, keeping a few cars lengths between them at all times. When Brody pulled into a hotel about ten minutes from Julia's house, he drove past it and pulled into a gas station, where he still had a good view of the hotel's entrance. Watching as Brody and Julia went inside, he smiled. *At least I'll be sleeping in a decent place with an ocean view tonight,* he thought.

CHAPTER 31

Brody walked into the precinct after dropping Julia off at the hotel and was immediately called in for a meeting with the Chief of Police. As he walked to the Chief's office, he felt the weight of the journal in his pocket and contemplated getting a second opinion on it.

"Brody," the Chief addressed him before he had even walked through the door. "I want this case solved immediately. The Mayor has been on me all morning. Apparently, Krystle Davis has been calling his office every other hour looking for an update on this case for her 'readers'. You know as well as I do that an unsolved case involving a missing, and possibly deceased, man who may have had connections to a drug cartel does not look good. He is running on the platform of how safe the community is under his leadership. We do not want to give his opponent any fodder."

"Of course, Sir. I understand. We are all doing the best we can." He pulled out the printed sheets that Mary had given him. "I have a few more sheets and numbers we might be able to decipher, and they might help us find a few leads that could help. Unfortunately, this case is full of twists and turns and it is taking us longer to follow all the new leads we are finding."

"We don't have a lot of time, Brody. The election is in a few months and the Mayor wants this case solved and forgotten by then. Tighten the screws on Mrs. Masterson if you need to. I have a feeling she knows more about her husband's activities than she is letting on. She is more than likely the key to his whereabouts, dead or alive. I want an update on my desk tomorrow, so I can give something to the reporters and get them off the Mayor's back."

Brody suspected the reporter he was talking about was Krystle Davis and he cursed her pushiness under his breath.

"I'm working on this case day and night, sir. Following any and all the leads that we get. I certainly appreciate the urgency the Mayor feels to get this solved, and believe me, I want to find Mr. Masterson as much as anyone. But I don't believe Julia is involved in any way, nor is she the key to his disappearance. The answer is out there somewhere, but not with her."

Daniel Wilson eyed Brody suspiciously. "I hope that you are not becoming too attached to Mrs. Masterson, Brody. I would hate to have to take you off the case and put someone else on it at this point."

Brody bristled at the suggestion that he was not being objective. "I have always handled all my cases in the most professional way I know how, and I don't intend to change that now. I believe my record speaks for itself, Chief. I follow the leads where they take me, and right now, they are not leading to Mrs. Masterson."

The Chief nodded at him. "Calm down, Brody, I'm just making sure we are on the same page. That you aren't letting your personal feelings cloud your judgment. I trust you, but the bottom line is, I want this case solved as soon as possible."

Brody took a deep breath, trying to stay calm. "I understand the pressure you are under to solve this case. I know that it would make a great story for Miss Davis to have a big arrest to write about, but I need to make sure that this case is solved correctly, and only the guilty people are arrested. As far as we know, this is still just a missing persons case. Krystle Davis is the one turning it into something more right now."

The Chief walked to the door and opened it, effectively ending the conversation. "You and I both know that Frank Masterson was more than likely involved in something illicit and is probably long dead already. Just solve this case Brody and solve it fast. I don't want to have to put someone else on the case."

Brody wanted to defend his case, but he bit his tongue and walked out. When he got to his desk, he took out the ledger and looked through it once again. He couldn't quite decipher the meaning of the codes and the numbers, but he could imagine that if someone had the key to the code, this ledger probably held a lot of information. He considered again if he should hand it over to forensics but was fairly certain that no one there at the local level had the expertise to break the codes.

The Chief clearly suspected Frank had been involved in the local drug cartel and believed Julia was part of it, or at the very least, been aware of what was happening. If he told the Chief that Mary had been instructed to hand this ledger over to Julia, it would make her look even more guilty. He wondered if the ledger was the reason why Julia's home was ransacked.

No, for now this little piece of information will be safer with me, he decided as he stuck the ledger back into his pocket.

Oceanside Palace was one of the most prestigious hotels on Longboat Key. It sat high overlooking an immaculate white sandy beach, which the hotel kept meticulously groomed for its guests. One call to the front desk would allow their guests to reserve an umbrella-covered deck chair with a hostess bringing over as many drinks as one wanted.

The minute Julia had arrived at the hotel, she laid down on the king-sized bed with its luxury sheets and fell into an uneasy sleep. She had the same dream of walking on the beach, trying to catch Frank. This time though, instead of trying to escape the ocean waves, she had been struggling to escape the clutches of an unkempt assailant. Once again, she had cried out for Frank to come and help her, and again he had turned away and left her to struggle on her own.

She had woken up from the nightmare drenched in sweat and had decided to take a long and invigorating shower. When she was finished, Julia wrapped herself in a white fluffy towel, stepped out onto the little balcony off her room and looked out over the vast ocean.

Earlier that morning, after seeing the destruction of her beach house, the ocean had seemed large, ominous and threatening. Now, looking out over the horizon from the safety of the hotel's luxury room, she could once again appreciate the beauty of it.

She had come to love the ocean and its different moods since she had moved to the Keys a few months ago. Even though she had just threatened to leave it all behind, she realized it was still the very place she wanted to be.

Julia sighed and slipped into a summer dress and a pair of sandals, hoping a walk on the beach would help her clear her mind. On her way past the concierge desk, she inquired about their laundry facilities, hoping to wash away the memories of her ransacked home.

After explaining her situation to the young woman behind the desk, the woman looked at her with sympathy. "We would be more than happy to launder as many of your things as you would like, Mrs. Masterson. It must have been so traumatizing to find your home invaded. We hope to make you feel as safe and comfortable while you stay here with us. Please just place the clothing in front of your door, and they will be returned to you fresh and ready to wear the next morning."

Julia smiled at her, grateful she did not need to go through her things herself. "Thank you so much. That would be so nice. I just want to forget about the whole incident and the fewer reminders of it I have, the better, I think. I'll gather some of my things later today. Right now, I think a walk on the beach might help to clear my head."

The concierge smiled kindly. "Please let me know if you would like me to reserve a chair for you when you return. We would be happy to serve you lunch on the beach if you like, or you are welcome to eat on our patio. Of course, we also have room service if you would prefer to dine in private."

Right now, all Julia wanted was to walk on the beach alone to think things through. She thanked the concierge and walked out to the water's edge.

She had brought her phone with her and she wondered if Brody would call and check in with her at all today. She was starting to look forward to his frequent calls and beginning to enjoy his regular company. The thought of seeing Brody later sent a little shiver of excitement through her in spite of all the turmoil going on in her life.

When was the last time I felt excited about seeing Frank? She thought. Now that she thought back on her and Frank's relationship, she really couldn't really remember the last time she felt that way.

Frank had been the one who would take care of her and give her a sense of belonging and security. How ironic, she thought to herself. When they met, he had felt like an anchor in an otherwise very scary and lonely world, and she had clung to him almost immediately. Now, she wondered how many warning signs she had overlooked in her desperation to not be alone and feel like she belonged somewhere.

She thought again of the wreckage that had been her home and shuddered slightly. Who would want to do something like that to her? What could they possibly have been looking for? After all she had learned about her husband over the last few days, she felt certain that the break-in had to be connected to Frank. She thought about what the Chief had said and wondered if it really could be true that Frank had somehow been involved in smuggling drugs.

Since her marriage to Frank, she had never had to struggle financially, but she had also never thought that they were rich. They had lived in a large and opulent house in Ohio, in a very nice neighborhood, but it had certainly not been the mansion that James Carson had referred to.

Frank had budgeted their money just like any other husband would have and she had always been very conservative when buying anything new for the house or herself. She had assumed that they were simply part of the upper-middle class that they were mostly associated with. In fact, a few times after meeting some of his wealthier friends at the country club Frank liked to frequent, Frank had seemed almost envious of their wealth.

Although he had never complained about it, she assumed that it had cost Frank a lot of money to take care of his girls over the years, and it would have been taking its toll on their finances. Now, knowing just how much money he had truly been spending, she wondered how he had been able to afford it.

Julia paused while walking and looked out over the ocean.

Could it really be possible that Frank had been dealing drugs throughout our marriage?

Julia tried to think back on the many dinner parties she had hosted over the last 25 years and if any of the guests had resembled the drug dealers she had seen in the movies. To her, they all seemed to have been average everyday businesspeople. Many of them had children, and their wives had been members of the local PTA groups. They had hosted playdates and the men had all gone golfing together – just ordinary middle-class families.

She then tried to picture Frank as a drug lord and found herself laughing at the thought. Frank had always been rather tall and awkward. He had dressed very conservatively; some might even say nerdy. The thought of him dealing drugs was absurd to her. He had always seemed perfectly at ease with his silly glasses perched on his nose, sitting behind a desk with a computer in front of him. Then, Julia remembered the gun case that she had found on his nightstand.

Could it be possible that Frank had been so different than how she remembered him? Could he really have carried a gun and been involved with drugs, all without her knowing?

Julia shook her head in denial and continued walking, heading towards a bend just a little further up the beach. No, she decided. There was just no way that Frank had been dealing drugs. He had managed to keep a multitude of secrets from her over the years, but this she was sure she would have known. There had to be another explanation for the gun case and for all the money Frank had earned.

Walking along the sand, Julia barely noticed her surroundings or the other beachgoers around her. She didn't notice the water that she was splashing through, nor the hot sun that was beating down on her head. She was lost in her own thoughts and struggling to come to grips with the idea that Frank had been a completely different person than the man she had married.

Behind her, the dark-haired man walked along slowly, stopping every now and then as if he were examining a shell or piece of sea glass. To any curious eyes, he looked just like another tourist, ambling carelessly on the beach and enjoying the Florida weather.

Just a little further, up around the bend and away from the hotel guests, he thought. There he would make his move quickly and efficiently. The detective was nowhere in sight, and it seemed like he would finally get a chance to make his move without interruption.

He glanced around him, gauging the distance of the other tourists and sped up slightly, trying to get as close as he could before she rounded the corner, and at the same time, stay as inconspicuous as possible. As he made his way slowly closer to Julia, he felt around in the pocket of his shorts for the bottle of chloroform he had hidden there. Suddenly he stopped abruptly, spotting an overdressed woman who was awkwardly making her way to Julia, calling out loudly.

"Mrs. Masterson, wait! Over here! Wait up a minute, please, I really need to talk to you!"

Krystle Davis cursed her choice of shoes this morning as she stopped and attempted to slip them off her feet. The heels were digging into the sand, and she almost toppled over. Once they were off, she started at a slow jog, calling out again and hoping that Julia would stop before she was completely out of breath.

Why did this woman always have to be on a beach? Krystle thought. *Can't she just wander around the city like any other civilized person?*

Julia thought she heard someone calling out her name and stopped to turn around, looking to see who it could be. At first, all she saw were several tourists, splashing in the water and collecting shells. Then, she spotted a woman in a business suit, clearly attempting to jog up to her, red-faced and out of breath, holding tightly onto a pair of high heels. Julia's heart sank. She recognized Krystle Davis immediately. She considered pretending she hadn't heard her and sprinting away quickly, she really did not feel up for a sparring match with the reporter right now.

As she stood, undecided, Krystle Davis waved and called out again. "I'm coming, Mrs. Masterson, almost there. I just need a minute of your time!"

Julia wanted to run around the bend to get away but she couldn't bring herself to be that rude, not even to the nosy reporter, so she stood still and waited for Krystle to catch up to her.

The dark-haired man watched as the woman in the suit caught up to Julia and started to shake her hand vigorously, at the same time, gesturing to a café that was close to where she had emerged from. He realized that he had missed his chance once again, and slowly melted back into the throng of beachgoers, blending in perfectly. Then, he turned around and headed back to the hotel.

It's only a matter of time Julia Masterson, he thought to himself. Your luck is bound to run out at one point, and I'll be waiting when it does.

*

Julia allowed Krystle to take her hand and shake it dramatically before finally pulling it away. She glanced around in desperation, looking for any excuse to get away, but saw only other beachgoers, and no one seemed to be paying any attention to her or the woman in the business suit.

She could hear Krystle saying something about heading to the little beach café, and Julia sighed in resignation, realizing there would be no easy escape from the reporter.

"I really would like to get your side of the story, Mrs. Masterson. I heard that your house was broken into and left in shambles. Understandably, the residents of our little town are alarmed. I feel we owe it to them to give them the full story and set their minds at ease. Please just come and join me so we can sit down and have a little chat in comfort." Krystle gestured again to the little café. "I'll be happy to buy you a cup of coffee, or anything else you would like. I just think we need to set the record straight for our readers."

Julia gave Krystle a cold look. "Like you did in your last article, where you as good as called me a husband killer, you mean?"

Krystle had the decency to look slightly chagrined but persisted. "Now, in fairness, Mrs. Masterson, I tried several times to get a hold of you and get your side of the story. When you refused to talk to me, I had no other option than to draw my own conclusions. If you come on up with me to talk now, I can get your side of the story and I won't have to draw my own conclusions."

Julia looked at Krystle in disgust. "I have nothing to say to you Miss Davis. There is no story for you to draw any conclusions from. My husband is missing, and as of right now, we don't know if he is dead or alive. He may be hurt somewhere or even being held against his will. For you to accuse me of murdering my own husband is unfounded and unforgivable." She tried to turn away from Krystle, but Krystle reached out and held onto her arm, preventing her from pulling away.

"Now, now, Mrs. Masterson. I didn't exactly accuse you of murder. I only brought a few likely scenarios to the forefront for my readers. Of course, I understand there is no proof yet whether or not your husband is deceased, but let's be honest here, the likelihood of the man still being alive after all this time is highly improbable."

Julia stared at Krystle in disbelief in response to the reporter's callous words, but Krystle continued on undeterred, "And since you wouldn't agree to an interview with me, what other conclusion was I supposed to draw? If you really want to find out what happened to your husband, it makes sense to talk to me so we can enlist the public's help. Quite frankly, staying silent just makes you look like you have something to hide." Krystle gave Julia a big but forced smile. "Of course, I am a very forgiving person. I understand you have been under a tremendous amount of stress, and I am more than happy to give you another chance to tell your side of the story. Let's just head on up, take a seat and let me get my little tape recorder out and you can tell me all about the break-in and who you think is responsible."

Julia stepped back and stared at the reporter. Surely this woman couldn't really believe that she would so much as give her the time of day, much less any kind of interview. "I believe that the made-up little fairytale in the last article you wrote has shown you to be a very untrustworthy and unscrupulous person. I have no idea who would want to break into my home, but even if I did, I would not jeopardize an ongoing police investigation by telling you anything. Please just leave me alone, and if you continue to slander my name or my reputation, I will be calling my lawyer."

Krystle shrugged her shoulders. "You can avoid me all you want, but in the end, the story will come out and I'm going to be the one to write it. I have my contacts within the department. You can hide all you want Mrs. Masterson, but the police will find out what you did with your husband and when they do, I will be there to watch as you are dragged off to jail. Trust me, it will be better for you to cooperate with me and allow me to tell your side of the story. It might help them go easier on you if you have the public on your side."

Julia looked dumbfounded at the reporter, at a total loss of what to say to such a crazy accusation. She wanted to scream at her that she had nothing to do with Frank's disappearance and she was as much in the dark as to what happened as anyone else. She wanted to defend herself and tell Krystle that she was wrong about her, and she would never do anything to hurt Frank, even after everything she had learned about him. Looking at Krystle's triumphant sneer however, Julia knew it would be useless to try and explain anything to her. Krystle was only after a story, not the truth and she didn't care if she destroyed Julia in her greed to get it.

After a few seconds, Julia collected herself and chose to just ignore Krystle, turning back to the hotel and walking quickly along the shoreline in the sand, knowing full well that Krystle would not be able to catch up to her.

CHAPTER 32

Brody sat back in his chair at his desk and looked at the papers strewn about him. He gathered the notes he had scribbled on throughout the day, deciding he needed a change of scenery. Most of the afternoon had been spent on the phone, and the various notes had been scribbled throughout the day on random pieces of paper. Now, as he gathered them up, he took one last look through them.

Just as he had suspected, the numbers and the accounts that Mary had printed out and given him had been a dead end. None of the accounts were active, and it was clear they had only been used as transitory accounts to help hide where the money was coming from or going to. The one thing that was apparent though. Frank Masterson was most likely involved in some kind of money laundering scheme. But until he could find a victim, or some evidence of theft or tax evasion, there was not much that Brody could do about it.

He had followed up on the information Jane had given him for Charlotte Taylor and found out that she did indeed, still live in Orlando, and when he called the number Jane had provided, Charlotte had answered. She had not wanted to talk to him at that moment because she had said her husband was home and he did not know about Frank. She promised to call back tonight when he left for his shift at work and talk with him then.

He had also tried to track down the third woman Frank's lawyer James Carson had told them about. Maria Martinez. Clearly she had moved around a lot, but Brody believed he finally had her current number. He had left a message for her to get back to him as soon as she could, so he could talk to her before he needed to go and track her down. Interestingly enough, from the number he found, it looked like Maria Martinez now resided in Miami.

He gathered all his scratched-on notes together and texted Julia, telling her he would be at the hotel to pick her up shortly and that he had several things to tell her over dinner. As he walked to his car, he felt some of the day's tension ease away and found he was really looking forward to seeing Julia and telling her what he had discovered. He started the car and when he heard his phone ding, he looked eagerly at his phone.

The text read.

I can't wait to hear what you found out. I would love to go to dinner, but I think you should call Becky and ask her to spend some time with you.

Brody smiled as he pulled out onto the street. After everything that had happened, she still had time to be concerned about the relationship between him and his daughter.

When he got to the hotel, he texted Julia to let her know he was at the door and then gave it three quick taps, eagerly waiting for her to open it. When she opened the door he was once again mesmerized by her natural beauty. Even though her long dark hair was tangled, and her eyes looked tired, when she smiled his heart softened.

Julia motioned for him to come inside, and when they were safely in the room he gave her a tight reassuring hug.

"So how was your day? Were you able to get any rest at all?" he asked as he walked across the room to the small balcony and looked outside. "Nice view by the way."

"Yes, it's such a nice room," said Julia. "I tried to get some sleep this morning but just ended up having more bad dreams, so I took a walk along the beach instead."

Brody smiled at her. "That's good then. You said the beach always relaxes you."

Julia perched on the edge of her bed and looked at him. "Yeah… until I ran into Krystle Davis. Or I should say she ran into me."

Brody frowned. "What did she want now?"

"She wanted to interview me. She knew all about the break-in at my house and wanted me to tell her my side of the story."

Brody's frown grew deeper. "Did you talk to her or tell her anything?"

"After what she wrote about me in her last article?" Julia shook her head, "Of course not! I have no intention of telling that woman anything."

Brody nodded in agreement and wondered how he had ever gotten involved with a women like her.

"I think you are right Brody." Julia continued. "She is definitely not someone to be trusted. She even said she had contacts at the police station though…and insinuated she could get information about me, even if I didn't talk to her."

Brody winced slightly and wondered if Krystle had been referring to him. Maybe he would call Krystle later and try and find out what she was up to.

He had enough pressure from the Chief to solve this case without her articles fueling rumors around town.

"Anyway, I spoke to the concierge earlier and they said they would launder all of my clothes, so I need to pick them up from the house and bring them here. Do you mind taking me? I don't really feel comfortable going there alone yet," Julia asked.

"Of course. That's nice of the hotel to agree to wash them for you. I contacted a cleaning crew and they can be there by the end of the week to help sort out the house. They said they could also provide a dumpster if you needed one." Brody felt his stomach growl. "Maybe we could go to dinner before we go to the house? I'm famished."

Julia smiled at him. The poor man always seemed to be hungry. "Oh, did you get a chance to call Becky yet? I feel like I am always taking you away from her. Do you think maybe she would want to come to dinner with us?"

Brody brightened. "I was going to call her later, but I think that's a great idea… if you don't mind?"

"By all means, call her now and see if she is free," Julia agreed.

"I have been thinking a lot about what you said. About just taking her out to have fun with no lectures or lessons. I would love to give that a try."

"I think this is as perfect a time as any to reconnect with Becky again. As long as she doesn't mind me tagging along with the both of you. Let me just go and straighten my hair and I'll be ready in a minute."

Julia walked into the luxurious bathroom, wanting to give Brody some privacy to call his daughter without her listening in. When she came back out a few minutes later, Brody was just putting his phone away.

The look on his face was brighter than Julia had seen in quite a while. "It's all set. She seemed thrilled to be invited along. Her only condition was that she gets to pick the restaurant." He looked at Julia apologetically. "I have a feeling I know what it will be… I hope you like Italian!"

Julia laughed along with him, feeling happy and lighthearted for the first time in months, and found she was really looking forward to the evening. She heard Brody's stomach growl again. "I love Italian. Let's head out and get Becky before you starve to death!"

As they exited the hotel, they failed to notice the dark-haired man sitting at the bar with a clear view of the hotel lobby entrance, frustrated once again that Detective Barker was always by her side.

168

CHAPTER 33

Becky was waiting in the driveway when they arrived and jumped eagerly into the car. "I'm starving," she exclaimed. "Can we go to Mario's, Daddy? Please? I swear they have the best lasagna in the world."

Brody looked at Julia with an *I told you so* grin, "I didn't know you were so worldly, but sure, Mario's sounds great."

Becky giggled and leaned back. "So, how's the search for your husband going Mrs. Masterson? I sure hope you find him soon. It must be so difficult for you to be going through this right now."

Leave it to a teenager to jump right in with the awkward questions, thought Brody.

"That's not exactly polite Becky. Maybe Julia doesn't want to talk about it right now."

"Oh sorry," Becky sank lower into her seat. "I guess I wasn't thinking."

"It's alright," chimed in Julia. She shot Brody a warning look. This dinner was supposed to be about connecting without any lectures. "It's a legitimate question. And please, call me Julia. Mrs. Masterson makes me sound so old."

Becky perked up in the back seat. "Ok Julia. Thanks, but you don't need to worry. You don't look old at all!" She smiled reflectively. "I didn't mean be rude.... I just really do feel bad for you. It must be, like, really scary to have a person you love go missing. I would go insane if my mom or dad just disappeared."

"Thank you for the concern. You're right. It hasn't been easy. Unfortunately, his disappearance has brought several things to light that I wasn't aware of during our marriage. It is making me think I didn't know Frank that well at all and I'm starting to wonder if, we ever do find him, what the future will look like for us anyway."

"Oh, I'm so sorry. I didn't know that." Becky shot Brody a cautious glance. "If you ever wanna talk about it, or even just spend some time shopping and hanging out, I'm your girl. I know I'm still young, but all my friends say I'm a great listener. And I have the whole summer free."

Julia shot Becky a grateful smile. *It might be fun to spend some time with the young woman,* she thought, and she certainly didn't have many other friends.

"I would love to spend some time shopping with you. As a matter of fact, someone seems to have thought it would be a great idea to destroy my home and wreck my furniture, so I think I have a lot of shopping to do anyway, that is if I plan to move back in any time soon."

Brody smiled over at Julia, secretly glad to hear her say she was planning to move back into her house. He hoped that she had given up the idea of moving back to Ohio, and if Becky could help convince her to stay, then all the better. He couldn't stop himself from commenting on Becky saying she was free the whole summer though.

"I think it's a great idea for you to help Julia, but I thought we had discussed you getting a job this summer to start saving up for college. Did you apply anywhere yet?"

Becky groaned, and Julia shot Brody another warning look.

Did this man ever stop lecturing? She thought.

"There's just not that much around here, Dad. All the cute little boutique shops have their regular summer help and I hate the thought of flipping burgers at the local fast-food joint all summer."

Brody looked back at Becky through his rearview mirror. "I think I could talk to Diane about getting you a job at the diner," he said.

Becky wrinkled her nose. "Ew, Dad. I'm going to smell like diner food all summer if I work there. Honestly, I just don't think that waitressing is my thing!"

Brody was just about to ask her exactly what she thought her thing was, when Julia spoke up.

"You know, I could probably use a little help with my business if you're interested Becky. I have a lot of people trying to make appointments and I'm having a hard time scheduling and keeping it all straight. On top of that, if I'm going to take on more clients, I think I will need some help with the billing and stuff. It would probably only be part-time work, but do you think you'd be interested in helping me?"

Becky's face beamed. "You do Reiki, right? How cool. I would love to help you. I'm great with schedules and numbers and it sure beats flipping burgers or bringing people coffee all day long! Do you think I could come along on some of your appointments and watch you work?"

Julia smiled back at her. "I think we could arrange that. I have to get my house back in order first, but as soon as I do, you can start coming over and giving me a hand."

Brody suspected that Julia had just made up the assistant position on the spot to help Becky, but if it would keep her here on Longboat for a while longer, he was happy to let Becky work with her.

When he pulled into the restaurant's parking lot, he gave both the girls a grin and opened their doors ushering them inside.

Maybe things were starting to look up in his private life after all. Now, if only he could solve the baffling case of the missing Frank Masterson, life would be good.

CHAPTER 34

The dark-haired man surveyed the mayhem around him and wondered if anything might have been overlooked. It seemed the team he had sent to canvass Julia's house had done a thorough job just like they had claimed, and he was frustrated that they had come up empty. He had decided to take this opportunity to see for himself if there was something or some spot they might have missed in their search.

He looked around at the nice but somewhat modest house that Frank Masterson had been sharing with his wife and shook his head in bewilderment. It was a nice home and had been tastefully decorated, but it was a relatively simple home and the man wondered once again at Frank's ability to keep his spending under control. With the money he and his associates had paid Frank over the years, he could easily have afforded one of the million-dollar homes he had seen further up the beach on the bluffs.

Clearly money had not been a motivating factor in Frank's life, as he seemed to enjoy leading a simpler life, and the man wondered again why Frank had decided to double cross them in the last few months. He shook his head in disgust. He, Frank and the rest of his associates had shared a very good and lucrative working relationship over the years. They had all come to trust Frank Masterson implicitly and he had been privy to a great deal of their operation. Even so, it was second nature for all of the associates to watch each other closely, and when one of them had discovered a few months ago that Frank was collecting information on them, they had all decided to act quickly.

The group had spent the last few weeks since discovering Frank's betrayal covering their tracks and erasing any connections to themselves that Frank might have divulged to anyone. They had all been waiting anxiously for the fall-out from his betrayal, but since then, all still seemed to be calm; they believed they had acted quickly enough before Frank could cause any great harm to the group. They were all starting to relax and felt they were once again cloaked in relative anonymity and out of any immediate danger. There was just one more loose end to tie up and Frank's wife Julia seemed to hold the key to that.

He wandered into the couple's bedroom and scoped the walls, looking behind pictures and even taking apart the wood frame of the couple's old wedding picture, admiring Frank's wife as he did so. She looked young and vulnerable in the picture, and he wondered how much Frank had shared with her about his true business dealings. It was a shame she had to be involved in this, he thought, but he couldn't afford to leave any loose ends. They had all worked too hard to build up their little group.

As he was looking around, his sharp ears heard the sound of a car pulling up in the driveway. He walked over to the front window and, cloaked behind the curtain that had been drawn shut, he looked out and saw Julia, the detective and another young woman exiting the detective's car. He silently cursed.

That detective is becoming almost as big a problem as Julia Masterson herself, he thought as he silently slipped out of the house. *He might need to be dealt with as well.*

*

Julia, Brody, and Becky had had a great time at dinner together, laughing almost throughout the whole meal. Becky had been entertaining them with stories of the typical high school drama and Brody wondered how he had never realized his daughter had a funny sense of humor. Julia, in turn, had relayed her own humorous stories of college life, and the group had spent most of the dinner laughing and enjoying each other's company.

Now, as they approached Julia's front door, however, Julia's mood had become somber and Becky was quiet, waiting to see the damage inside the beach house. Brody was the first to step in and turn on the lights. The house was in as much disarray as it had been this morning when they had walked in, and Brody wondered what he had expected.

Julia walked in after him and looked around with dismay. This morning, the mess had been devastating to her, but now, in the dark, the whole place took on an eerie feeling and Julia just wanted to quickly gather some clothes and leave.

Becky looked around in amazement. She had never seen a house in such disarray. It looked like it was a set for a horror movie. The couches and chairs were overturned and slashed wide open, along with the pillows and blankets.

She could see the open cupboards in the kitchen and the broken glass littering the floor. Even the pots and pans had been strewn about. "Oh Julia, this is horrible!" she exclaimed. "What do you think they were looking for?"

Julia surveyed the mess and shook her head sadly. "I haven't the slightest idea. No money or jewelry seems to be missing, and they could certainly have taken the computer and the iPad they stole without making such a mess." Brody thought of the ledger he had stashed safely in his apartment this morning and wondered again if that was the key to this mess.

"Daddy this is awful." Becky looked at her father. "We have to do something to help Julia clean up this mess and get her house back to being livable."

"I agree, Becky. I have already arranged to have a crew come clean up this week and start the process. Maybe you can be here with Julia when they come so she doesn't need to face this alone. If that's ok with you Julia." Brody looked over at Julia as he spoke.

Looking around again at the destruction of her home, Julia shuddered. "I would love for you to be here Becky. I'm not sure I want to be here alone anymore at all."

"I can't really blame you for that," Becky commented. "It's kind of creepy here. Let's come again in the morning and see if it looks any better. We can gather up anything that's still useable and take inventory." Becky was getting more and more animated as she spoke, and Brody was happy she showed such enthusiasm. He had a feeling that Julia was not that excited to come back in the morning, but he was determined to do what he could to convince her to stay in Longboat Key.

"If you think you have the time, I guess we could do that." Julia looked doubtful as she spoke. "I'm not sure that there is a lot to be salvaged though. I'm probably better off throwing everything away and start over somewhere else."

"Are you kidding me?!" exclaimed Becky. "This place is like a dream home. I can't wait to come back here in the morning and see what it all looks like during the day."

She walked over to Julia and hugged her. "If you pick me up, I'll make a picnic lunch for us to take down to the beach. We'll work really hard in the morning sorting through everything and then spend the rest of the afternoon lying on the beach. Maybe you can teach me some yoga poses?"

Julia couldn't help but smile at the young woman's enthusiasm. "Ok then, that sounds like a plan." Julia looked at Brody. "I think I'll get my car and drive myself over to the hotel so I have it in the morning."

Brody nodded in agreement. "Sounds good. Why don't you grab what you want to take with you, and I'll lock the place up nice and tight. We should all be getting some sleep anyway. It sounds like you two ladies have your work cut out for you tomorrow."

Julia smiled at Becky and gathered some of the clothes she wanted to have laundered and headed for the door. With the prospect of Becky helping her, the task of cleaning up the house suddenly didn't feel so daunting anymore.

As Julia drove her car to the hotel, her mind was racing through the events of the last few weeks and all she had learned about Frank. It was becoming clearer that the real Frank Masterson was not the man she had married and agreed to spend her life with. She had learned to live with his anger and his control issues, but she would never be able to forgive him for his infidelities and all the lying he had done. She doubted that Frank had ever truly loved her and she couldn't shake the feeling that she had completely wasted the last 25 years of her life. She knew that the marriage was over for her, and she decided that tomorrow she would call a divorce attorney. Even if they found Frank alive, she didn't think she would be able to live with him again.

The dark-haired man sat in his usual spot in the lounge bar where he could see the hotel entrance. He watched as Julia walked in and was happy to see she was finally alone. He saw her head to the hotel desk, speak with the clerk, and then watched as she lugged a suitcase toward the elevator.

It looks like she plans to stay awhile, he thought. That was good. That meant he still had some time to make his move. He looked around casually at the other hotel guests and noticed a middle-aged woman glancing over at him and smiling. He decided he would need to move soon though. People were starting to notice him.

Julia unlocked the room and went inside, looking all around suspiciously before she threw the suitcase on her bed and opened it. She knew she was probably just being paranoid, but she couldn't shake the feeling that someone was watching her. She transferred the clothing she had brought into the oversized laundry bag the concierge had given her and placed it outside her room. When she was done, she locked and bolted the door, and still not satisfied, she placed a chair under the knob for extra security. Then, she secured the balcony door with the bolt and door jamb provided by the hotel and looked around, satisfied that she was safe, at least for the night.

While Julia was making her preparations, the man with the dark hair went to his room and donned the jacket he had taken earlier from the laundry room. He looked in the mirror and decided that at first glance, he looked just like a hotel worker. He put on the gray wig he brought with him and fixed the mustache over his lip.

Perfect, he thought. *She'll never recognize me now.*

As he prepared himself and made his way down the hall towards Julia's room, Julia was busy filling the tub with water and the essential oils she had brought with her. She sunk deeper into the hot water, donned earplugs, tuned into her favorite station on the entertainment section of her phone; just wanting to shut out the outside world for a while. She sank further down into the water and lost herself in the music, not hearing the loud knocks on her door.

The man stood outside Julia's door and knocked again, louder this time. He could see the laundry bag outside her door and decided it would be the perfect excuse to convince her to open the door for him. After knocking for a few minutes, he put his ear to the door and listened, but could hear no sounds coming from the room, not even the sound of the television.

Maybe she went out to the balcony, he thought. He jiggled the door as quietly as he could, checking to see if she had locked it. Using the master key he had also procured earlier, he deftly unlocked the door and hoped she had not set the hotel bolt yet. But instead of the bolt being his only obstacle, he realized something was jamming the door from the inside.

As he cursed under his breath, the elevator door slid open just down the hall, and he quickly bent down and pretended to retrieve the laundry bag that was in front of Julia's door. Standing back up, holding the bag, his pulse quickened when he saw the woman who had eyed him earlier at the bar approaching. Evidently, his disguise was working, as the woman passed him with just a quick cursory glance. He dropped the bag quickly and after another try at opening Julia's door, he slipped quietly away towards his own room. Just as he closed his door, he thought he could see the outline of another hotel worker walking to Julia's room to retrieve the laundry bag he had just thrown back.

Julia slowly got out of the hotel bath and wrapped herself in the oversized towel it provided. She walked over to her bed and threw on a pair of shorts and a t-shirt, contemplating if she should call down to the front desk and request a glass of wine to help her sleep tonight. The bath had helped ease some of the tension from her body, but she was even more eager to call a lawyer in the morning and felt a little too wound up to sleep.

As she contemplated calling, her phone dinged. It was Brody, asking her if she had seen the local paper yet. Julia's blood instantly ran cold. The question could only mean one thing – Krystle Davis was at it again.

After she texted back that she had not seen it, the phone rang. Brody was on the other end.

"Hi Julia, sorry if I woke you. I just didn't want you to be caught unaware."

"No, I wasn't sleeping. I actually just got out of the bath. How do you already have tomorrow's paper?" she asked. "Did Krystle write something about me again?"

"I follow it online, so I get the news as soon as it's out, even before it's distributed sometimes." Brody was silent for a moment. "I think I should come up and show you in person. She didn't take very kindly to you refusing her interview request it seems."

Julia looked at her bed longingly, wishing she could just crawl in and fall asleep to get away from this never-ending nightmare. Then, she looked back down at her phone and said, "I doubt I will be getting any sleep tonight anyway, so you may as well come by and show me."

"I'll be over in a few minutes. Don't answer the door to anyone but me." He instructed. Julia smiled wryly. She doubted anyone else was going to come knocking at this hour, but she agreed to check and make sure it was him when he knocked.

"I'll be the guy with the wine," Brody joked.

About 15 minutes later, she heard the soft knock on her door and peeked out the peephole. True to his word, there stood Brody with a bottle of wine in one hand. As she dislodged the chair and unbolted the deadbolt to open the door for him, she noticed that the door was unlocked.

Strange, she thought. *I swear that I locked that.* Then, she opened the door the rest of the way and stepped back to let Brody in.

Brody strode in and quickly secured the door again, then headed over to the tiny bar and pulled out two glasses, pouring a generous portion into each glass.

"Is it that bad?" asked Julia, watching him pour.

Brody grimaced. "It's not good. I think that woman really has it out for you. She should have been a fiction writer."

Brody walked to the balcony, unlocking it as well and they sat down on the two chairs overlooking the ocean. He took out his phone and pulled up the article by Krystle Davis, handing the phone to Julia to read.

Julia paled slightly as she read the article, shaking her head in denial. "I don't understand. How could she know all of this? She couldn't have been at the house, so how is she making the same connection about a drug stash that the Chief made? He only said that this morning."

Brody glowered out over the ocean. "It seems like she wasn't lying when she said she had connections at the station, and believe me, I intend to find out who it is first thing tomorrow."

"I guess when you read the article, it makes me look like a drug dealer, and it follows I easily could have killed Frank and made him disappear. If I didn't know better, I would believe it myself." Julia sounded so defeated that Brody quickly leaned over and took her hand.

"Don't get discouraged, Julia. We'll find out what happened to Frank and then Krystle will have to eat her words. In fact, when we solve this, I'll make sure she issues a public apology for putting you through all of this."

Julia smiled. "You can do that?" she asked.

"I sure can, and I will," Brody answered. But secretly he thought to himself, until I do though, there will be hell to pay with the Chief tomorrow. He was sure Krystle's article was going to have the Mayor's phone ringing off the hook in the morning, and the pressure to solve this case was going to lay squarely with him again.

Down below standing on the beach, the dark-haired man hid in the shadows of the moonlight, silently watching the figures on the balcony of Julia's hotel room.

CHAPTER 35

The Chief looked angrily at Brody. His face was red, eyes bloodshot. "The Mayor got me out of bed this morning, that's how frustrated he is over this case. He wants this solved immediately, and if the Mayor wants it solved, so do I. If it means I need to take you off the case and put someone else on it, then so be it. I either want that man found, and his wife cleared, or I want an arrest. And I want it by the end of the week. Do I make myself clear?"

"Perfectly clear, sir." Brody looked coolly at the Chief. Brody suspected that Daniel Wilson's career was on the line as much as the Mayor's. He wished he could tell the Chief that this case wasn't like a deadline for a newspaper. He couldn't just work late, put in some overtime, and boom, the case was solved. But he knew better than to say anything right now. If someone else was put on the case, there was no telling what could happen to Julia, and Brody wasn't willing to risk that.

With a huff, the Chief slammed his office door shut, almost before Brody had even left the room.

Brody walked back to his desk and once again tried to leave a message for Maria Martinez. When she hadn't picked up the phone, he decided that he would not sit around and just wait for Maria to get back to him. He ordered a number of detectives check the schools in Miami, to see if they could find out where her son was enrolled and possibly find her location through him. Brody was determined to find and speak to Maria before the day was over.

Then, he left another message for Charlotte, telling her she needed to call him back. If she didn't, he would head down and speak to her in person, husband or no husband.

179

*

When Julia pulled into the driveway, Becky was already standing on her front porch with a picnic basket in hand, ready to go.

"Good morning, Becky. Are you ready to do some cleaning up?" Julia smiled warmly at the young woman.

"I'm ready, willing and able." Becky laughed as she jumped into the passenger seat. "I talked to Dad this morning and he says the cleanup crew is coming tomorrow morning with a dumpster, so let's get all the good stuff sorted and just pile up the ruined stuff for them to take."

Julia gave an involuntary shudder at the thought of all of her ruined belongings and Becky couldn't help but notice.

"I'm sorry Julia, that sounded really insensitive. You must feel awful about losing so many of your belongings."

"No, no, it's alright." Julia put on a smile. "You are absolutely right. That is the best way to approach cleaning up the house. I really do appreciate you volunteering to help me today. I don't think I would have been able to face going into the house by myself." She glanced gratefully over at Becky.

"I'm super happy to help. If there is any way to make this easier for you, I'm in. I saw that dreadful article that horrible reporter wrote, and I want you to know that not everyone here believes everything they read. Most of the people who live here are really nice."

Julia doubted that most people were as open-minded as Becky, but she smiled at her anyway. She really was grateful that Becky had agreed to help her sort through the mess. Julia was still uncertain if she would move back into the beach house, but the mess needed to be dealt with regardless. She was also happy she did not have to face it all by herself.

When they walked into the house, Becky went to the kitchen and set the basket on the table looking out over the ocean. "Oh Julia, this is just fantastic!" she gushed. "This view is to die for!"

Julia stood by Becky's side and looked out at the ocean with her. It truly was a magnificent view, and when she had first moved in, she had enjoyed the mornings spent sitting in the window watching as the waves rolled in.

"Oh, I can't wait to come here and work for you. Imagine just looking out over the ocean every day."

Julia didn't have the heart to tell Becky that she was still contemplating moving back to Ohio, so she just set to work sorting through and discarding the broken dishes.

As they worked their way through the kitchen, Becky asked questions about Julia's work in Reiki and how she had acquired her skills. She seemed genuinely fascinated and Julia couldn't help but smile when she remembered how Brody had first reacted when she had tried to explain what Reiki was all about.

They had moved on to the living room, and already had two garbage bags full of broken items when the doorbell rang.

Becky looked at Julia surprised. "I thought that the cleanup crew wasn't supposed to get here until tomorrow."

Julia looked at Becky, equally surprised. "I didn't think so either. I guess we had better go and see who it is."

Julia went to the front door, and just like she had promised Brody, she looked through her peephole to see who it was.

Standing in front of the door were several women and a couple of men, most of whom she recognized as her neighbors. With a bit of apprehension, Julia slowly opened the door.

A blonde-haired woman was the first to step forward. "Hi, Mrs. Masterson." She held out her hand in a greeting. "I'm Amanda Blakely and I live across the street." Julia took her hand and shook it, looking suspiciously at her and at the other people gathered on her doorstep. "I hope we aren't overstepping here, but we heard about what happened with your husband… and the break-in at your house."

Julia remained quiet, looking from one person to the other, assuming they had all read Krystle Davis's article. She wondered if they were here to drive her out of the neighborhood.

A red-haired man stepped up to stand next to Amanda. He saw the suspicion in Julia's face. "Yes, we read about what happened in the local paper. We all live in the area, and we just wanted you to know that we don't buy into what that horrible reporter wrote about you." He looked behind him and saw the others nodding along. "We know you are not dealing drugs, and don't think you had anything to do with your husbands' disappearance. We are all here to volunteer our help and support if you would like it."

Julia gasped in disbelief. "You all came over to help me?"

The blonde-haired woman smiled kindly. "Yes, that's right. I don't know if you remember, but when you first moved in, a package of mine was delivered to your house by accident, with some postage due on it. You paid the postage and set it over by my house without ever saying a word or asking for payment."

A short motherly-looking woman spoke up next. "A few months ago, my daughter was riding her bike along the road when she lost control and ran into your flowers. Instead of yelling at her for ruining your flowers, you helped her up, gave her a bandage for her cut, and then some lemonade. She had been so afraid you would be mad at her, and it meant the world to her that you helped her instead."

One by one, the neighbors stepped up and recounted a few of the nice things that Julia had done for the neighborhood in the last few months since moving in.

"We wanted to let you know that your small kindnesses did not go unnoticed, and now it's our turn to help you," said Amanda.

Julia was too overcome with emotion to say anything.

Becky gently stepped in front of Julia and opened the door wide. "Hi everyone, it's so nice to meet you all." She looked back at Julia who seemed relieved that she was speaking on her behalf. "Yes, we would so appreciate the help. As you can see, whoever did this made quite a mess and we sure could use all the helping hands we can get."

The small crowd entered the house, and under Becky's direction, were quickly put to work, sorting through Julia's belongings and carefully packing aside anything that was not yet broken. As the morning wore on, Julia started to feel at ease, and by lunchtime, everyone was talking and joking as if they had known each other their whole lives.

Amanda invited everyone to her house for lunch, with the agreement that they would all reconvene after a nice meal to finish sorting out Julia's house, in time for the cleanup crew's arrival in the morning. She wanted to make the house habitable again so Julia could move back in as quickly as possible.

Watching from the jeep down the road, the dark-haired man was having a hard time containing his frustration. He was speaking into his phone angrily.

"I have no idea who all these people are. Neighbors, I guess. I had planned to grab her today and take the other woman too if I needed to, but there's no way I'll go unnoticed with all these people around."

He listened to the voice on the other end of the phone, and replied angrily, "You are more than welcome to come on down here and give it a try yourself if you think you can do better. If Grant had just nabbed her back at the airport, I wouldn't need to be wasting all my time right now." With a last explicative, the man hung up the phone and quickly pulled away from the corner of the road where he was parked, for once not paying attention to his surroundings.

A few car lengths behind him, Brody Barker took note of the car's license plate and made a mental note of the man, wondering where he had seen him before. Then, Brody headed on down to Julia's house to see what all the commotion around her home was about.

When he walked in the door, he was surprised to see so many people all bustling around and trying to bring some order into the chaos that had been Julia's house that morning.

"Daddy!" Becky came running over to give him a big hug. "These people are all Julia's neighbors. They came over to show their support and to help us clean up. Isn't that fabulous?"

Becky introduced him to various people and Brody was trying his best to keep the names straight and thanking everyone. At the same time, he was looking around to see if he could spot Julia anywhere.

He finally saw her in the guest bedroom. She was with a blonde-haired woman who had a pad and a pencil in her hand and the two women seemed to be taking measurements. As Brody approached them, Julia spotted him and came running over full of excitement.

"Brody, what are you doing here? We weren't expecting to see you until tonight! Did you see all the people helping Becky and I? I never knew I had such a great group of neighbors around." As she spoke, she hugged him and then took his arm and steered him towards the woman with the notepad.

"Brody this is Amanda Blakely, one of my neighbors. She organized this whole thing! For everyone to come over and help."

Brody took the hand that Amanda extended and shook it warmly.

"How kind of you all to lend a helping hand," he said. "I was telling Julia that we had a great group of people in our town, and you and the rest of your neighbors are certainly proof of that."

Amanda smiled. "It's the least we can do. Julia has been a wonderful neighbor right from the moment she moved in, always doing kind little things for everyone around, often without saying anything." She turned to Julia and hugged her. "When we read that horrid article in the local paper, I felt that we had to come over and show our support."

Julia smiled at her, and then said excitedly to Brody, "Amanda is an interior designer. She offered to help me turn the guest room into a Reiki studio. That way, I can actually have people come here for their sessions."

Julia's eyes glowed, and Brody had never seen her so excited. He rejoiced at hearing her plans for the house. It sounded like she was planning to stay. He didn't want to ruin her good mood, he needed to share some information with her.

"That's wonderful. I'm sure it will be a great studio." He looked at Amanda. "I hate to interrupt, but I need to talk to Julia about some developments in her husband's case." Gently, he took Julia's arm. "Maybe we could take a quick walk down to the beach where we can talk away from all the commotion?"

Julia gave Brody a curious look, then turned to Amanda. "I'll be right back. If you see Becky, will you let her know where we are in case she needs anything?" She gave Amanda a spontaneous and heartfelt hug. "Thank you again for everything. You have no idea how much this means to me!" Then she quickly turned and led the way out the door and down to the beach.

CHAPTER 36

"What happened, Brody? Did you find Maria Martinez?"

Brody led them towards a rock formation overlooking the ocean. He wanted to make sure Julia was sitting before he gave her the news and figured that the rocks were as good a place as he would find on the beach.

"Yes, as a matter of fact, we did. She still hasn't returned my calls, but we were able to track down her address and I am leaving for Miami in the morning to pay her a surprise visit and ask her some questions."

Julia looked at him sadly, almost afraid to ask the question. "Do you think that the boy is also Frank's son, Brody?'"

Brody shook his head. "No Julia, I don't. The school records did not show Frank listed as the father, and from what Jane told us, the timeline doesn't fit either. It also seems that the payments to Maria started after her son was already born. I don't think the child belongs to Frank."

Julia nodded, relieved. She wasn't sure why she cared so much at this point, but it would have devastated her if she had discovered that Frank had yet another child she hadn't known about.

They had reached the rocks by this time, and Brody motioned for her to sit down on a rather flat one facing him, and then he sat down close to her, reaching for her hand.

Julia looked into his face, concerned. "Brody, what is it? What's wrong? Has something happened?"

Fearing that Krystle had written even more lies about her, she tried to give Brody a reassuring smile. After the show of support from her neighbors this morning, she didn't feel nearly as vulnerable to Krystle's inflammatory articles as she had yesterday.

Brody held on to her hand and looked her squarely in the face. "Julia, they found a body washed up on the shore, near South Point Beach. Apparently, some beachgoers noticed their dog sniffing around acting strange, and when they went to investigate, they found the body."

Julia looked at Brody, not registering what Brody was trying to tell her. "That's very sad of course, but what does that have to do with me?"

"They took the body back to the morgue and ran some DNA tests on it." He held Julia's hand tightly. "The DNA is a match for Frank, Julia. It was Frank's body that they found washed up."

Julia's face was blank, not registering any kind of emotion. Brody was afraid she might be going into shock, so he reached over and took her into his arms, holding her tight.

She finally pulled back from him and looked into his face. "There has to be some mistake. Why would Frank's body be in the water? That's not possible, Brody. He hated water. That can't be Frank." Julia was shaking her head in denial.

"There's no mistake, Julia. The body had been in the water a long time but there was enough DNA to take a sample and get a match. It is definitely Frank. There's more." Brody reached into his pocket and pulled out a photo. "This was found on his finger."

Julia hesitated to look at the photo for a few seconds, not wanting to look at a dead body. But what Brody showed her was the picture of a ring. When she finally recognized it, Julia gasped. "That's Frank's wedding ring. He always wore it. We picked them out shortly after we got engaged."

Julia cradled her head in her hands and leaned forward, letting them rest on her knees. "Oh dear God, it is Frank. He really is dead."

When she looked back up at Brody, tears were starting to form in her eyes. "I just can't believe it. He was always so invincible, so sure of everything. How can he be dead? What happened Brody, how did he die? Why was he found on a beach?"

Brody kept a grip on Julia's hand. "They are doing an autopsy now, and when they are done, we should know more. The lead investigators down there think he was on a boat out at sea when he died. That would explain why his body wasn't found until now. The beach he was found on is pretty popular, so they believe the body must have washed up fairly recently, probably with some of the rain we have been experiencing lately."

Julia stared out over the horizon, across the vast ocean. She tried to imagine what Frank's last moments would have been. Had he lost his balance and fallen overboard? That had always been one of his biggest fears. Why had he been out on the ocean anyway? Julia just couldn't wrap her head around the circumstances of his death.

Suddenly, she straightened up and looked Brody squarely in the face. "I want to go to Miami with you in the morning. I have to see him, Brody. I have to see his body for myself."

Brody grimaced. He had volunteered to go in and do an ID from the pictures she had provided to save Julia the trauma of having to go in and see his badly battered body, but he knew that the coroner would prefer a family member to identify the body.

"Ok Julia, if you're sure you're up to it, I'll arrange for them to let you go and ID his body. But Julia, you need to be prepared for what you're going to see. It's not going to be pretty."

"I understand Brody, but I need to see him for myself to make it real. I still can't wrap my head around the thought that he is really dead." Then, she looked at Brody in panic. "We need to let the girls know, don't we? We need to tell them that their father is dead."

Brody nodded. "Yes, we can decide after you go to the morgue tomorrow if you want to tell them or if you want me to. One more day isn't going to make a difference at this point. Tomorrow, they should have completed the autopsy anyway and we'll hopefully be able to give them the cause of death."

"Yes, you're right of course. They will want to know what happened. I just can't imagine why he would have been out on a boat in the first place." Julia shook her head in bewilderment.

Brody had his own ideas, but for now, he kept silent. He was fairly sure that Frank had somehow become a liability. Further investigations into Maria Martinez had shown indications that she had ties to the local mob in Miami. Brody was convinced that she held the key to what had happened to Frank Masterson.

As Julia and Brody sat on the rock, making plans to leave for Miami in the morning, the dark-haired man was already in the car speeding down US highway 1, making his own way to Miami. He had just received a frantic call from Maria, informing him that Frank's body had been found and he needed to come to Miami immediately. As he sped down the highway, he thought to himself, *I'll be back soon Julia Masterson. We still have some unfinished business.*

PART SIX

CHAPTER 37

Julia sat silently in the passenger seat and watched the miles slip by as Brody drove North on US Highway 1, speeding toward Miami. Normally, Julia loved riding in the car and taking in the scenery around her, but today, she wished he would drive slower, wanting to prolong the inevitable as long as she could.

She had not slept at all last night, and as a result, she felt groggy and exhausted. Thoughts of Frank and what she had discovered about him had been swirling around in her head all night.

When Brody had shown up bright and early to pick her up, she had already regretted her decision to join him. Now, all she could think about was the terrifying moment when she would need to go in and identify her husband's body.

When she first heard the news that Frank's body had been washed up on shore, she couldn't believe that he was really dead; in fact, she wanted to see him for herself.

Since last night, however, and all the sleepless hours she had spent reflecting on everything that had happened, the initial shock had worn off and left her with a weary acceptance of his demise. She desperately wanted to find out why he had been out on the ocean and what had happened to him, but at the same time, she was terrified of what she would find out.

To her dismay, shortly after they had left, Brody had also received a call from Charlotte Taylor agreeing to meet with him, which meant Julia would likely be meeting the other woman that Frank had had a child with.

Brody drove quickly, wanting to get to Miami as soon as possible. He had a lot of work to do and hoped that today would be the day that many of the unanswered questions about Frank's death would finally be answered.

Occasionally, he glanced sideways at Julia, who sat silent and rigid in the seat next to him. His heart ached for her, and he fervently wished he had not agreed to bring her along on this trip. He had understood her need to see things for herself, but seeing how pale and withdrawn she was this morning, he wondered if she would have the strength to make the identification.

"We'll be there soon, Julia. Do you want me to stop and get you a coffee or anything before we go in?" Brody looked over and watched as she shook her head silently.

"No, I doubt I can keep anything down. Let's just go and get this over with." Julia felt queasy and thought that anything she ate or drank was sure to come up as soon as she walked into the morgue. She had never actually been in one, and she wondered if it was anything like she had seen in the movies. "Have you ever been to the morgue before?" she asked Brody.

Brody glanced over and wondered if he should answer her truthfully. "I've had to go and ID victims a few times, yes. I'm sure it's very different when it's someone close to you though. Are you sure you want to do this? I can still call and tell them that you are not up for it."

Julia was tempted to accept his offer but shook her head. She feared that if she didn't go, she would regret it later. This would be the only opportunity she would have to see Frank, and she was afraid that her imagination could be worse than what she would actually see. When she had dozed off briefly last night, she had been woken up by a nightmare about a gruesome, waterlogged face staring silently at her. She didn't want to picture Frank like that for the rest of her life.

"Will they let you come in with me?" Julia asked, looking over at Brody with apprehension.

"Yes, I'll be right by your side the whole time." He reached over and took her hand in his. "It's ok Julia. We'll get through this together. It's almost over now. Hopefully, you can start a new life soon and leave this nightmare behind."

Julia leaned back in her seat and closed her eyes, but she kept Brody's hand in hers and held on tightly. For some reason, she found almost anything was possible if Brody was there.

Hopefully Brody was right, it would all be over soon. She wanted nothing more than to be able to move forward with her life. Even before they found his body, she had already decided that her future would not include Frank, but she was still shocked and sad that he was dead. Strangely though, she could imagine her life moving forward without Frank, but the thought of never seeing Brody again was something she didn't want to contemplate right now.

They pulled into the basement parking garage at the coroner's office and Brody walked over to get Julia, taking her securely under his arm and supporting her to the elevators and then to the morgue. As soon as the elevator doors opened, Julia's sense of smell was immediately assaulted by the mix of strong chemicals and she hesitated for a moment, leaning against Brody. He stopped and looked at her.

"Are you feeling alright? Do you want to sit down for a minute before we go in?"

Julia tried to rally and straightened herself up. "No I'm ok. Let's please just go in and get this over with."

*

"You must be Detective Brody Barker." The door opened and a kindly-looking older man stepped out. "I'm Bill Holden, Miami-Dade county's medical examiner."

Brody nodded as he extended his hand to meet a warm and friendly shake.

Bill looked over at Julia sympathetically, "And you must be the deceased's wife, Julia Masterson?" Julia weakly shook the hand he extended. "I'm deeply sorry for your loss, Mrs. Masterson. I'm afraid this is the part of the job that never gets easier for me. We will try to make this as quick as we can."

The coroner led the way to a room across from the elevator. There, in front of her, was a large window that was covered with a curtain.

"My assistant, Robert, is standing on the other side of the window Mrs. Masterson," Bill Holden explained. "When you're ready, I'll ask him to draw back the curtain. The body will be covered except for the head, and you will hopefully be able to make the identification. As soon as you do, we will cover him and close the curtain. That's it. It should be very quick, and any time you feel we need to stop, or you need to have a seat, just let me know and that's what we will do."

Julia stared at the closed curtain. *Frank is lying behind this curtain,* she thought.

"Just let me know when you feel you are ready. You don't need to say anything if you prefer. Just a little nod will do." The man held a small walkie-talkie, ready to let his assistant know when to draw the curtain open.

Brody held tightly onto Julia's arm, hoping she could draw strength from him, and watched her carefully, on the lookout for any sign she needed to sit down or even faint.

Julia stood for a minute, almost hearing the seconds tick by as she strove to garner her courage, and finally she said, almost in a whisper, "Ok. I'm ready."

The coroner just said, "Ok" into his walkie-talkie and, in a second, the curtain was drawn back.

Julia saw the body lying on the gurney just on the other side of the curtain. Just like the coroner had said, he was fully covered in a sheet, only his face was left exposed. The face looked somewhat puffy and discolored, but his eyes were closed and the man lying there looked peaceful, almost as if he had just closed his eyes for a brief rest.

She looked briefly up at Brody and then at the coroner, who was patiently watching her, waiting for the answer to his unasked question.

Julia looked back at the body and nodded. "That's him. That's my husband Frank Masterson."

The coroner gave a quick and silent nod to his assistant, and Robert immediately pulled the sheet over Frank's face and then closed the curtain to the examining room again.

Julia felt numb and she was afraid her legs would crumble beneath her. Brody could feel her leaning heavily on him, "Is there anywhere we can go where Mrs. Masterson could sit down for a minute?"

The medical examiner opened the door and led them down a short hallway into a small but neat little office. In front of the desk were two chairs, and Brody quickly helped Julia over to one of them, sitting her down and crouching in front of her.

Bill Holden opened a tiny refrigerator in the corner of the room and took out a bottle of water. He held it out for Julia, "Here, Mrs. Masterson, drink this and try and take some deep breaths. I know this must be extremely difficult for you. I really do appreciate you coming in to make the identification."

Julia accepted the water gratefully and took a few sips, trying to breathe and keep herself from passing out. The smell of the chemicals from the morgue seemed to etch in her brain, and intermingled with Frank's lifeless face, lying like a mannequin on that gurney.

Both men sat and waited until they thought that Julia had composed herself. Brody finally broke the silence. "Have you been able to determine the cause of death yet?"

Bill Holden looked at Julia cautiously before answering, "Yes, we were able to determine the cause of death. Are you sure you want to hear this, Mrs. Masterson?" he asked.

Julia took another deep breath and steeled herself. "Yes Mr. Holden, I'm ready. I need to know what happened to my husband."

The medical examiner opened a folder on his desk and glanced through his notes. "The immediate cause of death for Mr. Masterson was a gunshot wound to the back of the head. That is likely what caused him to either fall or be pushed into the water."

Julia gasped and turned even paler than she had already been. "Oh my God! What do you mean? Who would do did that to him? Why?"

Bill Holden looked at Julia with compassion. "We believe from the minimal amount of water in his lungs that he must have ended up in the water shortly after he was shot. According to what we found, the gunshot wound to the head caused his brain to stop functioning almost immediately. Please rest assured that your husband didn't suffer in his last moments."

Julia felt the bile once again threatening to come up and she fought valiantly against the nausea. Brody saw the look on her face and decided he needed to get her away from the morgue as quickly as possible. He stood up and addressed the coroner.

"I think I had better get Mrs. Masterson some fresh air. I would like to look at the details of the autopsy and see the caliber of the gun and all the details as soon as possible. I am sure there are some leads I want to follow up on while we are still here in Miami."

"Of course, detective." He handed a folder to Brody. "These are the copies we were going to forward to your precinct. You can take them with you now if you like and look them over right away. I'll have my assistant fax another set to your precinct early this afternoon."

Brody took the folder and thanked him, and then looked over at Julia, who sat frozen in her chair. "Come on Julia, let's go and get some fresh air."

Julia rose slowly and thanked the coroner quietly, then clung to Brody's arm and let herself be led back down into the basement parking garage. Brody settled her into her seat and carefully buckled her seat belt, then came around to the driver's seat and started the car, hoping the AC would help to drive the smell of the morgue away from both of them.

He pulled out of the garage and drove until he saw a small street lined with trees. There he pulled over under a huge old shade tree and opened every window in his car, allowing as much of the early morning air in as possible. When he looked over at Julia, she was pale and absent.

I should never have allowed her to go in there, he chastised himself. *She is not strong enough to handle something like this.*

They sat in silence for a few more moments, while Brody contemplated how best to help Julia.

"I have a hotel booked for us tonight. I am going to call and let them know that we will be arriving earlier, then I'll take you there so you can rest," he said, pulling out his phone to make the call.

Julia roused herself at the sound of his voice and looked at him with frightened eyes. "What are you going to do after you drop me off?" she asked. The thought of spending the next few hours by herself locked in a room terrified her.

"I have a meeting with Charlotte Taylor. She finally agreed to meet with me but insisted we meet at a rest stop outside the city. She wants to be as far away from her husband as possible."

The thought of spending hours in a hotel room by herself seemed unbearable.

"I'm coming," she said simply, looking at Brody resolutely.

Surprised, Brody looked at her curiously. "Are you sure Julia? I don't know how this meeting is going to go… so far Charlotte has not been the most friendly or cooperative person. You have already had a traumatic morning. I really think I should take you to the hotel."

Julia sat back in the seat and looked stubbornly ahead. "I'm not going to spend the afternoon alone. I would go crazy. I am going to go with you, wherever it is you need to go."

Brody hated the idea of putting her through any more suffering than she had already been through. He turned towards her and took her hand. "Julia…" he began, but Julia looked back at him with pleading eyes.

"Please Brody, I can't be alone today. I really need you there. I know it's a lot to ask, but I don't think I can get through the day without you."

Brody's heart melted at Julia's desperate plea, and he felt he had no choice but to relent and bring her with him. "Ok, ok. If that's what you want. But you need to promise me you'll let me know if at any point, it all becomes too much for you."

Julia sat back again in her seat. "I promise I'll let you know."

She closed her eyes and braced herself for what was coming next. She prayed she would hold it all together long enough to get the answers he needed from Charlotte Taylor.

CHAPTER 38

Brody spotted Charlotte the moment she walked into the little diner at the rest stop where they had agreed to meet. She was a voluptuous brunette and looked very much like the picture that James Carson, Julia's lawyer, had given him. She was dressed in a tight-fitting t-shirt with tight jeans and was getting some appreciative looks from a number of the truck drivers seated at the counter. When Brody stood up to wave her over, she walked over quickly, looking furtively around, as if she were afraid of being discovered.

"Please, sit down Mrs. Taylor. I really appreciate you taking time out of your busy day to come and talk to us." Brody laid the charm on hoping to put her in a more cooperative mood.

"The name is Smythe now, so if you're going to be all formal with all this Mrs. stuff then at least use the correct name, otherwise just call me Charlotte. Everyone else does." She shot Julia a nasty look. "You didn't tell me you were bringing her."

"Julia accompanied me to Miami unexpectedly this morning and we thought it best if she came along," said Brody, holding Charlotte's chair until she finally sat down.

"It's nice to finally meet you, Charlotte," Julia said softly, her eyes never wavering from Charlotte's face. "Jane has told us a lot about you."

"I bet she has," hissed Charlotte. "Don't you believe any of it. The jealous witch doesn't know the first thing about me. Why are you here anyway? I agreed to meet with the detective to help find Frank, not to meet you."

Julia gave Brody a pleading look and waited for him to fill Charlotte in. She was in no mood to recount what had happened in the morning to this hostile woman.

Brody ordered a coffee for Charlotte and then looked at her carefully, hoping to gauge her reaction to the news. "There have been a few developments in Frank's case. Julia came with me this morning to go to the coroner's office... to identify Frank's body."

Charlotte gasped as the color drained from her face. "Frank's dead?" she asked, her voice sounding just as shocked as her face looked.

"I'm afraid so Charlotte. His body just washed up on shore in Miami," Brody answered, trying to gauge whether her surprise was genuine or not.

"No! How? When?! I only saw him a few weeks ago. He was fine when he left me." Charlotte looked at Julia accusingly, "You did him in, didn't you? You found out about us and you killed him!"

Julia looked at her, stunned at her outburst. "How dare you accuse me of such a thing! I did not kill my husband. I didn't even know who you were until after he went missing. And I would never hurt Frank, regardless." She shot Charlotte an angry glance.

Brody looked on as the two women sat glaring at each other and decided it was time for him to step in. "You said that you just saw him, Charlotte? When was that?"

Charlotte broke her stare and looked over at Brody. "It was about 6 weeks ago." She gave Julia another disdainful look. "It must have been just a day or so before their anniversary, because he told me he needed to take care of his business quickly so he could get back in time."

Julia's veins felt as if they had ice running through them. *So, Frank really had intended to come back for their anniversary,* she thought. He had not planned on leaving her and he must have been killed before he could return. Somehow this realization made things even worse for Julia.

"Was it typical for Frank to come and visit you then?" asked Brody, thinking about how nervous Charlotte had been about her husband finding out she was talking to the detective.

Charlotte smiled arrogantly. "We saw each other as often as possible. It became much easier since his wife insisted they move to Florida."

"I'm surprised to hear that," Brody replied. "Jane told us that you had moved on and created a new life for yourself. She was under the impression that you and Frank were no longer in contact."

Charlotte shot Brody an angry look. "I told you she doesn't know anything about me. She's always acted so superior just because she was the first one to have his children. Of course, I wasn't going to be stupid enough to wait around for him like she did. I figured after he married her..." she threw Julia an angry look, "there was very little chance he was going to settle down with me. Anyway, I wanted my son to have a father, so when I met Joe and he proposed, I jumped at the chance."

"Does your son know that Frank was his father?" Julia asked quietly.

Charlotte looked at Julia as if deciding whether to answer or not, and finally said, "No. He was too young to remember the time before Joe and Joe wants him to believe he is his father, so I obviously went along with it. Joe legally adopted him and thinks of him as his own now. Frank didn't care and he happily signed his rights away. I was happy with the arrangement as long as the money kept coming and I still got to see Frank." She looked at Brody triumphantly. "See, it was a win-win for everyone."

Noting the secrecy Charlotte had insisted on maintaining about the meeting, Brody asked, "I take it that Joe does not know you were still seeing Frank?"

"Oh no, of course not! Joe would have probably killed both Frank and I if he ever found out. I made sure that Jane did not know I was still seeing Frank. I know how jealous she is, and I didn't want her squealing to Joe. I let her think she had won and had Frank all to herself." She looked again at Julia and said, "Except for her of course. She has been a thorn that neither one of us has been able to get rid of."

Julia stared down at her coffee. Both Charlotte and Jane had been so awful and she wandered how Frank could have ever dated either of them. Especially behind her back.

Charlotte sat back. "Jane tried to contact me a few times, but I told her I wanted to forget the past and just move on with my future. She bought it hook line and sinker. She's always been such a condescending know it all, she deserved it." Charlotte grinned at Brody. "She didn't know much about anything though. She never suspected that Frank and I were still seeing each other, and she didn't know about Maria either. She also never knew that her daughter Cynthia and I kept in touch."

"So, you knew about Maria?" asked Brody. "How long had Frank been seeing her?"

Charlotte shrugged her shoulders. "I'm not sure exactly. I found out about her a few years ago."

Julia could see the hurt in Charlotte's eyes and wondered if a lot of her bravado was actually just an act. "It must have been hard for you to find out that he had yet another woman on the side," she said gently.

"You would know, wouldn't you?" Charlotte replied snidely.

"No, I don't know. I never knew he was seeing you or Jane until after he disappeared. I never got a chance to confront him. For you, it must have been different?"

Charlotte realized that Julia really had been a fooled all these years, and it made her feel superior to have been trusted by Frank with so many of his secrets.

"Yes, it was hard. I knew why he had to stay with you, and I knew that he and Jane were together sometimes, but he said it was only because of the girls. Maria was a different story though. Her kid was not his and he shouldn't have needed yet another woman. I should have been enough for him." She looked at Brody sadly. "Maybe she's the one that killed him? I never trusted her. I told him to steer clear of her, that she was trouble, but he wouldn't listen." Charlotte took a napkin and dabbed at her eyes. "And now he's dead."

Looking at Brody silently for a minute, Charlotte finally asked, "How? How did Frank die?"

Brody decided to answer, thinking it would be all over the news soon anyway, and he hoped if he gave her the information she requested, she would continue to cooperate. "He was shot in the head, and then he either fell or was pushed into the ocean."

Charlotte's eyes were red, and it was clear she was fighting back her tears. "It was her, I'm sure of it. He told me he had a meeting with her, and he needed to see her right away because it was important. That's why he couldn't stay with me for very long."

"You mean Maria? He had a meeting scheduled with Maria Martinez right after he saw you?" Brody had brought out his ever-present notebook almost as soon as Charlotte had sat down and was now scribbling on it furiously.

Charlotte was nodding and still dabbing her eyes when he looked up at her.

"Isn't scheduling a meeting an odd way of referring to going to see his other girlfriend?" Brody asked.

Charlotte gave a cynical little laugh. "They were business partners as well as lovers," she said. "I imagine that's how they met. He gushed on and on about how smart and clever she was. I think that's partly what made her so attractive to him. He probably thought the rest of us were rather simple minded and pliable. Her spunk and brains were probably something new and exciting for him."

Julia cringed a little in response to her words, but she couldn't really disagree. They had certainly all acted like a bunch of foolish lovesick women, giving in to his every demand.

"Have you ever met Maria?" asked Brody.

Charlotte shook her head. "No, but he gushed on enough about her to me that I feel like I have. She is apparently quite well built and dark-haired as well. He seems to like dark hair, doesn't he?" she asked, glancing over at Julia.

Julia decided to ignore her. She wasn't ready to discuss her dead husband's preferences quite yet.

"Well, at any rate, no matter what he preferred in his type of women, he sure loved his secrets and his conspiracies. I think his daughter took after him with that trait, that's for sure."

Brody looked at Charlotte questioningly, "What do you mean? Which daughter took after him? Mary?"

Charlotte laughed harshly. "Hardly. She was a complete washcloth when it came to Frank. Whatever Daddy asked her to do, she did it without question. Cynthia on the other hand, had some spunk. She has a real backbone that one."

"So, Cynthia stood up to her father?" asked Brody.

"Stood up to him and even manipulated him. She had a real knack for getting what she wanted from him. She even convinced him to support her girlfriend! As straight-laced and conservative as Frank was, I can't believe she got him to accept her lifestyle, much less support it." Charlotte was shaking her head in disbelief as she spoke. "And she managed to keep it all a secret from her mother and her sister. That is one cunning woman if you ask me."

Julia looked at Charlotte, stunned, as she was speaking. *The number of secrets this family held from one another was astounding,* she thought.

"He was supporting Cynthia's lover?" asked Brody, wondering if this was the fourth mystery woman on the list. "Do you know her name by any chance?"

"I don't know exactly... but once last year I met Frank for dinner and Cynthia was with him. She mentioned her girlfriend... I think her name was Abby." She was silent for a moment, as if thinking back to that dinner.

"Now that I think about it, Frank seemed upset after she talked about her. I got the feeling he was not very happy about the relationship and I wondered even then how she had convinced him to give the woman money." Charlotte shrugged. "But like I already said, Cynthia was the master manipulator when it came to her father."

Julia was still trying to digest the news that Cynthia had a female lover. "Did Jane ever find out about Cynthia having a girlfriend?" she asked.

"I highly doubt it. Cynthia always let them believe she was dating a rich foreign guy who was out of the county a lot and that's why they couldn't meet him. She got a real kick out of fooling her mother."

Brody had been looking through his notebook, and finally, he found the names of the women that James Carson, Julia's lawyer had given them. There it was; Abigail Carpenter. At last, he had the identities of the women on Frank Masterson's payroll.

He wondered what would happen later on today when he called Cynthia to find out how to contact the woman. He imagined the phone call would not be a pleasant one.

Charlotte looked down at her watch and stood. "Well, I think I've given you enough information for now. I need to go or Joe is going to get suspicious. Please don't contact me again, detective." She looked at Brody with a warning glare.

"I'm afraid I can't promise you that Charlotte. We now have a murder investigation on our hands, and you were one of the last people to see Frank alive."

Charlotte paled as she realized the implications of what Brody was saying. "Please, you can't let Joe know that I was still seeing Frank. You have no idea what a temper he has. If he finds out I have been going behind his back, he'll kill me for sure."

Brody looked at her sympathetically. It seemed that Charlotte's choice in men had not improved much over the years. "I'll do my best not to involve your husband, but you are a key witness right now, and I can't rule you out as a suspect as of yet either. I'll need to check out your alibi as soon as we can determine the approximate time of death. I will ask the detective who contacts you to be discreet, but you will be contacted and you will be required to give us any of the information as to your whereabouts during the time of the murder."

Charlotte looked at him, stunned. "You can't be serious? Am I a suspect in Frank's murder? I came here willingly to talk to you. Do you think I would have done that if I killed him? For heaven's sake, I loved Frank! Or else I wouldn't have risked Joe's wrath sneaking around behind his back all these years." Her voice broke towards the end before she cleared her throat. "If you really want to know who killed Frank, I suggest you look at Maria Martinez and her shady cohorts. I have no reason to want him dead, but who knows what that group was involved in. I always warned Frank that they were trouble."

Watching as Charlotte's eyes filled with tears, Julia believed what she was saying. She couldn't imagine why after all these years Charlotte would have wanted to kill Frank. It seemed like she had known most of Frank's secrets, and if she had accepted them for this many years, Julia couldn't imagine why she would change now.

Brody stood up and thanked Charlotte, telling her he would be in touch and promising they would be as discreet as possible.

"Now what?" asked Julia, her shoulders slumped, clearly exhausted and looking defeated.

"Now we head back to Miami and give Maria Martinez a call," said Brody. "According to Charlotte, she is the key to Frank's murder."

"Do you believe her?" Julia motioned to the door that Charlotte had just exited. "I don't think she had anything to do with his murder. She seemed genuinely shaken."

"Maybe," Brody answered. "But until we can verify an alibi for the time of death, we can't rule her out. She still might be guilty. Who knows, maybe she finally just got tired of waiting around for Frank and snapped one day. Anything is possible."

Julia stood up slowly and wearily, making her way out the door and to the car. When she sat down and had buckled her seat belt, she waited for Brody to pull out onto the freeway.

"Do you think she was his favorite?" her voice sounded full of anguish.

Brody looked over at her, not sure how to answer. "Do you mean Charlotte?"

Julia nodded and looked out the window, trying to hide her tears. "It seems that out of all of us, she was his confidant, the keeper of all his secrets. She seems to know all about the rest of us, while we were all kept in the dark."

Brody reflected on what Julia had said but remained silent. If it were true that Charlotte had been the confidant, could she really have snapped one day and decided Frank had gone too far? Maybe the affair with Maria had been the final straw and pushed her over the edge. Brody accelerated slightly, eager to get back to Miami. He was convinced that he was getting very close to finally solving this case.

CHAPTER 39

Brody stood at the doorway of Julia's room and watched as she sat on the edge of the bed staring absently out the window. She hadn't eaten or spoken since they arrived back at the hotel. He was afraid the events of the day before had been too much for Julia and maybe she was going into shock. Maria had finally agreed to meet him, but now he was hesitant about leaving Julia all alone.

"Are you sure you are going to be alright?" he asked for the third time.

If they had been back at Longboat Key, he would have asked Becky to stay with her, but as it was, they were stuck in a hotel in Miami, and Brody had no one to watch over her.

"I'll be fine," Julia said, listlessly.

She stared out the window without seeing the panoramic view of the skyline. Brody had asked her if she wanted to come along to the interview with Maria, but she was in no mood to meet any more of Frank's mistresses.

Brody looked at her and debated what he should do next. He didn't want to leave her on her own, but he didn't want her to go with him. He had no idea how the meeting with Maria Martinez would go after Charlotte had alluded to her being tied in with the mob.

He glanced down at the time on his cell phone and decided if he would make his meeting with Maria, he had better get moving.

"Please stay here in your room, Julia. Until we know who murdered Frank and why, I don't want you to wander around on your own. We are not sure how the break-in in your home ties into all of this yet either. Order room service if you need anything, but don't forget to check who's at your door before opening it." Brody walked to the door and waited for Julia to get up to lock the door.

She nodded and dutifully walked over, waiting for him to exit and then bolted it behind him.

Walking back to the bed she had been sitting on, she spotted the minibar and decided she needed something to numb the pain. She grabbed a little bottle, and without even looking to see what it was, opened it and swallowed, coughing a little as the strong alcohol made its way down her throat.

Ever since they had met with Charlotte earlier, Julia fought a terrifying feeling of rage towards Frank. Scared of what might come out if she'd spoken, she had stayed quiet and tried to comprehend everything she had found out about her husband over the last few days.

The more she thought about it, the more enraged she became. Everyone had known everything about Frank and his infidelities except her. She had been left in the dark and played for a fool.

She thought about the smug and superior looks that both Charlotte and Jane had given her, and her blood boiled even more. Frank had confided more in his daughter Cynthia than he ever had in her, and it was clear after yesterday's conversation with Charlotte, that Frank had put more trust in her than his own wife.

She remembered how excited she had been when Frank had agreed to move to Florida, thinking how he was doing it solely for her and their marriage. Now she wondered if he had schemed all along, so that he could be closer to his other two love interests.

She reflected on how hard she had worked at making their little beach house a loving home, she now remembered how it had looked after it had been ransacked and destroyed.

She thought about how Cynthia, and even Mary, had accused her of causing Frank harm, and how Krystle Davis had written several articles accusing her of being a Black Widow. Even Brody had suspected she was involved in Frank's disappearance when they had first met.

All the awful and traumatic memories and events of the last few weeks were running through her head. She felt her stomach tighten and twist in rage at Frank for having lied to her for all these years and turning her once peaceful life, chaotic.

She could feel hot tears of shame, anger and frustration welling up in her eyes. He had taken her as a young and naive girl and used her, trampling on her feelings in the process.

Julia walked over to the minibar and took out another small liquor bottle, opening it and downing it all in one swallow. She wondered what meaning was left in her life. She had spent the last 25 years of it catering to a disloyal and manipulative man. She had spent over half her life committed to a marriage that was a sham.

Julia looked out the window at the setting sun, and the restlessness and anguish was suddenly too much for her to handle alone. She walked over to her suitcase and pulled out a simple pair of blue jeans and a t-shirt, not even glancing in the mirror as she grabbed her hotel key and exited the room.

She headed to the elevator and down to the hotel bar, determined to drink as much as she needed to, until, at least for tonight, she could forget the pain in her heart.

As she walked over to the bar, she barely noticed the other patrons or the appreciative glances she was getting from some of the single businessmen who had gathered for happy hour.

The dark-haired man sat alone and watched as she walked right by his table, not even glancing his way as she passed. He had been sitting here for the better part of the hour and had seen Brody exiting the hotel. He had been contemplating the best way to lure Julia from her room when she had emerged from the elevator and headed right to him.

Tonight is the night I take care of the final loose ends, he thought.

CHAPTER 40

Brody walked into the dingy bar Maria Martinez had chosen to meet in and looked around, waiting for his eyes to adjust in the dim light, trying to spot her in the crowd. He jumped when he felt a light touch on his arm from someone who had snuck up behind him.

"A bit jumpy tonight, aren't we, detective?" Maria gave him a sly, but coy smile, clearly pleased with herself that she had been able to catch him unaware.

He looked at the woman whose hand was still lingering on his, and he could see what Frank must have found so attractive. Just like Charlotte had said, the woman was very well built in all the right places and her hair was a glossy black color that shined even in the low light in the bar.

Charlotte had not mentioned the sparkling dark eyes twinkling out of a flawless olive complexion and the perfect pearly smile that was now being bestowed on him enticingly.

Maria Martinez exuded seductive confidence with just a hint of danger, and Brody could feel the attraction that most men would have for her. He knew that if he had met her under different circumstances, he himself might have easily fallen prey to those dark haunting eyes. As it was, he was grateful for the gun he had holstered under his jacket.

"Didn't your mother ever teach you that it's not nice to sneak up on men, Miss Martinez?" Brody spoke with a slightly flirtatious tone, guessing he would learn more from her if she thought he was not immune to her charms.

Maria gave him a wide smile, leaning in closer. "Just the opposite, detective. Mama taught me to always keep a man unaware and guessing."

Brody smiled at her back and took her arm, guiding her over to a small table in the back. "Let's sit here where it's a little more private, and maybe you can share some more of your Mama's wisdom with me."

He ordered them both a drink from the waitress who appeared almost instantly, and when they both had their drinks, he sat looking at her, trying to look casual and relaxed, waiting for her to speak. Maria took a dainty sip and sat back slightly, studying the man in front of her.

"So, I'm sure you didn't go through all this trouble to hunt me down just to flirt with me, detective. Am I right?" She gave him a slight, knowing smile.

Brody was silent for a moment, deciding if he should jump right in with the questioning or start slower, letting her feel she had the upper hand on him for a bit longer. He casually looked around the bar and then back at her.

"Nice place you chose for us to meet. Did you bring Frank here as well?" The place was full and rowdy, and Brody wanted to get answers before the next bar brawl broke out.

Maria was not quite ready yet to answer the questions though, and she found she liked the idea of toying with the detective a bit longer, hoping to keep the upper hand. She looked at him with wide innocent eyes. "Frank who?"

Brody looked over at two men about three tables away engaging in a shouting match that seemed to be escalating and decided he didn't want to waste any time on Maria Martinez and her games. What he really wanted was to get back to Julia, not play guessing games with his number one murder suspect.

He swirled the whiskey in his glass and took a slow sip, looking at Maria the entire time. "I've had a long day and I'm tired, Maria. You can answer my questions, here, in your playground, without any games, or I can bring you to my playground at the Miami-Dade police precinct and you can sit in a holding cell and answer my questions in the morning, after I've had a chance to rest. The choice is entirely up to you, and it's fine with me either way."

He could see Maria's smile falter slightly, but she managed to keep it fixed on her face. "You're not quite as charming as you first pretended to be, detective. I'm disappointed. But have it your way. If you want to be all boring and business, I'll answer your questions."

Brody pulled out his notebook and set it deliberately in front of him. "When was the last time you saw Frank Masterson?" he asked, cutting right down to the chase and losing any pretense of flirting.

Maria shrugged her shoulders. "I haven't seen Frank in over 2 or 3 months now. So, you see, I didn't have anything to do with his drowning."

Brody raised an eyebrow at her. "I didn't say he drowned. How did you know that?" He looked at her suspiciously, surprised she would slip up so early in the game.

Maria gave him a knowing smile and flipped open her phone. She shuffled through it for a moment, and then slid it across the table to him. It was a newspaper article from this morning, saying a man had been found washed up near South Point Beach, and that the police believed it to be the body of a man who had been missing from Longboat Key for several weeks.

Brody nodded, satisfied for now, and handed the phone back. "So, you naturally assumed it was Frank? Why?"

"Well, it was Frank, wasn't it? That's why you're here now and why you hunted me down for questioning, right?" She looked at him intensely; the smile was now gone from her face.

"You don't seem that upset, Maria. Why not? According to Charlotte, you and Frank had quite the affair going."

Maria scoffed. "Charlotte is a washed up and jealous old woman. She still hasn't gotten over the fact that Frank got bored and moved on." Then, her eyes softened slightly. "Poor old thing made the mistake of falling in love with the guy." She looked at Brody. "That's never a good idea, trust me, especially not with a man like Frank Masterson."

Brody watched her face as she spoke, "So, I take it you weren't in love with Frank then? What exactly was your relationship?"

Maria looked at him coyly. "Oh, we were just flinging it. Why not blend a little pleasure with business, am I right, detective?" She leaned forward suggestively and shot him a pouty little smile.

Brody ignored the come on and continued his questioning. "Charlotte said he went to see her right before he went missing, but he told her he couldn't stay because he was coming to see you on urgent business. You did see him right before he went missing, didn't you?"

Maria sat back in her chair and sent him a scathing look, disappointed her flirting was getting her nowhere. "That's where you're wrong, detective. I have not seen Frank in a few months, just like I said. She was right though. We were supposed to meet and go over a few business deals." Maria gave him another seductive smile. "And of course, I was looking forward to a little fun as well. But he never showed up."

Brody frowned. He was not sure he believed her, but if she was telling the truth, it seemed like he was heading toward yet another dead end.

"Did you try and contact him when he didn't show up? What about the people you and Frank were doing business with? Did they see him? By the way, I will need a list of names from them too."

This time the laugh that came out of Maria Martinez was genuine. "Are you kidding me, detective? Do you really think I have real names and contacts for those people? And even if I did have them, I would be signing my own death certificate if I gave them to you. I have a young son and I plan to be around to raise him."

Just then, the table of men that had been loudly brawling erupted, and Brody felt someone fall against him, slamming him forward and pushing him against the table they were sitting at. The last thing he saw before he rolled onto the floor was the figure of Maria Martinez, jumping up and running for the door.

CHAPTER 41

Brody rolled over and jumped up, barely avoiding a beer bottle that had been flung his way and ran to the back exit door where he had seen Maria escaping through. He could just glimpse a flash of her silver tank top in the light coming from the alley as she opened the door, setting off the security alarms.

Instead of dashing through it like he had expected, she paused and looked over her shoulder at him, gesturing at him to hurry and follow her. He quickly followed her across the street to a seedy 24-hour diner, where they entered, and she motioned for him to sit down at a booth. From their seats, they had a clear view of the bar across the street and watched as the police cars came squealing in, sirens blaring.

"Fools," said Maria, the disgust in her voice apparent. "You think they could keep their emotions under check enough not to land them in jail. That's the problem with people today, they have no self-control."

Brody just sat and looked at her in surprise. First, because he had expected her to make a run for it, and secondly, because she sat there as if this whole incident was just an everyday occurrence to her.

Maria calmly ordered them both a coffee and they sat in silence for a few moments, watching as the police across the street cleared out the bar and escorted the men from the rowdy table away in handcuffs.

Finally, she looked at him with a slight smile of amusement. "I hope you don't mind that I lured you away from the action. Now the cops are going to keep everyone in there for at least another hour or two, taking their statements and writing it all down in their little notebooks. Then they will leave and nothing will ever come of it anyway." She flipped her hair. "Quite frankly, I have better things to do with my evening and I imagine you do too. Am I right?"

Brody nodded in agreement. He wanted to ask why she went there if she was so disgusted with the place, but decided his time was better spent getting back to Frank's murder and what she knew about it.

"Let's continue where we left off then. What did you do when Frank didn't show up to your meeting?"

Maria looked at him carefully, deciding how much to tell him. "I called him a few times with no answer. Then I called my other associates and asked if they had seen him. I thought maybe they had all agreed to meet without me... I was really just a go between Frank and them, and I was expecting to be cut out of the loop at one point anyway."

Brody looked at her curiously. "What was Frank doing for these associates, exactly? I'm not after anyone for money laundering or tax evasion right now. That's not my department. I just want to know what Frank was up to and what led to his murder."

Maria sat contemplating and finally said, "At first glance, Frank looked like an ordinary guy, glasses, a little nerdy. I was honestly surprised when I found out he was hanging around a group of such powerful men." She smiled at the memory of her first impression of Frank. "As it turns out, the man was a genius. He could take dirty money and turn it into legit income, without anyone ever paying any taxes, like no one I have ever met before. He had the respect of a great many very powerful people and they started to really trust and depend on him to take care of all of their money issues."

"So, he was working for the mob?" Brody said.

Maria glanced away. "Let's just say the men he was doing business with were not working at the local Walmart. They needed to get their money clean and undetected, and Frank was the man who could arrange that for them."

"Is that what the business was about the night he didn't show up?"

Maria frowned. "Well, kind of. Some people in the group started suspecting him of gathering and saving too much information on them. They were starting to believe that he was trying to double cross them somehow."

Brody sat and waited for Maria to continue. "Look, I liked Frank. It turned out he could be quite charming and exciting when he felt like it. The group respected him and treated him like a king most of the time, and I liked being his girlfriend. Some of that respect even trickled down to me." She shook her head sadly. "But I have a son to think of. Frank was generous with his money, but I couldn't risk going against the rest of the group for him. When they asked me to lure him to a meeting where they could find out what he was up to, I didn't really have much choice but to go along with it."

Brody said quietly, "So you suspect this was a mob hit?"

Maria swirled the coffee around in her cup and contemplated his question. "I'm not really sure. I guess it's possible. I don't know why the fool thought he could get away with double crossing these people and I don't understand why he would try." She looked at Brody. "We had a good thing going. I think he liked being with me and he was definitely making more money than any man could ever spend." She shrugged. "Maybe he just got bored and decided he needed to shake things up a bit, or maybe he wanted even more control than he already had. He was always on a power trip, that's for sure."

She finished her coffee and motioned the waitress over to refill their cups.

"The thing is though, it just doesn't seem like the typical hit. Why would they take him all the way out in the ocean when it would have been just as easy to take him to some remote area and just deal with him there?" She sipped her coffee reflectively. "The men I deal with seemed surprised when Frank disappeared. Either they were in the dark as well, or the group really has nothing to do with Frank's murder."

As Brody was listening and taking notes, a thought came to his mind. "Were they watching his house and looking for him there by any chance?" He was thinking about the mysterious dark sedan and the rock that had been thrown through Julia's window.

Maria looked slightly chagrined. "Yeah, about that... I think I know what you're talking about. They should have never sent me anyway," she said defensively. "I'm not a surveillance expert and I told them that, but they thought I would be the least conspicuous if I was seen."

"Why the rock and the note? What was the point of that?" asked Brody.

Maria smiled, somewhat abashed. "That was a spur of the moment idea. I was getting tired of sitting around and watching the house and his wife for days. I wanted to get back to my son, so I thought I might try to stir things up and see what happens. I tried to make the note as menacing, but as vague as I could, so if she was hiding him, or if he was hiding nearby, it looked like we knew it and we could flush him out." She shrugged. "It didn't exactly go as planned though. The place was swarming with cops almost immediately, and I needed to get out of there fast."

"And the break in?" asked Brody. "Were you involved in that also?"

Maria now looked genuinely confused. "What break in? Sorry, but I don't know about that. It doesn't surprise me though. They have been looking for some kind of ledger ever since Frank went missing. In fact, I was supposed to sneak into the house and look for it, but I never did get the courage to do that. Sneaking around and watching someone is one thing but breaking and entering is a little more than I'm willing to do."

Brody thought about the ledger hidden in his desk drawer back home and wondered if the information inside it was worth someone's life. "I don't suppose you know what is in that ledger?"

"I have no idea and I don't want to know. The fewer secrets I know about, the safer I am. It is something they really seemed to want though, and I doubt they will give up looking for it any time soon. They are now pretty convinced that Frank must have given it to his wife before he was murdered."

Brody suddenly felt a chill pass through him, thinking of Julia sitting at the hotel alone and unprotected. He quickly sent her a message, asking her to let him know if she was alright.

Maria looked around. "Look, I've been sitting here with you long enough and the commotion across the street has died down. I'm all out in the open now. I need to get going." She started to stand up but seemed to change her mind and sat down again, looking him straight in the eye.

"This is bigger than you, or even your police department, detective. I don't know if they killed Frank or not, but it wouldn't be the first or the last time. I don't have names, and I don't want them, but Frank told me the people involved in this are at all levels. You aren't just talking a few two-bit mob boys here. From what he told me, some pretty high up government officials were involved, along with some high-level politicians. If they're the ones that killed him, you won't find them."

Maria gathered her purse and put some money on the table for the coffees. Then she looked at him. All pretense of flirtation was gone and there was a desperate and pleading look on her face. "Please detective, for the sake of my son, don't contact me again. I truly have told you everything I know, and given you more information than I safely should have. I can't help you anymore. I just want to stay alive for my son. These people aren't above killing me, or even you, if we get in their way."

She stood up again to leave, but before she did, a thought passed through her mind, "You know, I was supposed to pick him up that day, but he told me not to. He said his daughter was picking him up and he had a few personal things he needed to take care of. You might want to ask her or her girlfriend a few questions about that day." Maria gave him one last look as she walked away.

CHAPTER 42

Julia was on her sixth drink of the night, three of them having been purchased by the two men whose attention she had been enjoying for the evening. Tonight, she felt like the life of the party. She only had to open her mouth and say something, and the two men seemed to find her the most fascinating and witty woman they had ever met. Frank had never found her conversations enthralling or funny and she was enjoying every minute of the attention.

The dark-haired man sat at his corner table watching the proceedings with disgust. He would have liked to intervene and send them both on their way. He decided to bide his time for now though. It was better to let them do all the work and get her drunk. They would get the attention of the rest of the bar patrons, and when he took Julia later, the witnesses were sure to remember the two men. He could then disappear into oblivion, unnoticed.

Julia laughed at the joke the tall blonde man had just told, but her laugh was forced. Their jokes and conversation were becoming distasteful, and she was starting to tire. She also knew she was getting drunk, and the inner voice she had never fully been able to shut off was now screaming at her to stop drinking and make her way back up to her hotel room.

The one with the long beard started to order another round of drinks when Julia put up her hand to decline. "Thank you so much for the fun evening gentlemen, but I believe I've had more than enough for the night. It's been a long day and I need to be up early in the morning."

"Awww, come on Julia. You said you wanted to spend the night forgetting all your problems. Steve and I can help you with that." The blonde-haired man then put his arm on her, pushing her back onto the bar stool in an attempt to detain her.

The bearded man leaned in toward Julia, close enough she could smell the alcohol and sweat emanating off him, making her want to gag. "You just relax Julia. Let's all just enjoy a few more drinks, and Dennis and I are going to show you a real good time tonight. We'll make sure you forget all your problems and everything else. That's a promise little lady." Then, he gestured to the bartender to bring them all another round.

Julia felt nauseous and now she felt a twinge of fear starting in her gut. She looked around and spotted the sign for the restrooms. Excusing herself, she quickly hurried over to the bathroom and shut the door firmly behind her. Once inside, she splashed some water on her face, trying to clear the muddled fog in her brain. Just outside, the two men stood waiting for her.

"I think she's trying to ghost us, Steve," sighed the blonde-haired guy.

Steve let out a laugh. "Ha! No way I'm letting her go that easy. She's so drunk it won't take much to get her upstairs. Besides…" He gave his friend a wink. "I slipped a little something in that last drink. When she comes out you take one arm and I'll take the other. The elevators are right there. We'll just tell her we're helping her to her room and instead we all have ourselves a little fun."

The blonde man looked at him doubtfully, but when Julia exited the bathroom, he did as instructed and took one arm.

Julia found it hard to stand straight and focus. She tried to think of an excuse to get away, but her words came out slurred and slow. "I really need to be getting back now. I have someone waiting for me upstairs and he'll start to wonder where I am if I don't go up right now."

The bearded man just smiled a wicked smirk and leaned in close. "That's alright Julia. We'll just help you over to the elevator and make sure you get to your room nice and safe. We wouldn't want anything happening to our new little friend now, would we?"

Julia could smell the repugnant odor of whiskey coming strongly from his breath, but she couldn't get her thoughts together enough to figure out a way to make it to her room herself.

Steve looked over at his friend with a grin of greedy anticipation and didn't notice the dark-haired man until he almost stumbled right into him.

"Just where is it that you two think you are taking the lady?" The dark-haired man asked, looking at the two men with a cold and menacing stare.

"It's all ok mister, we are just gonna help our friend here up to her room," said Dennis, looking over at Steve uncertainly.

The dark-haired man stepped forward and grabbed Julia by the waist, pulling her quickly away from the two men and slightly behind him. "I think I'll just take over from here," he said.

"Hold on there, buddy!" said Steve angrily. "This one is ours. You go find yourself someone else for the night." He stepped forward, attempting to grab at Julia.

The dark-haired man took a quick step back and kicked out at his feet. It caught the man by surprise, and he found himself on the floor staring up at a very menacing and deadly face.

"Like I said, I'll take over from here. You two disappear and consider yourselves lucky that I'm letting you off with only a hurt ego."

The dark-haired man then shifted Julia around and attempted to balance her upright as he walked to the exit. Julia tried to focus on what was going on but was having a tough time staying aware and registering her surroundings.

"What's going on? Who are you?" she asked, trying to pull herself away and get a clear look. Her words sounded fuzzy even to her own ears.

"It's going to be fine now Mrs. Masterson. I'm just going to make sure that those two men don't hurt you. Just come along with me and you'll be safe."

Julia looked at him and gave him a grateful smile. She didn't know if she would have been able to get away from the men on her own. "I owe you a big thank you. You're my hero tonight," she slurred while leaning heavily on him as he guided her to the back exit.

CHAPTER 43

Moments after Brody had pulled into the hotel parking lot, he watched as the dark-haired man exited the hotel carrying Julia, who seemed to be severely incapacitated. His gut clenched in anger, and he quietly made his way over to the man, going in just off to his side and out of sight. He felt the reassuring weight of the Glock 22 in his hand as he silently made his way close to the man.

He slowly raised his gun to the man's head.

"Put her down very gently and very slowly, then turn away from me and put your hands behind your back." Brody pressed the gun to the man's temple, letting him know that he meant business.

The dark-haired man's eyes registered a slight surprise, but he held tightly onto Julia and turned slowly to face Brody.

"I'm afraid I won't be able to do that Detective Barker. I've been waiting a long time to get a chance to talk to Mrs. Masterson, and my associates will not take kindly to me giving up just yet."

Brody clicked the hammer of the Glock. "I don't think you understood me. You don't have a choice. Put her down or you are a dead man."

The dark-haired man smiled slightly at Brody. "I don't think that's in your rule book, detective. You can't just go around shooting people in the head. That would be an awful lot of bad press for the men in blue, wouldn't it?"

Brody was getting impatient with the man and worried about Julia and what the man had done to incapacitate her. "I'm not concerned with what the press, or anyone else thinks right now. What have you done to her? If you have hurt her at all, I'll kill you anyway."

The man looked Brody in the eye. "I see you've become a bit too

215

personally involved with this case, detective. That's never a good idea, but it does change things a bit, doesn't it? I think we need to talk before you make a mistake you may very well live to regret."

"We can talk once I have you in handcuffs and I have made sure that Julia is alright. Now, do as I say. I am starting to lose my patience."

The man shifted Julia slightly and smiled again at Brody. "Relax, detective. Your little beauty is just sleeping. It seems the object of your concern has had a little too much to drink tonight, thanks to two very attentive gentlemen. You should really be thanking me for saving her from them."

Brody narrowed his eyes slightly and looked at Julia closely. He could see that she was having a hard time staying on her feet and just barely hanging onto the man's arm, but she did seem to be breathing normally.

"What do you want from her anyway?" asked Brody. "Since you've already murdered her husband why not leave her alone? She didn't know anything about what he was up to."

The dark-haired man looked at Brody in surprise. "Sorry detective, but you're mistaken. We didn't have anything to do with Frank Masterson's murder. I've been looking for him myself for weeks now, trying to get what I need."

"I don't believe you." Brody looked at the man coldly. "You murdered him for double-crossing you and now you are after his wife. I just can't figure out why."

The man shook his head again. "I just found out he was dead the same time you did, detective. If I had known he was dead before, I would have grabbed his wife weeks ago and gotten the information I needed from her."

The man looked around the dark parking lot, gauging whether he could get the upper hand on the detective while still managing to carry Julia away.

"Look, detective. This business goes way deeper than either you or me, or even Mrs. Masterson here. You may be able to kill me and save her tonight, but someone else will come to get her after me. Frank should never have given her sensitive information. Now that he's dead and can't answer for himself, he has doomed his wife as well."

Brody felt a cold chill coursing through his body, and he knew instinctively that the man was telling the truth. He adjusted his gun and considered where he could hide out with Julia if he shot the man and made his escape.

He had known as soon as he saw Julia in danger that he loved her, and even if it meant hiding with her for the rest of his life, he would do whatever it took to protect her.

"You and I don't need to die tonight, detective. And trust me, I won't go without a fight. You can just walk away while I deliver Mrs. Masterson to the group, and they tie up the last of their loose ends and eliminate any risks. If Frank had just given them the ledger before he died without showing it to her, we might have been able to avoid all of this. I believe you have three nice kids who you are proud of, don't you? It would be a shame if we needed to involve such a nice family in these messy affairs. Let's just end it here, and you move on and live a happy life with your kids."

Brody glared at the man coldly, wondering if he should shoot him directly in the forehead are right through his menacing eyes.

"I'll even throw you a bone, detective. I'll lead you in the direction of Frank's real killer. That way you can solve the case and be the hero. We make sure that Mrs. Masterson won't talk to the wrong people, and we all live happily ever after."

Brody contemplated his options and then really comprehended what the man had said he wanted from Julia.

"What if I told you that Julia has no idea what's in that ledger? As a matter of fact, she has never even seen it. Frank never did succeed in getting it to her, and he apparently disappeared before he was ever able to talk to her about it."

The man narrowed his eyes suspiciously but looked at Brody with interest. "How do you know so much about this ledger, if she never had it?"

"Let's just say it fell into my hands by mistake. I had no idea what it was or if it was even important, so I held onto it. I thought Julia had enough to worry about at the time, so I never showed it to her. Would she have known what it was if I had showed her?" Brody asked.

The man nodded. "We assume so. Frank was a genius at covert operations and moving money, but he bragged about his wife's ability to come up with the codes. He used to play games with her, the two of them coming up with secret codes just for fun. He told her it was just to keep her mind sharp, but he used a lot of them to keep track of a lot of secret information. I'm certain that if she had seen the ledger, she would recognize the codes as her own and be able to crack them."

Brody lowered his gun slightly. "Then, it's a good thing that I never showed it to her. I have the ledger."

The man looked at Brody with interest. "Where is it?"

"It's hidden. If we can make a deal, I can make sure that you get it. Julia needs to stay out of it and stay safe though."

As the man considered what Brody was proposing, they both heard a shout coming from the hotel entrance.

"Hey, you!" The two men from the bar had consumed a few more drinks at the bar and were now feeling braver than they had earlier.

One of them yelled out, "We're not letting you get away that easy. I don't know who you are, but you can't talk to us that way. We expect an apology, and while you are busy apologizing, you might just want to hand over the little lady as well." Steve pulled out a switchblade knife and stumbled toward Brody and the dark-haired man.

Brody sighed with annoyance and moved point the gun at the two men, when the dark-haired man grabbed his arm, forcing him to lower it.

"If we end up making a deal, we don't need any police attention on us, and that gun is going to bring the whole Miami PD down on us."

Brody looked at the man holding his arm, then back at the two men slowly approaching them and stuck the Glock back in his holster.

The dark-haired man quickly handed a limp Julia over to Brody and said, "They're just amateurs. Let's quickly get this over with and head upstairs to talk about the details."

Brody shifted Julia gently over to his left arm, and was able to get a good shot at the blonde-haired man with his right fist, sending him sprawling, before the dark-haired man leaned into both of the men like a whirlwind.

With a few well-placed jabs, both men were quickly on the ground, moaning and writhing in pain.

When he was done, the dark-haired man looked at Brody with a slight grin, "Ok, let's get going before anyone finds them."

Brody took Julia and cradled her gently in his arms, heading for the hotel's back entrance and up to his room. He laid her carefully on the bed when they got there, checked her vitals, and stroked her hair back off her forehead. The dark-haired man watched with interest.

"You really care about her, don't you?" He walked to the door and stood beside it, crossing his arms. "Let's hope what you said was the truth and we can come up with an agreement, so you and Mrs. Masterson here get the chance to enjoy your lives."

Brody stood up and faced the man; his hand ready to fly to the Glock he still had stashed in his holster.

"I have the ledger hidden, just like I said. I can arrange for it to be in Julia's house 3 days after we get back. Before then, the house will be filled with a clean-up crew, and I want to make sure no one interrupts you when you go in."

The dark-haired man frowned slightly at the delay, but decided he had already waited this long and if he could avoid any more violence, it would be worth the wait.

"Okay, in three days, I'll be back in Frank's house. Leave it in his old office on the desk. I'll let myself in and out quickly. You make sure no one is there and if you are telling the truth and you don't double cross me, you and the woman walk away."

Brody nodded, satisfied with the deal. He would have made a deal with the devil himself if it meant keeping Julia safe.

"Now, what about the lead you were going to give me on Frank's murder? What do you know about that?"

The man smiled slyly. "You seem to have been barking up all the wrong trees Detective Barker," he jibed. "You need to find Abigail Carpenter and put some pressure on her. She'll have all the answers you need."

"Abigail Carpenter?" Brody said, surprised. "What would Cynthia's girlfriend have to do with Frank's murder?"

The man opened the door to leave. "The question you need to ask detective, is what does Cynthia have to do with Frank's murder."

CHAPTER 44

Brody sat next to Julia on the bed and held a cold washcloth to her head. He had already plied her with aspirin, Alka-Seltzer and lots of water. Last night, he had vigilantly watched over her while she slept, laughing to himself as she let out a few light and dainty snores. He had known as soon as he saw her in danger that despite his best efforts, he had fallen head over heels in love with her.

He also knew that it was much too soon for Julia to feel the same. He had decided last night, while keeping watch over her, that he would take it slow and give her time to heal from the traumas she had endured. He had every intention of being there right by her side until she did.

Julia sat up and looked at Brody, ashamed that she was once again hungover in his presence. "You really must think I'm a complete alcoholic," she moaned. "I can't remember anything, apart from a couple drinks at the bar."

Brody smiled at her gently. "That must have been around the time I brought you up to bed then," he said.

She grimaced. "It's lucky for me that you came when you did then." She smiled at him. "You do always seem to swoop in just in time to save me, don't you? Thank you, Brody. I really am grateful."

Brody gave her a slight kiss on the head and stood up, as Julia looked at him in surprise.

"I need to go to the Miami Dade precinct," he explained. "They brought in Abigail Carpenter last night and she has been stewing in a jail cell all night, waiting for me to question her about Frank's murder. I really need to get in there and see what she has to say."

Julia gasped. "Abigail Carpenter? That's Cynthia's girlfriend, isn't she? The other woman that Frank was giving money to? What would she have to do with Frank's murder?"

Brody put on his jacket and headed for the door. "That's what I'm going to find out." He turned around and looked at Julia sternly. "Lock the door and get some sleep now. I called room service and they brought up some food for you, so when you're ready to eat, it's already here. Don't open the door for anyone." Then, he grinned at her as he was leaving and said, "And for goodness sake Julia, no more drinking!"

After he left, Julia leaned back against the pillow and fought a slight wave of nausea. She tried to remember last night's events, but after she had gone to the ladies' room, it was just a blur of images. She did remember being cradled and gently carried, and when she woke up Brody had been leaning over her, holding a cold washcloth to her head. Smiling, she laid down and closed her eyes. Brody did seem to be her Knight in Shining Armor.

*

The woman sitting behind the small, sparse table in the interview room at the precinct was slight and timid looking. Abigail Carpenter threw Brody a scared look as he strode into the room, trying to look as big and intimidating as he possibly could.

"Alright Abigail, you already know why you're here so we might as well cut right to the chase. What do you know about the murder of Frank Masterson and how were you involved?"

Abigail was visibly shaking but she gave one last attempt at bravado. "I have no idea who or what you are talking about."

Brody gave her a withering look and sat down on the small chair across from her, leaning in close. "Cut it out, Abigail. The jig is up. We know you are in a relationship with Cynthia Masterson, and we know that Frank Masterson was sending you money regularly. We have proof, so please don't waste my time with your lame denials."

Abigail visibly paled. "I was afraid you would come for me after that terrifying man made me tell him everything."

Brody remained still, knowing who she was referring to but not wanting the officers on the other side of the mirror watching to catch any slight movement.

He could see that Abigail was terrified and decided to go in strong, using a little bit of creative narration to urge her to talk.

"Cynthia has been more than helpful in providing us with all the details, Abigail. According to her, you were the mastermind in this whole relationship, but I'm not so sure that's true."

He could see the young woman across from him start to tremble.

"Cynthia told you that? That's not true! Cynthia called all the shots in our relationship! I always did what she told me to do. I can't believe she would try to blame all this on me. I wasn't even there when she killed her father!"

Brody's ears perked up, did he hear that right?

"That's not at all the story she told us, Abigail. One of you must be lying. Why don't you tell me your version of the events, and we can compare them and see who is telling the truth. Remember, we can verify anything you tell us, so make sure you aren't hiding anything."

Abigail's hands shook as she picked up the glass of water and took a drink. "Where do you want me to start? What did she tell you?"

"Just start at the beginning, Abigail. When did you meet and why was Frank sending you money?"

"I met Cynthia like six years ago. It was all so wonderful when it started. She was so kind and giving. I had made some terrible financial choices and she helped me out of them. She came and visited me often, but then she started demanding more of my time, and I was finding it hard to balance both being with her and keeping my job."

"And that's where Frank and his money came in?" Brody asked.

Abigail nodded. "Yes. At the time, I didn't know what she told him. Cynthia just told me to quit my job and her father would take care of me."

"Did you ever meet Frank?"

"Yes, but not till much later. It turns out that Cynthia had told Frank I was blackmailing her about our relationship. Threatening to go to her mother and tell her about Cynthia and me being together. The money Frank sent me at first was supposed to be hush money… although I had no idea until a few years later."

Brody kept his eyes on her as he asked, "How did you find out what she had told him?"

"Several years later, a private eye knocked on my door and Frank Masterson was with him. He had started to suspect that Cynthia and I were still seeing each other, and he had us followed. He wanted to know from me what she was up to, and that was when I found out the story she had told him."

"Okay, what happened then?" Brody asked.

Abigail just shrugged. "Not that much… we all sat together and yelled and cried for a while, then we decided to forgive each other and move on. Frank agreed to keep sending me money for the time being, but he said to both of us that he would only support us for another year, and then we would be on our own."

Abigail shook her head sadly, thinking back to that night.

"I should have known right then what kind of person she was, but I was in love and had become so dependent on her both financially and emotionally. Anyway, Frank kept sending the money, even as the years went by. Occasionally, we all went out to dinner together."

Brody gave her a quizzical look. "He just kept sending you money? It sounds like Frank was very generous with the two of you?"

Abigail nodded. "He was. I really grew to like him."

"Then why did you murder him?" Brody looked her squarely in the eye as he asked the question.

Abigail gasped and let out a slight sob. "I didn't murder him!" she cried. "I begged Cynthia not to carry out her plan, but she was adamant we had no choice. She wanted me to go with them on the boat that day, but I refused. I didn't want to see the man who had been so kind to me, killed. I didn't want to see the love of my life kill her own father!"

Brody was baffled. "Why did Cynthia need to kill her father?"

"I don't know what she told you, but she told me her father was involved with some dangerous men and that they were paying him to help them cover the tracks for some illegal money they were receiving. I guess he was involved in some kind of money laundering scheme." She looked at Brody and continued, "I liked Frank and I didn't really care what he did to earn his money, as long as he kept sending me checks. Cynthia told me he was about to cut us off, but she had figured out a plan to blackmail him so he would keep the money coming."

"What plan?" asked Brody, extremely curious how this all tied into Frank's murder.

"She was collecting information behind his back about some of his associates. I think her idea was to tell him she would take the information to the police if he didn't continue to support me, and I'm sure she was asking for some extra money for herself as well. It was harder than she thought to gather enough information though because Frank was so good at covering his tracks. Finally, she found a ledger in his briefcase when she was snooping through it. She was convinced it was the key she needed to blackmail him."

Brody sat silent and waited for her to continue, thinking again of the ledger he had hidden in his apartment and how it was turning out to be the key to this entire investigation.

"She met up with him in Ohio and confronted him, and I guess things turned pretty ugly between the two of them. Frank told her she was playing with fire and threatening some very dangerous men. These men knew that someone had been gathering their information and they were not happy about it... She told me later he looked really scared. Frank told her he would do what he could to ease things over with his associates, but he wasn't going to take the fall for her. If necessary, he would tell them exactly who had been digging around in their business."

"She thought Frank was going to turn her in?" Brody asked.

"She was convinced he would," said Abigail. "I told her she was crazy, that her father would never do that, but when he told her he was coming to Miami to meet up with the group and try to straighten out the mess she had caused, she panicked."

Brody was piecing together what had happened in his mind.

"Cynthia thought she needed to kill Frank before he had a chance to tell anyone it was her… that she was the one who had been gathering information. She was sure that if he told them what she had been up to, they would kill her, and she had no choice but to kill him first."

"How did she convince Frank to go out on a boat with her if things were so tense between them?"

"She called him and convinced him she was being followed, and the only secure place they could talk was out on the ocean where they knew no one else could see them. She told him to bring the gun that she had bought for him a few years back for protection."

"She bought the gun for him?" asked Brody.

Abigail nodded and said, "She bought it for his birthday as some kind of sick joke. Everyone knew how Frank felt about guns, but since she acted like she did it out of concern for his safety, he kept it only to make her happy. She'd laugh about it to me occasionally, saying how she was sure it was nagging at him, having a gun in his nightstand and keeping it secret from his wife."

"So, she convinced him to bring it with him?" Brody asked, waiting for her to continue.

"Yes, she was already here in Miami by then, and I was listening in on her side of the conversation. She told him she was really scared, and he needed to come immediately. That's when she told him to bring the gun for their safety." Abigail looked down crestfallen.

"Did she tell you what happened when she finally did meet up with Frank?"

"Unfortunately, yes. Although I wish she hadn't. They apparently had some trouble getting a boat without an ID and Frank was getting impatient. He was afraid he would be late for the meeting he had set up for later in the afternoon. Cynthia finally got desperate and used the driver's license I'd left in the car to rent a boat from a small rental place."

Brody was sure that the men behind the mirror were already checking to see if any boats had been rented that day under Abigail Carpenter's name.

Abigail shuddered slightly but continued, "Once they were finally out on the water and far enough away, Cynthia asked her dad for the gun. She said she wanted to keep it for her own safety, knowing Frank would be happy to be rid of it. She told me that she pretended to show him something by the rail… and when he turned to look where she had pointed, she shot him point-blank in the back of the head. As soon as she did it, she pushed him into the ocean so there wouldn't be any blood on the boat. Then she drove around a bit and returned the boat to the slip without checking in."

Brody sat silent for a moment, contemplating what Frank Masterson's last moments must have been like and how much he should tell Julia about what Abigail had said.

"And what about the ledger that started all of this? Did Cynthia tell you what happened to that?"

"I don't know. I guess she was so focused on killing him she didn't think of it. If he did have it on him, it's probably floating somewhere at the bottom of the ocean about now."

Brody stood up, hoping the detectives behind the glass also believed the ledger was gone and at the bottom of the ocean. Now that he finally had the whole story to Frank Masterson's demise, he felt exhausted and just wanted to get back to Julia.

"Thank you, Abigail, I appreciate you telling us the truth. I'm sure it will go a long way in keeping you out of jail. The local PD will have a few more questions for you about Cynthia shortly."

Brody tried to wrap his head around the senseless murder of a man by his own daughter. Julia's husband had certainly been no saint, but Brody didn't think anyone deserved what Cynthia had done.

He exited the room, nodding at the two detectives who walked in to take his place.

EPILOGUE

Three days later

Julia leaned against Brody's strong shoulders, soaking in the warm sun and relishing the feel of Brody's arms around her. She closed her eyes and took in the sounds of the ocean lapping against the shore.

Turning, she gave Brody a slight smile and a small peck on his cheek, then turned back to the ocean shyly. She still wasn't sure about the new feelings she had for Brody or where they would lead, but for now, she was willing to take it slow and see where things would go.

"What was that for?" Brody smiled down at her.

She pulled his arms around her even tighter, "For being there for me through all of this. I don't think I could have faced all this mess without you at my side." She looked up at him gratefully.

Brody held her tightly and looked over her shoulder at the beach house she had once shared with Frank. The cleaners and her neighbor's had spent countless hours repairing the house back to normal. The only input Brody had given was to insist that Frank's office remain as it had been until they started the renovations.

Tomorrow, he would accompany Julia to Ohio, where Frank Masterson would be laid to rest beside his parents in a small, private ceremony. Brody doubted that Jane would show up for the funeral, but they received a phone call from Mary saying that she would like to be there to say a final goodbye.

Cynthia had been arrested and charged with her father's murder.

As far as the police chief was concerned, the Frank Masterson case was closed and shelved, and he and the mayor could now go on unhindered into the upcoming election.

Julia looked down at the local newspaper she held in her hands and smiled at the article that Krystle Davis had published - a public retraction of all past stories about Julia.

Brody pulled Julia in close, hugging her into his chest.

"Hmmm. This is nice," said Julia. "Be careful, Brody Barker, or you may never get rid of me."

Brody smiled down at her. "That just might be my plan, Julia."

As he stroked the top of her head, he glanced up towards the house and spotted a man with dark hair walking quickly away from the window where Frank's office was located. When the man was almost to the road, he turned around and looked directly at Brody. He held his hand up with a slight wave, and in it, Brody could see a small, bound ledger. The man gave him a slight nod of his head and disappeared out of sight.

Brody leaned down into the top of Julia's head and breathed in the scent of her jasmine shampoo, holding her against him even tighter.

He knew now that the deadly legacy Frank Masterson had left for his wife was over, and she now had all the time she needed to rebuild her life slowly.

A life that he had every intention of being part of.

ABOUT THE AUTHOR

NOTE FROM SAGE PARKER

Hi lovelies.

I love writing sweet and clean contemporary romance novels. I was born and raised in a small town in South Carolina, but you can almost always find me at the beach…usually reading a book. I hope my writing brings joy and inspiration to everyone that uses their precious time to read my stories.

Thanks for stopping by!
Stay safe and happy x

Keep in touch! If you would like to say hello, you can e-mail me at: hello@sageparkerauthor.com   or
Follow me on Amazon [Sage Parker] to get updated whenever I release a new book!

MORE BY SAGE PARKER

A COASTLINE RETREAT Feels Like Home Series

LAST RESORT ON THE COAST Search For Truth Series

NEW IN CLIFFS POINT Cliffs Point Series

THE BEACHSIDE CAFE Saltwater Secrets Series